Savage Assassin
A Dark Mafia Romance

The Savage Trilogy
Book 1

M. James

PNK Publishing

Elena

In all the years I've known him, my father has rarely ever raised his voice.

It's terrifying to hear him raise it now. Especially to my mother.

I'm crouched outside the heavy wooden double doors that lead into his office, listening as they argue. It feels even worse than a normal argument because they're arguing about me.

"This is real danger, Lupé," I hear my father say, his voice low and urgent. "Diego isn't going to stop. He's not *ever* going to stop, not until he's dealt with or we give him what he wants. We're on the verge of all-out war–and I refuse to give him my daughter."

"*Our* daughter," my mother hisses. "This is Isabella's fault. The match was perfectly suitable; it just wasn't what she wanted. She ran off with that Irishman, all because of her selfish decisions, and now we're left to pick up the pieces. *Elena* is left to pick up the pieces."

A jolt of fear pierces through me. I don't fully understand what she means, but I can feel the tension in the air, seeping out from the room until my stomach feels like a series of cold knots, my heart beating hard in my chest.

"You are right about that," I hear my father say tiredly. "Diego wants her to make up for losing Isabella. But I'm not giving in to those fucking demands. He can't have her. It's not an option, no matter what he threatens–"

"You might consider that it's possible to make it work." My mother's voice is taut and haughty, the tone I've always heard her use when she's insistent that she be listened to. But I can hear a thread of fear in it too, and I know she's scared.

We're *all* scared. Ever since Isabella left, it's been nothing but fear. We all heard how Diego sent her to the bride-tamer for her insolence, for how she'd refused to give in to him. It had only been a few days later when my father had received the first threat from him, and we'd found out that she'd escaped.

The communication from the Kings had come a little while later, and we'd known then that the Irishman had saved her and taken her to Boston. She's safe now, far away from here.

We're anything but.

"He could make assurances that he won't hurt her," my mother insists, her voice carrying louder now. "Make that a term of the deal. Her safety. That he treats her the way a husband should treat his wife."

"You're out of your mind, Lupé." My father's voice is rougher now, angrier. "What will we do if we make that deal, and he goes back on it? How would we enforce that? How would we protect her? He'll have her then, and we'll still be where we are now–weaker than ever, because he'll have the threat of her life to hold over us."

There's a moment of silence, and I can see in my mind's eye the way my father must be shaking his head, his arms crossed stubbornly over his chest. I've seen it before, when I've caught sight of them arguing.

"I'm not going to throw her to the wolves like that," he says, so quietly that I almost don't hear it. "It's not going to happen. We'll find another way."

"He's going to kill us," my mother murmurs, and this time I can hear the panic clearly in her voice. "You have to *do* something, Ricardo. We can't rely on the Irish–"

The same panic floods through me, and I clench my fists against my stomach as I crouch there, listening, my blood turning to ice.

I miss Isabella. I miss her so much. She would know what to do, what to say–

It might be objectively true that she's the reason we're in this position, but I don't blame her, not like our mother does. How could I? She had always been the wilder one, the braver one, not much older than me, but enough for me to look up to her. To want to be as brave as she was.

As she *is*.

She'd gotten everything that she wanted, everything that we'd both been too afraid to dream of for our future. She'd gone out and claimed it for her own, seduced the Irishman, and he'd fallen in love with her. He saved her and took her far away from here, like some kind of fairytale. It was exactly the kind of adventure, the kind of romance that we'd whispered about once upon a time, a story that had never ever seemed like it could come true.

I want my own happy ending now. But I can see that it's not going to happen.

The best I can hope for is that somehow, my father will keep me out of Diego Gonzalez's clutches. That he'll keep him from claiming me as restitution for Isabella–for his lost bride.

I can't help wondering, as I listen to my parents fight over my fate, if Isabella knows what's happening. If she would have done things differently if she'd known that Diego would come for me next.

I hope that she wouldn't. I want her to be happy–and I want my own happiness, too.

The right-side door to the office flings open suddenly, so quickly that I jump and tumble backward onto my ass, letting out what my mother would term a very unladylike squeak of shock.

It's my mother who is storming out of the office, and she pauses, her face tight with anger as she looks down at me sprawled on the stone tile floor.

"I see you were eavesdropping," she says icily, her eyes narrowing. "What did I do, to be cursed with no sons and two such rebellious daughters who–"

"Lupé, that's enough." My father's voice booms past her as he pushes open the other door, stepping around my mother as he reaches out to help me up from the floor. "Elena is scared. We all are. There's no need to make that worse."

It's meant to be reassurance, but somehow hearing my father say that he's scared, lumping himself in with the *we all are*, makes this all feel a hundred thousand times worse. I can see it on his face, as I get to my feet slowly, dusting myself off. His expression is as composed as ever, but I can see the fear in his eyes, lurking there.

Throughout all my life, my father has always been the steadfast rock, the one I knew could keep us safe from anything. I always felt secure that he loved Isabella and me, that he would protect us, and I knew we were lucky in that regard. In our world, daughters could be nothing more than a means to make alliances. They are only valuable because they could be used as a bargaining chip.

I knew our father had never seen us like that. Even when he'd felt forced to promise Isabella to Diego Gonzalez, it hadn't been because he'd wanted it. It hadn't been because he'd thought that was her *purpose*.

And now, he's trying to protect me from the same thing.

"Lupé, go upstairs." His voice is colder than I've ever heard speaking to my mother. "Let's take some time to cool down. We'll talk about this later."

I see her mouth tighten angrily. She hates when my father orders her around; I've always known that. But surprisingly, she doesn't argue.

"Are you alright?" He brushes off my arms, looking at me with clear concern. "How much did you hear?"

I press my lips together, feeling a little sheepish now that he's caught me eavesdropping–but I'm also still terrified. "Everything," I admit quietly, looking up at him. "Is Diego really going to–"

"No," he says sharply, cutting me off as he pulls me in for a hug, wrapping his arms around me in the embrace that I've always found so comforting, all my life. "I'm not going to let that happen, Elena. I'll keep you and your mother safe. I promise."

"But–what can you do to get him to stop? You said he won't–"

"I know what I said." My father lets out a sigh, reaching up to stroke my hair as he looks at me ruefully. "I wish you and your sister never had to grow up, you know? It was so much easier when you were children. No one wanted to take you from me. Isabella was still willful–but you were always good. You both would listen better, then. There was less for you to fear. More for you to dream of–"

He lets out a sigh, running one hand through his hair as he looks down at me, his face taut with worry now. "I can't blame your sister for trying to escape him. I *do* blame her for the mess of things that she made with that Irishman, but she's safe with him in Boston now, so perhaps she knew what she was doing all along."

"But *Mama* feels like she left us to pick up the pieces." I bite my lower lip. "Is that how you feel, too?"

"Your sister should never have had to shoulder the responsibility of keeping this family safe. It's unfair that she should ever have had to do so. I don't want the same to happen to you."

"I don't want to marry Diego." I feel a cold shudder go through me just at the thought. "He won't be kind to me, no matter what you make him promise—"

"I know. He'll take his anger at Isabella out on you. That's why he wants you. And that's why I won't allow it."

Gently, my father reaches for my upper arm, steering me towards the stairs that lead up to the floor where my bedroom is. "I think it's better if you're upstairs in your room for now, though, Elena. I have work to do, and I'll feel better if I know where you are, with José patrolling."

"Diego isn't going to come here—"

"I hope not." My father catches the expression on my face and winces. "I shouldn't be so honest with you. I don't want to frighten you."

"I'm twenty years old." I look up at him, wrinkling my nose. "I'm not a child for you to keep secrets from anymore."

He laughs ruefully. "Twenty is still a child, Elena. You'll understand that one day. And you're still mine to protect, for now. So I intend to do that."

José is coming around the corner as we walk up, making his rounds of the upper floor. He catches sight of me and my father, and stops, inclining his head respectfully. "*Señor* Santiago. Is there something you need?"

"Just for Elena to stay in her room for tonight. I have business to take care of, and I'll feel better if I know she's here, safe and sound."

"Of course."

José looks at me with an unfathomable expression on his face, something darker than I'm accustomed to seeing from him. Not so long ago, when Isabella was still here, he was always in a lighter mood, teasing us and mildly flirting with my sister. However, he was always quick to shut it down when she pushed it too far. We'd both always had a bit of a crush on him—it was hard not to. He's extraordinarily handsome, deeply tanned with buzz-cut black hair, dark eyes, a strong jaw, and a muscled body that his fatigued cargo pants and tech shirt cling to more tightly than they really have any right to.

But recently, he's been quieter, more sullen. He nods tightly to my father, who smiles at me as he pushes my door open. "Goodnight, Elena," my father says pointedly, letting me know that he expects me to stay put, as he said.

Where would I go, anyway? It's not as if I have the nerve to leave the compound in search of adventure or an escape the way my sister did. It's not as if I could go anywhere at all. The most I might do is wander to the library upstairs or go out to the garden, and it's not a terrible loss to be unable to do that tonight. I can curl up in bed with one of my books and float far away from here, into some kind of adventure that I'll never be able to live in real life.

I'm about to close the door when José's arm pushes against it, stopping me as he glares down at me with a bitter expression on his face. "Don't make me have to chase you down," José says irritably, once my father is out of earshot. "Just stay in your room like a good girl, alright? Don't make my life any fucking harder than it already is."

"I hadn't planned on it." I can hear a bite to my own words that isn't usually there—it's been a long and scary night, and I don't quite understand why he's been like this recently. "Is there something you want to tell me, José? It's not as if we haven't known each other for a long time."

"Why would I want to tell you anything?" he asks irritably. "It's my job to keep you safe, not talk to you."

Something about the way he says it makes me feel more upset than before. "No one is making you," I snap back, retreating further into my room. "I'm sorry I asked."

He turns away, but before he does, I hear him mutter under his breath.

"Spoiled brat."

I'm at the door in an instant, shoving it open wider as I glare at his back. "I heard you," I snap accusingly, and I see his shoulders shake for an instant, almost as if he's laughing–or as if he's very angry.

Slowly, he turns around, his expression dark and hard. "I don't care if you heard me," José says evenly. "In fact, I'll say it again. You're a spoiled fucking brat, and your father should have handed you over to Diego Gonzalez long before this."

I can feel myself start to tremble, a fine shaking spreading through me, but I tilt my chin up, staring him down. "I'm sure he'd love to hear you say that to his face."

"It shouldn't come as a surprise that I feel that way, if I did." José steps closer to my door, his muscled bulk almost filling the doorway. There was a time when I would have felt my pulse leap at him being so close, but now I just feel afraid. It's clear he's angry, and I don't entirely understand why.

"My brother died in the fight with the Gonzalez cartel when he took Isabella," José says evenly, his every word tight and harsh. "All to protect the Santiago princesses. And I'll be expected to do the same, if it comes to it. While you face no consequences for not doing *your* duty."

He glares down at me. "Your sister should have married Diego like she was supposed to, and none of this would have happened. If she'd done her duty, my brother would be alive. There would be no war going on. And you–"

His gaze slides up and down me, in a way that feels far too personal for who he is and who I am. "You wouldn't be in danger of following in her footsteps."

The words are low and threatening, and he smiles tightly down at me, his eyes still hard and cold. "Goodnight, *princesa*," he murmurs. "Sweet dreams."

I manage to stay upright until he shuts the door, harder than he needed to. I stumble backward, feeling my pulse pounding in my throat as I sink down onto the edge of my bed, feeling that same terror that I'd felt earlier, threatening to overwhelm me all over again.

Diego Gonzalez is coming for my family. For *me*, just like he had my sister.

Isabella had Niall to save her.

Who is going to save me?

Levin

"We owe them the men we promised."

Liam is standing at the head of the table, next to Connor, and the tension in the room is palpable. It generally is, in times like these, when all the heads of the various members of the families are assembled for a crisis. The entire table of the Kings is present, including Jacob, Connor's right hand, who is now a member, the same as Niall is for Liam. They sit on either side of the two men, the rest of the Kings flanking down, with seats left for Viktor and me, and Luca, who is short his right-hand man for this meeting.

They've all been talking now for a long time, in circles, as men like this are often to do when they don't have an answer for the problem they're trying to address. This time, the problem is the alliance with the Santiago cartel, and the deal that Niall had made in exchange for trade with them.

"We agreed that I'd rescue Isabella and that we'd send men for backup," Niall says sharply, his voice rising. "I accomplished the first part. The Santiago cartel has opened up trade with us. We've been doing good business. So now we need to do the rest of our part."

"There won't be any fuckin' trade if the Gonzalez cartel decimates them," one of the older Kings says, slapping his hand down on the table. "I say we wait and see what happens."

"The entire point of sending men is to ensure that doesn't happen," Liam retorts. "We're supposed to be men of our word. We've waited too long already."

"We sent men. Half of them fuckin' died—"

"We sent a handful. A few from the Romano mafia, a few from the Kings, a few from the Andreyev Bratva. Nothing close to what we agreed. It's been too long—"

"Seems like a shit deal," another of the Kings speaks up. "Niall made that deal because he wanted the woman. He got what he wanted, and the rest of our men get what? Sent to their fuckin' deaths?"

"I made the deal to save her," Niall says tightly. "I didn't do it to make her mine. I wasn't interested in that, then. But her father wanted her saved, and Liam and Connor wanted an alliance. So I made that happen. Now you want to renege on our word, like Liam is saying? On *my* word?"

I feel Viktor glance at me, and I know what he's thinking—likely the same thing that I am. There's not likely to be an easy resolution to this. The only way that there will be one at all is if Connor puts his foot down as he so often does, and reminds the table that while his brother Liam might still prefer to run things as a democracy, he does not. He might not be the sort to favor men with money or family names to sit at the table over men who he feels have earned it, but he's also not a man to have his voice overruled if he decides he's come to a decision.

"Look," Liam says, his voice tight with an irritation that's rarely there in my experience, and speaks to the fact that he's also getting exhausted with the entire ordeal. "We have information that Diego Gonzalez is demanding Elena Santiago as payment. Her father is refusing. I don't think there's a man here who isn't aware of what consequences that's likely to have for the Santiago family."

"And that's our problem?" Another of the Kings speaks up sharply. "We've got our own families, too. If the Santiago cartel falls and the Gonzalez family takes more power, it's better if we're not on the losing side. What does that girl's marriage have to do with us? That wasn't part of the deal."

"*That girl* is my sister-in-law," Niall growls. "So I'd say at least someone at this table has a vested interest in what happens to her."

"That sounds like a personal issue."

"I don't agree that it's not our problem at all," Luca speaks up, his smooth, cultured voice rising above the others. "But I'd agree that we do have to think about our own families in this—the consequences of war with the cartels. I have my children; Viktor has his. Isabella is pregnant again, as is Saoirse. Ana and Liam have their child. There's hardly a man among us not married or with children of his own to think of, except Jacob, Levin, and a few others."

Jacob snorts. "I'll do what the McGregor tells me to, as I'm used to doing," he says roughly, his accent thickening. "But I'm hardly of a mind to think that I should be riskin' my neck for the girl just because I have no children of my own to come back to."

"If we abandon the Santiago cartel," Viktor says calmly, "we will have broken our word. That matters, gentlemen. Our word will be useless with the cartels going forward—and perhaps for others, too, if they hear about it. Furthermore, if we do send the kind of force that was promised to back up the Santiago cartel, it's entirely possible that they may be able to beat back Diego Gonzalez. We will benefit, in that case."

"And what if the Gonzalez cartel is a more likely bet?" one of the Kings calls out from further down the table.

"Diego Gonzalez is not the sort of man that I think most of us wish to ally with," Luca says calmly. "Now, I understand the reservations. But as several of us have said, we gave our word. I will provide men to go, from my mafia, along with those that the rest of you are willing to offer up."

"Elena needs to be removed from the situation," Niall says sharply. "She can't stay in the middle of what is effectively a war zone, when she's the prize to be won. We need to get her out of there and to safety. Here, to Boston."

"Is that you or your lass speaking?"

Niall glares at the King across the table from him. "It's me that's fuckin speaking," he snaps. "I'm not willing to leave the lass there. So we get her out when we send the men. That's my opinion."

"I'm inclined to agree." Liam glances at Connor. "I expect that you'll have something different to say, brother."

Connor frowns. "Surprisingly, no. I agree with Niall, as much as it pains me to say it. If Elena is left there, she's a card that Diego can play. All he has to do is get ahold of her, and he can use that to his advantage. We all know Ricardo Santiago will fold if his daughter is threatened–from experience." He looks at Niall, who shrugs.

"Aye, and it's not a negative character trait, in my opinion," Niall says dryly.

"Well then, who should go?"

The other Kings start to speak up at once, the voices rising in a din of conversation. "Niall!" is called out more than once, and there's a murmur of assent. "Aye, send him back. If he's so worried about his wife's sister, let him rescue the lass."

"Isabella is pregnant. Luca just said that."

All of the heads at the table turn towards me as I speak–the first time I've spoken up throughout this meeting–purely because it didn't seem to me that there was much for me to add.

"It's my opinion," I say coolly, glancing around the table, "that we do not send a man with a pregnant wife into what the rest of you have termed a 'war zone.'"

There's a moment's silence, and then one of the Kings gestures at me.

"Aye, and are you volunteering to go yourself?"

"I am."

The words come out before I'm entirely certain that I want to say them, but it's hardly a surprise–to me or to anyone else. I'm not inclined to take them back.

"Well, that's not unexpected," Connor says dryly. "If there were ever a man with a soft spot for damsels in distress, it's you, Volkov. You've already helped save Anastasia and Sasha. Are you going for the trifecta now?"

I refuse to take the bait, though I know he's doing his damnedest. Connor and I aren't enemies, but we're also not the best of friends.

"I'd agree with Jacob that no man should be volunteered for a job like this simply because he doesn't have a wife and children at home to come back to. An empty bed is still a bed most men would like to live to pass another night in. But I'm saying that, as a man without those things, I'll go, so another doesn't have to."

"Just to be clear, you're saying that–"

"I'll go to Mexico, extract Elena, and bring her back here to Boston, where she can be safe and with her sister. Is that clear enough?"

"Viktor, what do you think? It's your right-hand man who is volunteering himself." Connor glances at Viktor. "Is this something you find acceptable?"

"I think I can speak for myself." My tone is icy. "But by all means, run it past Viktor."

Viktor smirks. "I'm hard-pressed to send a man like you into danger, it's true," he says grimly. "But you're your own man, Levin. I'm not Vladimir, to tell you where to go and what to do, and where your loyalties should lie. If this is something you think you should do–" he gestures, shrugging. "Then I have no doubt you're the best man for the job."

"Niall?" Connor glances at him. "You'll trust Volkov with this task?"

Niall nods. "Aye, of course. I'd trust him to have my back any fuckin' day, and I'd trust him with Elena, for certain."

"Well then." Connor looks around the table. "It's settled then, men? We send backup to the Santiagos, and Levin uses that opportunity to get Elena out and back here to Boston. We'll inform Ricardo of the plan shortly before he arrives, so he's aware."

There's a murmur of assent, and I can see relief on Connor's face, as well as most of the others. It's been a long day, and it's good to have the matter settled.

It's not until I'm back in my hotel room, alone with a glass of vodka that I'm able to really think about what it is that I've signed myself up for–the job that I've agreed to do.

I know that it's nothing that I'm not capable of. It's dangerous, but I've done more dangerous things. It's more the impulse that concerns me, the way I'd spoken up before I'd even really considered whether I wanted to be taking on this job.

Connor was right, of course. I've long had a knee-jerk reaction to women in need of help–especially a woman as young and innocent as Elena Santiago. I'd gamble that there are not many who would deserve Diego Gonzalez as their fate, but I feel confident that she doesn't.

Still, it *was* an impulse, and one that will take me back to a place that I'd thought I wouldn't return to.

It was one thing to go to Greece, to Tokyo, to Paris in search of Anastasia, when Liam needed help finding the woman he loved. It was one thing to go back to Moscow to try and help Max save Sasha, to follow them to Italy and back to Santorini. But Mexico–

There are plenty of countries with memories of her, both good and bad. Moscow was the worst–but Moscow had been my home long before her. Tokyo, too, was a place where I can't shake her ghost, even if I wanted to. I'd gone there because I'd had to, because I was already on the hunt, and it was too late to turn back.

It's hard to say where I'd fallen in love with Lidiya, exactly. But I know of all the places that I'd least wanted to return to, to revisit the ghosts of the past; Mexico was the one that came to mind first.

"You'd want me to help." I lay on my back, looking up at the ceiling as I tip the glass of vodka to my lips, an old familiar ache filling me at the memory of her. "You're the reason I keep doing this. I see you, always. Needing me."

Blonde hair and blue eyes. A laugh that could lift a man's spirits in the worst of times, a sharp wit, and a sharper attitude. Words that could cut to the bone or ripple like silk over the skin. Desire so strong it hurt.

Happiness and grief, in equal measure.

I know it's been too long for me to still talk to her aloud like this, in the dark silence of the night. Too often, I make sure that there's someone else in the bed with me, so I don't have to remember. So that there's no silence to fill.

So that I can pretend that I'm a young man again, before I met her. So I can imagine that all of that is still yet to come.

All of the love and all of the pain. A pain so strong that sometimes, I wonder if I might have never done it at all, if I'd known how much it would hurt.

And then I remember her, every moment–on white hotel sheets and crisp golden sand, on a moonlit Tokyo night with drops of water from the onsen clinging to her skin. I know I'd do it all again, no matter how much it broke me.

No matter how clearly it divided my life in two–into the man I was before Lidiya Petrovna, and who I was after.

Elena

I know that things must be bad when my breakfast is sent up to me in my room, instead of my going downstairs for it. One of the maids brings it, looking pale and nervous, and leaves it by my bed. I catch a glimpse of José outside the door as she leaves, grabbing the maid's arm as he whispers something to her in a low voice.

The atmosphere in the house is tense, like thunderclouds gathering before a storm. I can feel it even from inside my room, like a low hum that sets my teeth on edge and makes me feel fidgety and unable to concentrate on anything, even one of the new books I had delivered a few days ago.

I spend some of the morning pacing, picking at the food on my tray, and opening my bedroom window to try and get some kind of breeze, as the room gets hot and stuffy with the warmth of the oncoming afternoon. I find myself starting to wish *something* would happen just to break up the monotony.

If Isabella were here, we would have snuck out to the garden by now. She could never stand being cooped up like this, and she would never have listened to the supposed need to stay where she'd been put. But without her, I don't have the gumption to sneak off on my own.

So I stay in my room, growing steadily and steadily more anxious, until I hear a sharp knock at my door. I know it's my mother before she even opens it and walks in—I know how she knocks after all these years, quick and impatient, as if she resents even that much of her time being taken up.

"Your father wants to see you, Elena," she says stiffly. I know that she hasn't forgiven me for last night–or for not begging my father to send me to Diego to make up for Isabella failing to become his wife. "He asked for you to come down to his office."

"For what?" I stand up, feeling my stomach tighten into a knot, and she purses her lips.

"Well, he didn't tell *me*," she says archly, stepping back out of the doorway. "Just come along. And try to do as you're told."

She doesn't say another word to me all the way down the stairs and to the doorway of my father's office. It hurts, though I do my best not to let on. Neither Isabella nor I ever felt particularly loved by our mother. Still, she'd always treated me with a bit more affection. It feels as if I've lost even those crumbs now, and it makes my chest ache with a lonely, grasping pang.

"Try not to make things worse," she says dismissively as I walk into the office. I can tell, from the look on her face as I shut the door behind me, that she resents not being a part of whatever conversation my father wants to have with me.

"Elena. Come sit down."

My father is behind his long mahogany desk, looking as if he's aged even more than he had in the time since Isabella was taken. His forehead is lined, his mouth turned down, his eyes shadowed, and I could swear that there's more grey at his temples and in his close-trimmed beard than there was before.

I walk to one of the leather seats in front of the desk and sink into it, feeling a wave of anxiety. My father's office used to feel like a safe place for me, with the huge windows behind the desk that open out onto the garden with sunlight streaming through, the floor-to-ceiling bookshelves stuffed with books of all kinds, and the warm scents of leather and wood and vanilla tobacco suffusing every part of it. But now, all I feel is a heavy sense of foreboding, as if the oncoming storm has centered here, and I'm about to be swept up in it.

"I need to tell you something." My father rubs his hand over his mouth, more exhausted than I've ever seen him.

"Is it about Diego?" I try not to let my voice tremble, but I can't help it.

"In a way." He lets out a sigh. "You were eavesdropping at the door last night, Elena. You heard what I was talking to your mother about. We spoke about it on the way upstairs."

"Diego wants me as his wife, to make up for Isabella." The words come out rote and numb. "And *Mama* wants you to give me to him, so he stops harassing and attacking our family and shipments and home."

"That's the sum of it." He sits back in his chair, looking at me tiredly. "I'm sorry that you have to hear about these things at all, Elena. I'm sorry—"

"That I'm having to grow up so fast." I parrot his words from last night back at him. "I know. And you know that I'm twenty years old. I can handle it. Just tell me what's happening."

My father nods, his Adam's apple bobbing in his throat as he swallows hard. "There was a deal made, when that Irishman—Niall—went after your sister. We made an alliance with some of the mob families in the States for trade, and in exchange, they said they'd send us backup. Men, to help defend our position here."

A cold feeling drifts through my veins at that. "And they've backed out?"

"No, actually." My father's mouth twitches. "Though I thought they might. They're sending the men, as promised. And they're sending someone else with them–to get you out of here."

I stare at him, startled. "What do you mean?"

"You'll be going back to Boston with him. To stay with Isabella and her husband until all of this blows over–or for as long as you want."

"I'm leaving you? *Mama?*" My throat tightens instantly with emotion, and my stomach knots. The idea of going so far away sends a different kind of panic through me, especially knowing the danger that my home and family are facing right now. *What if I never see them again?*

"You'll be with Isabella. You'll be safe, and I know you've missed your sister–"

"Well, yes, but–"

I can feel tears welling up in my eyes, my chest constricting with grief. The thought of seeing Isabella again is a happy one–I *have* missed her, more than I could ever possibly express with words. But I don't want to leave my family. Even when I'd thought of who I'd marry one day, I'd always assumed I'd be close enough that I could see them often. I'd never imagined that I'd end up going so far away–and that I might not come back or that they might not still be alive when I do.

That the danger could be so great that they'd have to send me away.

"Can't I stay here? With the others they're sending, it'll be safer–" The tremor in my voice is stronger now, and I'm trying desperately not to burst into tears.

"Not safe enough." He looks at me, his expression sad. "Elena, *querida*, it's for the best. We'll see each other again, I promise."

He stands up then, walking around the desk to put his hands on my shoulders reassuringly. "Dealing with Diego Gonzalez, putting an end to this threat, Elena, is not going to be easy. If I know you're safe, far away from where he can get ahold of you and use you against me, I'll be able to better focus on the fight that's coming."

I can feel the tears starting to spill down my face as my father reaches for my arm, gently tugging me up out of the chair so he can wrap his arms around me in a hug. I lean into his chest, breathing in the scents of smoke and cologne, wishing more than anything that I could be a small child again, when he could hold me close, and I could believe that nothing bad would ever happen so long as he was there.

But I'm not a child any longer. I know what's coming for me–for all of us–and I know that none of it is good. I also know that as much as I hate it, as much as it frightens me, my father is right.

If I'm out of harm's way, it's one less thing for him to worry about. One less thing keeping him up at night.

"Don't cry, *querida*," he murmurs, brushing the tears away from my cheeks. "I know you're scared, Elena. But I've been promised that the man who is coming to get you is the best at what he does. He'll get you to Boston, and he'll make sure you're safe. And this will all be over before we know it, and then, if you still want to, you can home, *niña*."

I know the decision has been made. It's even clearer that it's been made that night at dinner, when my mother sits next to my father at the table with a sour, angry expression that tells me he's filled her in on the plan.

"It's a bad idea to send Elena to Isabella," she hisses at him as we sit there, me picking anxiously at my food as she sips her wine. "If Isabella had done her duty instead of running away and then running off with that man, we wouldn't be in this position. Isabella will be a bad influence on her."

"Niall is the reason that we have backup coming at all," my father says crisply. "So while yes, their elopement caused some–problems– it hasn't been all for nothing. Aside from the fact that, as far as I've been told, Isabella is happy. We have a grandchild, Lupé. Another one on the way, apparently, I was told when I spoke with them today."

"A son-in-law who barely brings anything to the table and two grandchildren far away from us. Hardly the illustrious match that we'd hoped to make for our oldest daughter." My mother wrinkles her nose. "However you try to dress it up, Ricardo, Isabella damaged this family. Now you want to send Elena to learn from her example?"

"I want to send Elena where she'll be safe."

"This threat wouldn't exist if she'd just marry—"

"Enough!" My father slams his palm down on the dining table, his jaw tightening. "I've made the decision, Lupé. Elena is going to Boston. I want her out of Diego's reach and out of harm's way. I'm not going to change my mind."

The rest of dinner is a tense, quiet affair. I excuse myself as quickly as I can after the dessert course, my stomach so knotted with anxiety that I barely ate anything. I hurry upstairs, going straight to my room, thankfully not seeing José before I'm inside. I don't think I can deal with his mood tonight, and despite how exhausted I am, I don't know if I'm going to be able to sleep.

When I do finally drift off, it's far from peaceful. I dream of gunfire and flames licking at the walls of the house, of screams and Diego's grinning face looming over mine. *You're going to be my bride, little one*, he whispers in my ear, his hands plucking at the front of my clothes, tugging them down as they start to roam, his hot breath on my face—

I jerk awake to that same feeling. Someone's hands are on me, warm breath against my cheek, and I freeze in place for a second in sheer terror before I realize that I'm awake and that it's not a dream.

For one chilling second, I think that it *is* Diego, that he's gotten into the house somehow, that it's his hands and mouth on me, ready to force me into being his.

Somehow, that thought catalyzes into action, flooding me with adrenaline as I buck wildly underneath the person holding me, kicking and slapping as I open my mouth to scream.

The instant that I feel a hard hand over my mouth, I know that it's not Diego. I hear a voice in my ear, murmuring quietly, and shock jolts through me.

"Lie still, little one," José murmurs, his lips brushing against the shell of my ear. "I thought I might take you to Diego and get a reward for everything I've lost trying to protect this fucking family. But if you please me, maybe I'll think of something else—"

"Fuck you!" I scream from behind his palm, the shriek muffled as I try to drive a knee into his stomach. His other hand is busy pulling the blankets down, grabbing at my nightgown as he tries to wrestle me into submission, but I'm determined not to make it easy for him. I twist my head, biting at his hand, and he yelps as my teeth sink into the side of it, jolting backward a little as he tries to pin me in place.

This time, I don't miss the opportunity to scream.

"Fucking *bitch*!" José grabs me by the shoulders, wrestling me upwards out of the bed. "Fine. I'm taking you to fucking Diego. You can enjoy losing your virginity to him, you little—"

"Don't fucking move."

A male voice comes from the door, and José freezes, his hands digging into my arms as he swallows hard.

"Let go of her, and I won't shoot you where you stand right now. You can try pleading your case to *señor* Santiago, though I don't think it'll help you."

There are already footsteps moving into my room, other guards striding in to grab José as he hesitates, pulling him away from me. I snatch the blankets back up, covering myself as they haul him cursing out of the room, almost at the point of hyperventilating as I sit there in stunned shock. It had all happened so fast that I still barely have time to process it all.

I press one hand to my chest, trying to catch my breath as the sounds of the guards dragging José downstairs drift up to me, trying not to burst into hysterical tears. I'm shaking all over, and I nearly jump out of my skin when I hear footsteps at the door, before I realize a second later that it's my mother coming into the room.

"What happened?" she asks crisply, pulling her robe tighter around her as she walks to the edge of my bed. She reaches for the light, flicking it on as she scans me quickly. "What did that boy do?"

From the expression on her face, I can instantly tell that what's going through her head isn't sympathetic or anything to do with how to give me the comfort I desperately need at this moment. I know she's still hoping that my father might change his mind and give me to Diego, and in the same vein, she's worried that José might have damaged my value for that in some way.

"He didn't get far, if you're worried about whether or not I can still be sold off for my virginity," I tell her crossly, wrapping my arms around myself as I try to calm the chattering of my teeth. "He just got his hands on me, that's all. Nothing serious."

"Consider yourself very fortunate, then." Her jaw tightens as she looks down at me. "If you'd do what the family needs, Elena, you wouldn't be in these positions. You'd already be at Diego's, preparing to be his wife, and José would never have gotten his hands on you."

"You're blaming *me* for this?" I stare at her. "I was *sleeping—*"

"I can't believe I have two such ungrateful daughters." My mother's hands flutter in front of her, her lips pressed thinly together. "Your duty was always to marry to help this family, as was Isabella's. But neither of you is willing to do what needs to be done. So now you're going to abandon us—"

"What will happen to him?" I interrupt her, forcing the words out past the lump in my throat. "José. What will happen?"

"He'll be killed, most likely," my mother says crisply. "For touching one of the Santiago girls. As he should be. But that doesn't change the fact that if you'd done as you were told—"

"No one told me to marry Diego." The words sound strangled as they come out. "He asked for me, and *Papa* said no. So what am I supposed to do? Go there myself and offer to marry him?"

"You should have told your father that you wanted to do your duty." She glares down her nose at me. "But it doesn't matter now. The best we can do is hope that nothing is said about this, regardless of what happened, and that your father has a change of heart before this man comes and takes you back to Boston." She sniffs, crossing her arms over her chest. "I'd make the arrangements with Diego myself, if I didn't think your father would kill me for it."

"You wouldn't," I whisper, staring at her in shock. "You wouldn't do that—"

"Oh, stop acting like you're being sent to a firing squad. A woman's job in this world, in families like ours, is to marry and have children. That's all there is to it."

Someone shouts my mother's name from downstairs, and I see her mouth form a thin line again. "Go back to sleep, Elena. Consider yourself lucky that someone got up here before it was too late."

Of course, there's no chance that I'm going to be able to sleep again. I sit there, huddled in the middle of my bed, trying to stop the tears and the shaking as I hear her footsteps recede down the hall.

I know I should stay in my room. But when the house falls silent again, I can't stop myself. I slip out of bed, tossing on a robe and wrapping it tightly around myself as I quietly creep out of my bedroom door, slinking down the hall to the stairs.

I'm not sure why I feel like I need to know. It's not my fault that José attacked me; I know that much, regardless of whether or not my mother might like to paint my failure to agree to marry Diego as the cause of my being here for it. But I feel an overwhelming, morbid curiosity. I sneak downstairs and out into the courtyard, keeping to the shadows until I hear voices.

My blood runs cold as I hear my father's voice, stern and commanding. I crouch down behind one of the large SUVs parked in the courtyard, peering around it as I see several of my father's security dragging José out into the middle of the courtyard just before they force him to his knees in the dust.

I shouldn't feel any sympathy for him at all. He attacked me, and I know what awful things he would have done to me, even if he hadn't taken me to Diego. And who knows what would have happened if he'd tried to keep me for himself? He might have sold me off to another cartel when he got bored of me, or worse. There's no telling, but none of it would have been good.

He'd wanted to hurt me. There's no forgiveness for that, not really. But I've known José for years, laughed with him, been teased by him and teased back, pulled pranks on him with Isabella, and clumsily flirted with him. I thought I could trust him. Our father had always trusted him with guarding Isabella and me, with our *lives*, and the thought that that trust had been misplaced makes me feel sick, betrayed.

I see my father hold out his hand, and I clap a hand over my mouth as I see one of the guards hand him a gun. He pushes the muzzle against José's temple, and I swallow hard as I see José glare up at him defiantly. I expect him to ask for mercy, to beg my father not to kill him, but he doesn't say a word.

"What," my father says, his voice deadly quiet, "made you think that you could put your hands on my daughter and get away with it?"

"My brother is dead because of her and her sister," José hisses. "He died protecting your rotten family. So fuck off, Santiago."

"If that's the way you feel, then I'm sure you won't object to joining him, then."

When the gunshot goes off, I nearly scream. I stare with wide, horrified eyes as José's body slumps to one side, falling into the dust as my father hands the gun back, staring down at the lifeless body.

A part of me wishes I hadn't seen it. And the other is glad that I did.

I understand now, just how dangerous the situation has become. I understand exactly how dire it is, that there's no one I can really trust now except my own family–and after what my mother said, maybe not even that.

There's no choice for me, except to do what my father has told me to–and maybe there never was.

I have to go to Boston.

Levin

The travel to Mexico is made slightly better by the fact that we get to take the Kings' private jet, which all of the men going with me for Santiago's backup find to be an excellent way to sweeten the deal they've been made a part of. I keep to myself for most of the flight, tucked away in a window seat with a book, trying to calm my mind before we arrive.

I don't know how difficult it will be to get Elena out. It might be as easy as leaving with her after I meet with her father, or it might be a fight, depending on what moves the Gonzalez cartel is making.

I've tried not to think about Lidiya today. I don't want to remember the night on the beach in Mexico, the waves crashing behind us as she'd kissed me standing in the sand, the way her hands had felt on me, the way we'd ended up in the sand together before we'd realized what we were doing, and gone back to my hotel.

It had been our first time, something that had been building and building, a spark that turned into a conflagration of dangerous desire. I'd known what it could cost us both, and I'd done it anyway. And if I'd known how it would end–

When I drift off to sleep on the plane, I dream of her. It's impossible not to when she feels so close right now.

Her hands in my hair, palms smoothing over the side of my face, her lips finding mine eagerly. Her body arched against mine, the sound of her laughter in my ear as we'd tumbled into bed, feeling as if we were protected there, as if the danger only miles away was a universe away instead. As if love alone could protect us from all the evils of the world.

I should have known better. I did *know better. Even in my dreams, I know better. I kiss her lips to stop myself from saying the words that I know I should–that she should go back to Grisha, that I can't mix business and pleasure, that the danger loving me puts her in isn't worth the happiness it could bring us both. That I wish more than anything that someone else had been sent to pick her up that day in the train station, and that, at the same time, I wouldn't change it for the world–because loving her had changed me in every way, because only I would have kept her safe, even as I've endangered her every day since with wanting her.*

I see her, beautiful and slender and, in my view, the most magical thing I've ever seen as she walks towards me in our quiet room in Tokyo, the scent of flowers and fresh breeze coming through the open window as her warm, damp skin presses against mine, as we tangle together in clean white sheets, sheets covered in–

–blood. So much blood. The dream darkens, twists, and I'm standing in my own house, in my own bedroom, staring down at sheets meant to be clean and white, sheets that she'd picked out because she said they reminded her of all the hotel rooms we'd ever made love in, sheets now drenched in so much blood that I don't know how it could have all come from one body.

Her body, opened up, the dream we'd so briefly shared murdered along with her. I can't make sense of what I'm seeing, the carnage, the horrifying sight of it all, even as a man who has seen more horrible things, more blood, more carnage than most.

Sunlight on her diamond ring, on the blood, on her face. She's beautiful, even in death. So fucking beautiful that it hurts, and I go to her, reach for her, because I know that very soon I'll never hold her again–

I jerk awake in my seat, jaw clenched so hard that it hurts, my chest seizing with a pain that's years old, but still feels fresh and new. I've never been able to kill or drink or fuck it away, no matter how hard I've tried, and *fuck*, I've tried.

I can hide from it, for a little while. But it always comes back.

There's still vodka in the glass sitting next to me, left when I fell asleep, and I reach for it, draining it in one deep drink as I close my eyes. *I can't think of you right now, Lidiya. I can't miss you. I can't afford to be distracted here. Not when this job is so important.*

She'd want me to do my job well; I know that. To protect the innocent girl that I'm going to be entrusted with. To keep her safe.

I'm glad when we finally land. I can focus on work, on putting one foot in front of the other until I can finally leave with Elena, get her back to Boston, and return to the familiar routine that enables me to live my life.

There are several black SUVs with tinted glass waiting to take us to the compound. I slide into one, watching the landscape pass by as we drive, already counting the hours until I can be back on a plane, headed back in the direction from which I came.

There's a handful of places in the world I don't want to go back to, but this one especially.

I have a bad feeling lingering in my gut about all of this, but I try to shrug it off. *It's the memories, that's all. There's no reason to think this job will go bad. All things considered, it's fairly straightforward.*

The minute we get to the compound, I'm escorted directly to Ricardo Santiago's mansion. As we approach, get out of the SUVs, and walk to the house, I see the evidence of a recent attack–gunshot markings on the walls of the compound, bloodstains left in the sand, and shells that haven't been cleaned up yet. It speaks to the danger that they're all in. The uneasy feeling in my gut only strengthens, the instinct honed over many long years of work as an assassin and spy, setting off alarm bells all the way until I walk through the double doors of Santiago's office.

He's standing with his back to me when I walk in, the guard next to me stiffening and announcing in a loud voice, "Levin Volkov to see you, *señor*."

"Thank you. You can go."

Ricardo's voice is smooth and cultured, surprisingly calm for a man whose entire family and livelihood is being assaulted. He waits a moment, then turns to face me, and it's then that I can see clearly the toll that all of this has taken on him. He looks as if he hasn't slept in months–possibly not since Isabella was taken away.

"Things didn't look well outside," I say flatly. "Didn't do much for the morale of the men I brought here, I'll say that."

"There was another attack last night. A squad of Gonzalez' men. Not enough to make any real headway, which means he sacrificed some of his men just to make a point, just to let me know that he's not going to stop." A muscle leaps in Ricardo's jaw. "What kind of man does that?"

"Not a good one." I regard him from the other side of the room, my expression impassive. "I hope you have a plan. I'll let you know that the meeting of the Kings, the mafia, and the Bratva was a long one, and it was very close to sending no one at all. In the end, keeping their word prevailed, but–" I shrug, one-shouldered. "I don't think there will be a second wave of backup, Santiago."

"All the more reason for you to get my daughter out of here," he says tightly. "The rest, I'll deal with. But I want her out of harm's way. Diego wants her, and if he gets his hands on her, he knows I'll do anything to keep her safe. So he'll target her first."

"Of course. That's a common enough strategy. I'm surprised he hasn't gotten to her yet."

The muscle in Ricardo's jaw leaps again. "I've kept her as far out of harm's way as I can. But I can't do it forever. And the more worried

I am about her, the less I can focus on putting a stop to this war before it really gets started."

"From what I saw outside, it's already started."

"Diego is trying to frighten me into giving her up."

"Is it working?"

The two of us regard each other from across the room, and Ricardo lets out a breath, his hand rubbing over his mouth as his shoulders slump slightly.

"I'm not going to hand her over to him," he says firmly. "But I know what the cost of that will be. I need her safe, and that's why you're here."

"I'm surprised you'd trust me. A man you don't know. Why not send one of yours?"

"I need all of my men here. You're right that I don't know you." His jaw clenches. "But what choice do I have? I made an alliance, and you're the one they sent. So this is what I have to work with. I looked into you, Levin Volkov. Your background. You're not what some might call a *good* man, but you're not without a sense of honor. So yes. I'm entrusting Elena to you."

The door opens then, and another guard walks in. "I brought her down, *señor*," he says crisply, and Ricardo nods.

"I've filled Elena in on the plan," he tells me. "It's not what she wants, exactly, but she understands the necessity of it. I thought it best for the two of you to meet before it's time for you to leave."

I turn as he finishes the sentence, just in time for the girl in question to walk into the room.

The first thing I'm struck by is her bearing. It's clear just by looking at her that she's frightened; I can see it in her eyes. She looks young, innocent, someone that's been sheltered and kept safe all her life, as one would expect from a cartel princess. But at the same time, I can see strength in her, too. She's doing her best to hide her fear, to keep her shoulders squared, her chin up, to meet whatever is coming head-on, rather than cowering from it. It's impressive, especially for someone who I'm certain has never faced anything like this before.

It's hard not to think of Lidiya when that comes to mind. She'd been faced with an impossible choice, a terrifying circumstance that she could have cowered from. But she'd been brave—in the face of me and all I represented, in the face of everything that had come after.

I hadn't been there when she died. But I have no doubt that she was brave then, too. Lidiya was always courageous.

Elena, the girl who walks into the room, is also stunningly beautiful. Thick, black wavy hair pulled back away from her tanned heart-shaped face, with deep brown doe's eyes and a figure just curvy enough that it would make any man ache to have his hands on her. I can see the resemblance to her sister, but there's something softer, sweeter about her. Isabella, the few times I've met her, has always given off an air of sultry defiance. But Elena has a gentler demeanor.

A man like Diego Gonzalez should never be allowed near her. The ways in which he would break someone like Elena would be unconscionable.

"Hello." She forces a smile, stepping up to greet me and holding out her hand. "I'm Elena Santiago."

"Levin Volkov." I take her hand, and it feels small and warm in mine, her fingers instinctively curling against my palm as if she trusts me already.

The moment I touch her, I'm seized with a not-unsurprising desire to protect her. It's not as if I didn't see it coming—Connor was right when he'd said I have a soft spot for innocent women in need of help, even if he'd meant it disparagingly, as if he were calling out a knight's complex. I'd taken the job precisely because I'd known I would be devoted to doing it well, as much or more so than anyone else.

But as I look at her face, into her soft dark eyes, it feels more like a need than a desire. The thought of her being hurt, of the Gonzalez boss forcing her into marriage, of *anything* happening to her that I could prevent, feels horrifying.

I've failed before, in the past. I won't fail this time.

"You're the one taking me to Boston?"

Her clear, musical voice cuts through my thoughts, making me realize I've been holding onto her hand for too long. I let go, clearing my throat as I take a step back and nod. "The Irish Kings and their associates sent me, yes. I'll be escorting you to your sister."

"Tomorrow evening," Ricardo speaks up. "If the meeting with Diego goes poorly."

I frown, glancing over at him. "You have a meeting set?"

He nods. "He asked to meet with me, to have a parlay of sorts. To try to come to terms. I agreed to meet. If we can find a satisfactory way to end this, then sending Elena to Boston might not be necessary. But I'm afraid that it's a long shot."

There's no real reason for me to disagree with him. If he chooses to keep Elena here, it's a danger and a mission that I don't have to deal with. But the moment he says it, I feel a knot in my gut, a surge of protective emotion rushing through me as I raise an eyebrow at him.

"That doesn't sound like a shot at all. Even if Diego agrees to terms that have nothing to do with marrying Elena, how can you expect that he'll keep his word? You're better off sending her to where she's safe."

Ricardo starts to speak, but Elena cuts him off, looking up at me with a defiant expression on her face.

"*I* want to stay here if I can. So if my father thinks that there's a possibility, *I* want him to explore that first. If there's no other option, then I'll go with you."

I try to keep my expression neutral, but I can't help but be impressed by her. It's easy for me to read others—years of training as a spy and assassin will do that—and I can hear the faint tremor in her voice, see the way her lips tremble slightly. She's afraid, but she's not collapsing from it. She's strong, despite how sheltered she's been all her life.

If given the chance, she'll be an incredible woman, if a man like Diego doesn't crush her.

"Are you finished telling me how to handle my affairs?" Ricardo asks dryly, and I turn back to him as he speaks. "I brought you here to hear the plan, to meet Elena, and prepare yourself to act accordingly. I'll meet with Diego tomorrow. If he remains on his current course of action and refuses to come to terms, then I will have no choice but to send my daughter with you on a plane to Boston tomorrow night." He pauses. "In the meantime, you're welcome here. There's plenty of room for guests, and I would invite you to eat dinner with us at our table tonight and stay here until tomorrow."

Personally, I would be more comfortable in a hotel, with absolute privacy and the peace that comes with that. But I'm well aware that I can't turn down the hospitality without being rude, so I nod, giving Ricardo Santiago a tight smile.

"Thank you. I appreciate your generosity."

"Well." He claps his hands together, his expression as tautly pleasant as mine. "If you want to get refreshed, one of the staff can show you upstairs. Dinner is at seven, and we'll be pleased to have you."

I know when I'm dismissed. I nod again, turning to walk past Elena. I catch her gaze as she glances toward me, and I see something in her eyes that I don't entirely understand. Curiosity, maybe, which I can understand. But there's a flicker of something else, too, an interest that piques mine—and instantly sets me on edge.

I'm curious about her, too, but I shouldn't be. I don't need to know anything about her to get her safely to Boston. All I need to do is my job.

I glance at my watch as I walk past her and out of the office, forcing myself to tune out the quiet sounds of her and her father talking as I leave. If I get upstairs and shower soon, I might have time for a short nap before dinner.

This time, with any luck, I won't dream.

Elena

I feel as if I'm waiting for the hammer to fall.

Dinner had been mostly silent, punctuated by my father attempting to make small talk with Levin, who had answered fairly perfunctorily. I can't get a good impression of him—if this taciturn personality is how he usually is or if he's uncomfortable being here. I know I shouldn't really care either way.

His job is to get me to Boston, if I have to go. My father trusts him to take care of that task, so I do as well. But I can't help but be curious about him.

It had shocked me how handsome I'd found him. I don't know what I'd expected, exactly. Someone older, maybe? Levin Volkov certainly isn't a *young* man—though I didn't see grey in his dark hair, he looks as if he's been around for a while, with a few lines around his sharp blue eyes, set in a chiseled face.

I tried not to look at him too often as we ate dinner, but all it did was make the tension I felt even more palpable. I didn't want to stare by accident, but I also wanted to take a good look at him. He'd shown up to my father's office in grey chinos and a black leather jacket, but for dinner, he swapped it out for more formal clothes–slacks and a charcoal button-down rolled up to expose muscled and tattooed forearms. He seems to be tattooed all over–I'd seen them extending down the backs of his hands and up the sides of his throat, and it made me wonder how much of the rest of his body was inked as well.

Which was a train of thought I did *not* need to go down.

I hadn't expected the man I was going to be entrusted with to be so attractive, plain and simple. He didn't seem like a boss, but not ordinary muscle, either. Something about the way he moved had a predatory grace, and I could sense, from the moment we were introduced, that there was something dangerous about him.

Something *exciting*.

I chastised myself all through dinner for it, telling myself I was being ridiculous. But now, as I go upstairs to my room after being excused, I still can't stop thinking about it.

He's handsome and dangerous and exciting, like a hero in a romance novel. So why wouldn't you fantasize about him? Just don't take it seriously.

I flop down onto my bed, letting out a sigh. I can hear the footsteps of the guard outside, someone who replaced José that I don't recognize. I wait for his steps to fade off and let my hand wander, tracing a path over my breasts through the thin dress and bra that I'm wearing, feeling my nipples stiffen instantly.

What happens if I go to Boston? Can I meet someone? Am I still expected to agree to some arranged marriage, eventually?

I've been a good girl all my life. I might have flirted with José or some of the other cute guards, or thought about what it would be like if I could choose my own husband, but I would never have gone as far as Isabella did. I've never been brave enough to take my own future into my hands like that, to decide that *I'm* going to choose the man I lose my virginity to.

I'd been jealous of her when I realized that she'd succeeded in that. When she managed not only to make her own choice–but to make him fall in love with her, too, and marry her. *Her* life had turned out to be every bit as exciting as she could have ever hoped it would be.

The only *good* excitement I can hope to have is inside the pages of a book.

I let out a sigh, letting my hand fall to the side, slapping against the duvet. My own fingers and a blurry fantasy isn't what I want tonight, and I know I won't be able to stop myself from Levin slipping into my thoughts–which is exactly what I don't need.

I'm not sure how long I'm asleep before a sound wakes me up–a sharp, repetitive cracking noise from outside, over and over again, combined with a rattle that makes me jerk awake and upright in bed, my heart pounding instinctively despite the fact that I have no idea what's actually happening.

And then I see the glow coming from outside, orange and red in the darkness.

I fling back the covers, leaping out of bed as I go to the window, pulling back the curtain to look outside.

Just beyond the house, the other buildings in the courtyard are on fire. I can hear shouts, and more of what I realize now is gunfire, rattling across the courtyard.

I catch a glimpse of men in black fatigues and leap backward, letting the curtain fall back into place as I retreat to the bed, my heart pounding. *What is happening?*

I already know before the thought even really has a chance to enter my mind. It's Diego. The meeting with my father was a ruse, a means to get him to drop his guard just a little, and now Diego has taken full advantage.

My home is under assault.

The fear is choking. For a moment, all I can do is freeze in place, wanting to hide underneath the duvet and disappear, as if that might change any of this. As if it could save me, or any of us.

The paralysis lasts for only a moment. Heart in my throat, I dart for my closet, flinging clothes aside in an effort to find something to put on that isn't my nightclothes or a robe. I grab one of the first things I find, a green short-sleeved cotton dress with a tie at the waist, and scramble out of the shorts and tank top I'd been wearing, leaving them discarded on the floor as I pull the dress over my head.

My mother would kill me for leaving my clothes in a mess like this.

The thought almost makes me laugh. There's much worse coming after me now. Something that would have yesterday felt like a cause to be anxious now feels absolutely ridiculous, in the face of what's happening outside.

There's another rattle of gunfire, this time closer to the house, and then I hear the sudden sound of hard banging from downstairs, from what sounds like the front door.

Fuck.

I swallow hard, unsure of what to do. I know what my father would tell me to do–to stay put until someone comes for me, but the fear rising up in my throat is almost unbearable. I feel like I'm going to implode from it, shatter into a million pieces, and it feels as if the only way to fight it is to *do* something.

I just don't know what.

There are screams from downstairs, feminine screams and a man's shout, and my chest cramps from how hard my heart is pounding. I creep towards the door, my hands shaking as I reach for the knob– and I hear gunfire downstairs.

What if my father is dead? What if he can't come to tell me what to do because he's dead? What if they're all *dead?*

There's a door in the wine cellar downstairs; I know that. An old exit, one made hundreds of years ago for an escape exactly like this, except I'd never thought it would be necessary to use it. I know where it is–my mother and Isabella and I all did, but Isabella and I always made a joke out of it. It seemed ridiculous that we would ever have to run from something so dramatically, underground like frightened rabbits.

Now, I'm not so sure.

I yank the door open with one sharp gesture, that spark of courage all I can summon for a moment. *Just hang on, and there will be another.* I try to breathe through my nose and out of my mouth, interrupted by every sound of gunfire from downstairs.

My mother will be at the stairs to the wine cellar. Down there already. She didn't come get me because–

I can't think of any reason for it that doesn't make me want to burst into hysterical tears. So instead, I force myself to stop thinking about it, to stop thinking about anything other than the next step forward, the next breath, the next spark of courage that can get me to the edge of the stairs and starting to go down, looking around wildly as I crouch low for anyone who might spot me and try to attack.

"Elena!"

I nearly scream before I realize that it's my father's voice. A wave of relief washes over me, so strongly that I'm almost dizzy, before there's the sound of more gunshots. I feel as if I'm about to come out of my skin all over again.

"Volkov, quickly!"

I see Levin appear behind my father; his face is taut and determined, his jaw set as he steps quickly up the stairs, reaching for my arm. "We've got to get out of here, Elena," he says calmly, and I look up at him, feeling slightly dazed.

There's a smear of soot on his jaw, and a red mark on his throat, as if someone clawed at him with fingernails. However, he still has that devastatingly quiet danger about him that sparked my curiosity earlier, that would make my heart race if it weren't already beating at full capacity. His hand closes around my upper arm, broad and strong but gentle, and he tugs me carefully towards the side of the stairs that will lead me around my father and down. "We need to go," he repeats, and I shudder, twisting around to look at my father.

"No, I can't! I can't leave you—"

It had been bad enough to imagine leaving when we'd spoken about it yesterday or the day before, when the sun had been shining brightly enough to wash away the memories of the guerrilla attacks from Diego's men, José's attack on me, or the countless threats that have come our way since Isabella ran away with Niall. Now, with parts of my home on fire and the sound of gunfire in my ears, a look of fear on my father's face that he can't entirely hide, it feels impossible.

"Elena. *Querida.* You have to." My father reaches for me, briefly pulling me out of Levin's grasp as he puts his hands on my arms gently, looking at me with the expression of love that I've grown so used to over the years, trusted so deeply. "You're not safe here. You know that. Volkov will get you out. You can trust him, but you *must* do as he says. Do you understand me?"

My throat is so choked with tears that I can't speak. All I can do is shake my head, a wordless plea not to be sent away, and I see my father's face fall as he pulls me into his arms, embracing me tightly.

"*Querida,* please. Don't make me watch another of my daughters go to the hands of a man like Diego, or worse. Please go."

He leans back, stroking my hair with both hands as he looks into my eyes. "*Joya,* I love you. I'll see you again, I swear. But I need to know you're safe."

He stands, passing me off to Levin as he starts to walk back down the stairs, two at a time, and I see with a sudden shock that there's a gun in his hand. Somehow that chokes me up even more, knowing that he's going into danger, defending himself and the others in the house, in the compound, and I can feel tears streaming down my cheeks.

I want to be sick. I feel alternately numb and as if my entire body is vibrating with fear. It takes me a minute to realize that Levin's hand is gently on my arm again, guiding me down the stairs.

"You'll be safe," he says, his voice full of a calm reassurance that I find astounding in the present situation. "Your father told me where to go. All will be well, Elena–"

There's another burst of gunfire, and Levin spins, pushing me behind him as he levels a gun that I never even saw him reach for. I clap a hand over my mouth to muffle a scream, freezing in place as I watch him scan the area around us, head turning slowly before he lowers the gun and nudges me in the direction that I know leads towards the wine cellar.

"Quickly," he says, staying just slightly behind me. "We have to get out of here."

From the corner of my eye, I see the doorway that leads into the formal living room, and the flicker of flames from just beyond it. My entire body tightens with fear, and I feel myself shrink closer to Levin instinctively as I realize that the house itself is being set on fire.

"Stay close to me," he says tersely. "You'll be safe."

Somehow, despite the fact that I met him only yesterday, I believe him. It's something about the way he holds himself, the calm confidence with which he moves, looking around every corner and gauging our next steps before he guides me forward. His hand touches the small of my back, urging me towards the stairs that lead down to the wine cellar, and I feel a jolt go through me.

No one has ever touched me like that before. No one would have ever dared–except José, and that was nothing like this. I feel my breath catch in my throat for an entirely different reason, but before I can think too much about it, Levin is gently pushing me forward.

"The fire is going to spread. We need to move."

The words are terrifying, but his voice is so calm, so certain, that it doesn't inspire the kind of horror that I would have thought.

"Keep moving, and we'll be fine, Elena. I've got you."

I've got you. I feel a pinpoint of calm in my stomach, spreading outwards. I have a brief moment to wonder if that's normal or if I'm somehow going into shock, before I suddenly feel Levin push me forward a little harder and the swift movement of him spinning to face away from me.

The sound of the gunshots deafens me for a moment. I let out a surprised shriek, and I only know what Levin shouts to me because I see the motion of his mouth as he yells out, *"Run!"*

This time I don't hesitate. I get one glimpse of bodies on the stairs before I bolt for the wine cellar door, fumbling madly with it before I rush inside, leaving the door ajar for Levin.

Dimly, I hear footsteps behind me, and I hope they're his. I hope so even more when I hear the door slam, and I turn just as I reach the trapdoor at the back of the cellar, heart in my throat as I wait to see who is going to come around the row of shelves.

What do I do if it's not him? I don't have a weapon. I don't think I could punch anyone. I know I should go down the trapdoor and out into the escape, but if I go alone, what then? Without Levin, I have no idea where I'm meant to go after I emerge. Only he knows the rest of the plan–I just knew that I was supposed to go with him.

A shape lunges from around the tall shelf, burly and male, and I know in an instant that it's not Levin. I scream, staggering backward, away from the trapdoor in hopes that he won't notice the escape route, that I can somehow–

Somehow what? Where is Levin? Is he dead already? What kind of protector did they send if he's already–

The man is lurching towards me, a cruel smile twisting his mouth as he reaches out, his eyes dark with violence and lust. "Come here, pretty bird," he growls, his tongue running over his lower lip. "Boss says you come back untouched, but I think I can have a taste—"

Memories of José's attack flood me, turning my blood to ice, and I fumble numbly behind me for something, anything to use as a weapon. Anything to keep this man's hands off of me, to give me just a moment to escape–

My hand closes around a wine bottle, and I bring it forward, smashing it hard against the side of the man's face. He yowls in shock and pain, and before he can recover, I grab for another one, smashing it just as hard as I push past him, running back for the trapdoor. All thoughts of waiting for Levin are forgotten, and all I can think is that I have to get out. That I have to get away.

The man rounds the corner after me, face bleeding with shards of glass stuck in his face as he shouts incoherently at me, reeling. Terrified, I grab for another bottle, darting backward as I throw it directly towards his head.

The bottle shatters against his arms as he throws them up, liquid splashing across the floor. I watch in horrified fascination as he slips, crashing to the ground with an awful sound as he lands on shattered glass.

I don't wait to see what happens next. I turn and bolt for the trapdoor, adrenaline flooding me–and then I hear another gunshot behind me.

Quickly, I pivot, darting into one of the rows of shelves as I grab for another bottle of wine in each hand. Holding them aloft, ready to fling, I round the corner, only to hear a familiar voice call out to me.

"Elena! Stop, it's me!"

My entire body is shaking. I freeze in place the instant I hear Levin's voice, and I can't move, relief flooding me as I see him step over the now-dead body of the man who had attacked me, striding towards me quickly.

"Easy there," he says in that same calm and soothing tone, reaching for the bottles in my hands. He takes them away, turning one so he can see the label. He grins down at me.

"That's a rare vintage right there. Can't go breaking that over anyone's head."

Something about the combination of the easy smile on his face in the midst of so much chaos and the joke breaks something loose in me. I feel myself go limp, my muscles giving way as my knees turn to water, and I start to sink to the floor.

"Hey! Easy there."

He reaches for me instantly, scooping me up with one arm as he holds the gun in his other hand, glancing behind us. "Let's go. We're almost out."

"My parents—"

"I don't know," he says honestly. "But your father is a tough man, Elena, and a brave one. I'm sure he's doing his best to stay safe and keep your mother safe too."

It's not exactly reassurance, but I find to my surprise, that I appreciate it. He's not lying to me, not pretending that everything is fine when it very well could not be. He'd delivered the truth in the easiest way possible, and I look up at him, feeling soothed despite myself.

"You can put me down," I tell him, as calmly as I can manage. "I can walk. I'm fine. I just had a moment, that's all."

"Are you sure?" He's already backing towards the trapdoor, gun still half-raised, ready to shoot at any moment. "I can carry you. It's no trouble."

Of course, it's not. I can feel how strong he is, his muscled arm wrapped around me, holding me against his chest as if I were a feather. Truthfully, I want nothing more than to curl against him, to hide my face in his shirt and block everything out. He smells of warm skin, clean laundry, and the hint of a salty, citrusy cologne that lights a spark somewhere deep inside of me, one that I don't have the time or energy to investigate too closely.

But I also don't want to be the damsel in distress, carried out of danger. I want to stand on my own two feet.

My sister was brave enough to fight back against Diego Gonzalez, against the bride tamer, against every expectation held for her. I can be brave enough to walk out of here on my own.

"I'm sure," I manage, and Levin hesitates briefly, then nods.

"Far be it from me to tell you what to do," he says with a half-grin, as he nods towards the trapdoor. "Go. Get a headstart, and I'll follow, make sure no one is coming after us."

I swallow hard, moving quickly towards it. I undo the latch, hauling it up as I grab the ladder, scaling it downwards as fast as I can without falling. I've always hated ladders and had very few occasions to be on one, except when I needed a book from a very high shelf in the library–and those ladders are attached much better than this one is.

I don't feel as if I can breathe again until I get to the bottom. When my feet hit hard ground, I back up, watching for Levin to descend after me. I see him at the mouth of the trapdoor a moment later, glancing back once more before he starts to follow me down.

We're alright. We must be.

I hardly have that thought before I hear a door slamming from above and more footsteps.

"Bladya!" Levin curses in Russian, and something about the harsh bite of it sends that spark flickering through me again, in the instant

before he leaps down to the ground in front of me, turning that cool blue stare onto me and making a shiver ripple down my spine.

"Run, Elena."

His tone is flat and emotionless, and somehow that makes it worse. I try to swallow past the lump in my throat as I turn and run headlong down the long, underground hallway, fighting back tears of panic as I do. I've never been so terrified in all my life. I can hear footsteps, what sounds like more than just Levin's, but I don't dare look back.

I hear shouts, cursing in Spanish, and I grit my teeth, forcing myself to keep going. I want to burst into sobs, crumple to the ground, and give up, but I can't. *I can't.* If I stop now–

A rough hand grabs me, spinning me around as I gasp. I see a tall man in fatigues leaning over me, lifting me up as he throws me over one shoulder, heading back the way I came. I can still hear the sounds of fighting, and I kick and scream, punching him in the back as I try to kick for his gut, his balls, his thighs, anything I can reach.

"*Mierda!*" The man curses as he tightens his hold on me, jabbing me in the side with the butt of his gun as he strides forward. "I can explain away a few bruises, *princesa*. Stop struggling, or I'll find an explanation for the boss as to why you're black and blue."

I'm not entirely sure I believe him–I don't think Diego Gonzalez is the type of man to pause to listen as to whether the bearer of bad news was the cause of it or not–but I'm also not sure that I want to test that theory. And in a moment, it doesn't matter, because as the man strides closer to the ladder, passing the fighting in the hall as I squirm in his grasp, I see Levin engaged in hand-to-hand combat with three other men.

"Elena!" He barks out my name, twisting sideways as he punches one of the men squarely in the nose, sending him down in a gout of blood. "*Bladya*, Elena!"

I'm no longer concerned with the beating I might receive. I kick and punch, twisting to try to bite the man holding me as Levin tries to disengage from the fight he's in, but he can't quite get away. I hear him cursing, see him wheel on the two men that are left, and I realize with a sudden, sickening certainty that he's not going to get to me in time.

The man tosses me down from his shoulder in front of him like a sack of potatoes, driving the muzzle of his gun sharply into my back. "Climb the ladder, *princesa*," he says sharply, and I whip my head around to glare at him.

"Or what? You can't kill me."

The man grins, the expression spreading across his face toothily until I feel sick. "No, I can't. But I can make you hurt. I can think of a few creative ways that the boss might not even know about. And I'll do it right here while you watch your Russian friend get beaten to death. Or, you can climb the ladder like a good girl, and you'll be in the comfort of your new home all the sooner, with far fewer bruises."

I doubt that Diego's home will offer me many comforts, at least until we're married. But I also don't believe that the threats are idle. I look back at Levin, who is grappling one man as another lunges at him from behind, and utter a brief, whispered prayer that I'm making the right choice.

I don't know what other choice I have, really.

If he makes it out of this, without a distraction from me, he'll come after me. Surely he will.

I swallow hard, nodding as I start to ascend the ladder. I want nothing more than to squeeze my eyes tightly shut, to cover my ears with my hands so that I don't have to hear the sickening sounds of the fight, but I need both my eyes and my hands to get out of here.

I'm no sooner back up on the cellar floor than the man hoists himself up behind me, scooping me up and throwing me over his shoulder again. "I can *walk*!" I snap, driving my knee into his ribs, and I'm rewarded with a swift jab of his hand in mine.

"Sure you can, *princesa*. But this way, I know for sure that I don't have to chase you." He glances towards three more men walking towards the trapdoor, guns in hand. "The Russian is still down there. Finish him off."

"No!" I scream, but a moment later, I see someone else coming towards me, another of the men in fatigues, a smirk on his face and a syringe in his hand.

I know what's going to happen before the needle even moves toward my neck. I scream, twisting in the grasp of my captor, but the man holding the drugs grabs my hair, twisting my head to one side as he slides the needle into my neck.

"Good night, *princesa*," he taunts, still smirking as I blink, my mouth turning to cotton.

And then everything goes dark.

Levin

This entire place has gone to fucking hell.

I've fought worse odds in my life than two-on-one, but when the other three men start making their way down the ladder, I begin to get a little fucking nervous.

Not just for myself, but for Elena.

I'm furious that one of them managed to get past me, furious that one of them managed to take her, and worried that I won't be able to put an end to the fight until she's already gone. I still think I can win it and get out of here with my life, but even that starts to look a little dicey when I see that all three of them are already aiming.

I duck as the first bullet flies, driving my fist up into the gut of the man in front of me. The one to my right dives in to grab me, but I manage to wrestle the other man's gun free of his hand as he doubles over, driving a second punch right after the first to keep him that way as I pivot to one side, aiming the gun at his head and hoping against fucking hope that there are enough bullets left to do what I need to do.

He drops when I shoot, and I swing around, feinting away from the gunshots coming from the three men at the base of the ladder. I've got a loaded gun again, and as long as that holds out, I've got a fucking chance of getting out of here.

I pull the trigger again, the bullet grazing the neck of the man next to me. Blood spurts out, spraying the wall, and as he pitches forward, I catch him, using him as a shield as another round of gunfire goes off, grabbing for his gun with my other hand.

The minute the bullets stop coming for a second, I whirl towards the other three, both guns aimed as I start to shoot, going towards them instead of away. They do exactly as I hoped, flinching momentarily at the realization that I'm walking *toward* their fire instead of running from it.

That moment is all I need. A pull of the triggers and two men drop. All that's left is the one, and he gets a shot off before I can, the bullet grazing my arm as it goes wide.

White-hot pain shoots up my arm, and I feel the warm spill of blood down my skin, but I know without looking that I've taken worse. I'll deal with it later, but at the moment, all I'm focused on is that last shot, the gun aimed at the man's face as it goes slack, realizing with horror that he doesn't have enough time.

That he's fucking done.

He drops, and I bolt for the ladder.

I don't know how many bullets are left, but I hope it's enough to get me out of here. I know before I've even reached the stairs of the wine cellar that Elena isn't down here any longer, that she might not even still be in the house. I have to move fast, or history is going to repeat itself, and another Santiago daughter will be in Diego Gonzalez's clutches.

I get to the top, pushing the door open a crack, and I'm instantly assaulted with the smell of smoke, the sound of further-off shouting, and the crackling of fire too close for comfort.

Fuck.

Going back through the house is too dangerous. The only real option I have is to go back the way I came, down the trapdoor and through the underground exit, and hope that Ricardo's information about where it leads is correct–past the outer wall of the compound, so I can regroup without running into any more of Diego's men.

I spin on my heel, rushing back down the stairs. There are no more footsteps, no sounds of more men coming towards the cellar door, and that tells me more than anything else that Elena is likely already gone. If they have what they'd come for, there's no reason to stay.

Quickly, I go back down the ladder, past the bodies I'd left, further down the hall. Guilt swamps me, cramping my gut as I clench my teeth, forcing back the thought pounding in my head–that I'd failed. I'd failed at what should have been a simple task.

Get the Santiago girl out. Get her to safety. I've done harder jobs. More dangerous jobs. Jobs that should have gotten me killed and didn't.

But this one has gone completely awry.

I keep going, all the way until I reach a dead end and another ladder, leading up to another trapdoor.

For fuck's sake, don't let this spit me out in the middle of the compound, surrounded by a dozen men.

That is precisely how my luck would turn out, based on how the night has gone so far.

To my relief, when I'm above ground again, I am about a hundred yards out from the outer wall of the Santiago compound. I can see black SUVs driving away from it, and I crouch down, watching them as the dust billows out from the tires, undoubtedly taking Elena with them.

Time to go.

If I'm going to follow them and try to find out what the hell Gonzalez's next move is, now is the time. They won't expect to be followed in the wake of the attack, and I'm relatively certain that they're expecting me to be dead. I'm also almost sure that Gonzalez has no reason to know who I am. As far as the attackers are concerned, I'm just another of Santiago's grunts. Meat to be put through the grinder on their way to Elena.

I have a motorcycle stashed a little ways out, and I head towards it, moving quick and low as I keep an eye out for anyone still patrolling the area, gun ready in my hand. My mind is already two steps ahead, thinking of what I will do after I reach the bike and how I will get the information I need. It comes as naturally as breathing after so long. It keeps me calm as I cross the distance, straddling it quickly as I do another quick sweep of the surrounding area and then turn the key.

The engine roars to life, and I put it into gear, pulling out onto the road in the direction that the SUVs went, giving enough space that there's not any chance of coming into their view. I can see the tail end of the last one, and I keep my headlight off, relying on the faint light from the moon to get me where I need to go without crashing. It's not safe by a long shot, but the likelihood of anyone else being out on these roads is low, and I'm more concerned with being spotted by Gonzalez's men.

It's a long drive to the compound. I hang back as far as I can without losing them, and when I see the SUVs start to approach the driveway leading to the gate, I turn off the road, stashing the motorcycle and grabbing my bag so I can sneak to the walls and hopefully get in.

Over the years, I've learned a simple rule when it comes to missions like this–ones that involve spying especially–plan for what could go wrong, but don't think about it while you're in the middle of it all.

It's served me well, and I'm still alive, so I see no reason to change it up now.

I make it to the edge of the wall undetected and skirt along the side, looking for some way in that isn't over. I don't know Gonzalez's patrols like I would if I'd been able to do reconnaissance, so going over is a last resort. It's just as likely to leave me in the middle of a patrol squad as it is home-free.

I'm nearly all the way around the back of the compound when I find a thin gap, covered by a barred gate that is just barely wide enough for me to fit through. I have no idea what it's fucking used for, but it's the best shot I have at getting in.

I crouch down, peering through to see if there are any patrols nearby. No one is within my sightline for now, so I rummage in my bag, pulling out a torch and bolt cutters, and set to work.

It's not the quickest method, but it works. Like the rest of this, it's second nature. When the metal is hot enough, I cut through it with the bolt cutters, snapping it cleanly off and carefully removing the gate and setting it aside. They'll know someone broke in, but it's not as if things can get any hotter for the Santiago family.

Slowly, I slip through the opening, moving forward quickly and quietly as I approach the main house. I have no idea where Elena might be—or, once again, the layout—and I'm cursing myself inwardly for going along with the Kings' and Santiago's plans without giving any input of my own. I've been working with Viktor, who I trust implicitly, for too long. If I'd come sooner, I might have been able to do some recon in the event that things went pear-shaped—exactly as they have.

And then, I have a stroke of luck at last.

I catch sight of a group gathered near the front of the house. I see a flash of long dark hair, and I realize that it's Elena, struggling against the men holding her as a corpulent man with greying hair approaches.

"*Bastard!*" she spits out as he gets closer—literally. I see her spit in his face, and in the next instant, his hand flashes out, striking her cheek hard enough to fling her head sideways.

I expect her to slump back then, but she tilts her chin up, glaring ferociously back at him as he crosses the last steps towards her, paying enough attention only to her that I'm able to move closer, keeping hidden by the hedges near the house as I listen carefully for whatever it is that he might say to her, anything that might give me a clue as to what his next move is.

"Your sister tried these same tricks," he hisses, reaching out to grab her chin firmly in his hand as he glares down at her. "She was just as defiant. So defiant, in fact, that I sent her to the bride tamer to learn how to be a proper wife."

"And how did that work out for you?" Elena's retort is partially muffled by his grip on her chin, but she gets the words out anyway, still giving him the same furious expression. "She's not here now."

"No, she's not." He smiles cruelly. "Which is why you are. But you're not going to take her place at my side and in my bed as my wife."

Elena falters the tiniest bit. I can catch a glimpse of the confusion on her face, and Diego has a front-row seat to it. His smile widens, and I feel in that moment as if I would give anything to be able to punch it off of his face without consequences.

"I don't understand." Her voice shakes the tiniest bit. "You told my father you wanted to marry me."

"I did." His smile doesn't falter. "But then your father decided to make things difficult for me. He decided to attempt to force my hand, refusing to give you over. He was stupid enough to think that I would actually attempt to meet with him to come to terms, as if I would give that insolent *perro* an inch. So a greater punishment is needed, I think."

Elena's face goes ashen, and I grit my teeth, forcing myself to stay still. It takes everything in me not to bolt out of my hiding spot and towards her, to shoot every single one of the fuckers who have their hands on her right now, and Diego Gonzalez too, for whatever fucked-up thing he's about to say to her. But I know how that ends.

It ends with me dead, and probably her too. There are more men here than I could hope to take on my own. If I'm going to get Elena out, it'll have to be by other means.

But first, I need to know what Diego is planning.

"I'm not going to marry you at all," he continues, with an edge of pride to his voice, as if he's thrilled to be unveiling his plan to her at last. "I'm going to keep you here for a day or two, until all my friends and associates can get here. The richest men I know."

He leans in a little closer to her, and I have to strain to try to hear what he's saying, but I manage to make it out, just barely.

"I'm going to throw a massive party for them. I'm going to auction you off, along with the other women I have held for sale—but they won't hold a candle to you, *bonita*. You'll be the centerpiece of the entire affair—and that will be my revenge on the Santiago family for refusing me not one, but *two* brides."

He grins so widely that I think it might split his face as he steps back, surveying her horrified expression. "I trust you're still a virgin, though I'll have someone check. You'll make me rich—richer than I already am," he adds with a curt laugh, "and I'll break the Santiago family in the bargain. Your father will never recover from this."

Diego nods to the men then, and they push her forward, not towards the main house, but towards the left of it—the direction that I came. I shrink back into my hiding place, wishing that I could signal to her somehow that I'm here, that I know what's happening to her, and that I'll do my best to help.

But it will help no one if I'm caught.

I wait until they pass, making note of the building where they're taking her, and until Gonzalez and his personal security have retreated into the house. When the coast appears to be clear, I retreat back the way I came, making my way out through the gate. I force it back into place—someone will eventually look at it and see the marks where it was cut, but it will be a while.

I let out a breath as I retreat from the compound, watching for any sign that I've been spotted as I go. This is the easiest part—all I have to do is get back to the motorcycle, and I'm free to return to the Santiago mansion—or what's left of it.

What's left of it is an apt description, when I reach the gate. Smoke is still billowing from a number of buildings, including the main mansion, and there are bodies everywhere. Santiago's men are working to clean up, and I walk past them, picking my way through the courtyard until I find Ricardo near the mansion, trying to soothe his sobbing wife, who is sitting on a low wall near some shrubbery with her robe wrapped tightly around herself.

"If you'd just given Elena to him in the first place—" I hear her say in a low, shaking voice, and I grit my teeth against the retort that I want so badly to say.

Ricardo turns as he hears my footsteps, glancing back quickly at his wife. "I'll be back, Lupé," he says quietly, then strides towards me, his face taut and anxious.

"Elena isn't with you?"

I shake my head. "They got her away from me after we were already underground."

"I saw them leaving with her, but I couldn't get there in time." The guilt wracking Ricardo's face and voice make mine pale in comparison. "I'd hoped you might have—"

"They were already at Gonzalez's compound before I could get to her." I let out a breath. "I managed to get information, though. I know what he has planned for her."

Without waiting, I plunge into the explanation, telling Ricardo exactly what I'd heard Diego say to Elena. His face goes more and more ashen as I speak, until he's looking at me in a stunned silence.

"Maybe Lupé was right," he says quietly, when he can manage to speak again. "Maybe I should have given her to him when he asked at first."

"No," I tell him curtly, my jaw tightening. "You should have let me leave with her earlier today when I arrived, instead of putting it off for a meeting that he was never going to honor. But," I add, before Ricardo can speak, "there's no point in arguing about that now. Elena will be put up for auction in two days. All that's left to do is decide what we're going to do about that."

Ricardo presses his lips thinly together, clearly thinking. At last, he lets out a sigh, glancing at me.

"Did anyone important see you? Anyone who might recognize you?"

I shake my head. "Just foot soldiers. I doubt any of them got a good enough look for me to stick in their heads."

"And Diego Gonzalez? Does he know who you are?"

"He has no reason to. Not by appearance and probably not by name. Why?" I narrow my eyes at him. "What are you thinking?"

Ricardo frowns. "I think we find a way to get you an invitation to this party, under an assumed name, with my funds at your disposal. You go to the auction and bid on Elena, making certain you win her no matter the cost. And then, once she's in your possession, you take her and go to Boston. No more stalling, no other plans. Just get her out of here."

My gut reaction, the moment I understand where he's going with this, is one of sickened shock—and the instant urge to tell him no, *absolutely fucking not.*

I've done a lot of bad things in my life. My hands will never be clean of the amount of blood I've shed. But I've never hurt a woman, or violated a woman, and I sure as *fuck* haven't ever bought an unwilling one. The closest I've come is paying an escort for sex, and that isn't anything like buying a kidnapped woman at an auction.

Ricardo must be able to read my expression, because he lets out a sigh, shaking his head. "It's not real, Volkov. You'll bid on her, win her, take her to Boston, and hand her over to her sister. Aren't you supposed to be good at faking identities?"

"It's harder to fake not having a moral conundrum over something that vile," I tell him tightly. "But I'm aware it's fake. I'm also aware that it's the easiest way out of this. Storming the compound isn't a viable option, and breaking in to rescue her isn't good either. So since this seems to be the best path we have, I'll do it."

"Good man." Relief washes over Ricardo's face. "There will be a plane ready at the hangar you were supposed to take her to before. Just get her out of there and out of the country. I'll deal with whatever fallout comes later."

I nod. "I'll do my best."

"Your best is getting it done, Volkov," he says sharply, and I feel the words straight down to my core.

More than anything, I don't want to fail Elena. I want to get her to safety, because if her being in Diego's hands was a horrifying fate, this is worse. I can only imagine what one of the overstuffed pricks who buy women from men like Diego Gonzalez will do to her–and I don't *want* to imagine it.

"Just get me an invitation," I tell Ricardo. "And I'll get your daughter out and to safety."

I hope that this time, it's a promise I can keep.

Elena

I'm so terrified I can barely think straight.

I'd expected to be taken to Diego's mansion, to meet him and be lectured about how I'm meant to marry him to take my sister's place, peppered with lewd comments about how he can't wait to have me in his bed. I'd steeled myself for all of that, and then to be bundled off to some room where I'd be told to sleep and get ready for preparations for a wedding sooner rather than later.

I could never, ever have expected this.

I'm too stunned to keep fighting as the men march me towards a large building on the left side of the compound, tripping over my feet as I try to keep up with their brisk pace. All I can hear is Diego's voice, over and over again in my head, telling me that I'm going to be auctioned off.

I'd been so close to escaping, too. Just a little further, a hundred yards maybe, and I could have gotten out. I could have gotten out past the walls and kept running. Even if I had no idea where to go, even if I ended up in some town without Levin or a plan or a way to get back home, it would be better than this.

This is so much worse than what I'd thought would happen. Marrying Diego would have been bad enough, but the auction is a fate so terrible that I can't fully comprehend it. As Diego's wife, I would have had some measure of protection—it wouldn't have kept him from abusing me emotionally or physically. Still, he would have had to treat me with *some* care, as the wife of an eminent cartel boss and the mother of his children. It would have been miserable in so many ways, but compared to this—

There will be no protections from what the man who buys me will do to me, and no shortage of rich men eager to violate and debase Ricardo Santiago's daughter and pay handsomely for the privilege. Being sold to one of them won't stop my purchaser from taking money from the others to share me—once he's gotten the prize of my virginity, of course. I'll be passed around until they're done with me, then sold off again to a brothel—or worse, killed.

I'm not sure which fate is worse. And I know that whatever happens between the end of the auction and how this all ends, it will be more terrible than I can imagine—and I have a vivid imagination.

Too vivid for a circumstance like this.

The door to the building I'm taken to is flung open, and I'm marched inside to a row of cells. Most of them are filled with women dressed in short, silky slips, all of them in varying stages of cleanliness. Several of the cells have multiple women in them, but I'm taken to a cell of my own, at the very end.

"Enjoy the accommodations, *princesa*," the guard holding my arm says sarcastically as he shoves me into the cell, slamming the door shut and locking it before I can even think of trying to bolt out—as if that would do me any good. If I couldn't escape my own home, I can't escape this.

The other women are gathering at the front of their cells as the guards walk away, looking at me curiously. They're all young—a few look older than me, but some look considerably younger. That's all they have in common—otherwise, there's so much variety that I know Diego was telling the truth. These are all women he plans to traffick, that he's been waiting to sell at his planned auction–where I'm going to take center stage.

That's the moment when I can't keep from being sick any longer.

All there is in the cell is a metal bucket on a floor that doesn't look as if it was cleaned anytime recently. It's not filthy, exactly, but the stone surface looks damp, with brackish-looking water pooling against the edges of the walls from where the building is leaking. The vague scent of mold only makes my stomach rebel harder as I end up on my knees in front of the bucket, vomiting out everything left in my stomach as I grip the edge of it to keep it from tipping over.

"You look pretty," one of the women from across the aisle calls out, her voice vaguely mocking. "You must be someone important. Too good to be in here with us."

I can tell that it's meant to get a rise out of me, but I don't have the strength to respond, even if I could think of something. I half-crouch, half-kneel in front of the bucket, painfully aware of how I must look as I try to figure out if I'm done throwing up or not.

There's a bottle of water on a rickety side table next to the wall, and I go for it immediately, rinsing out my mouth and spitting it into the bucket as I try to ignore all of the eyes on me, staring at me like I'm some kind of zoo animal. The water is warm and stale-tasting, as if the bottle has been sitting here for a long time, but it's better than nothing.

Other than the side table and the bucket, the only other furniture in the room is a cot-like bed with a thin mattress, pillow and blanket. It's otherwise entirely empty.

"What's your name?" one of the other women calls out, and I turn around slowly, trying to calm my racing heart and decide what to do next, what to say.

There's no harm in telling them the truth, so far as I can tell. They're in the same predicament I'm in. I can't understand why they seem so hostile—we have a common enemy and a common fear.

I walk to the edge of the bars on my cell, gingerly setting my fingers against them as I look at the women across the aisle. There are three blonde women, a redhead, and two brunettes all shoved into the cell directly across from me—not much larger than mine, but with six cots arranged in it and still only the one bucket. I don't see any bottles of water in their cell, which instantly makes me feel guilty.

"I'm Elena Santiago." I motion toward the half-full water bottle. "I could try to reach over and hand this to you? I don't know if it's too far—or I could try to shove it."

The tall blonde woman nearest the bars laughs, a sound that's almost a cackle. "Aww, isn't that sweet. The cartel boss's daughter offering us some water. How generous of you."

I blink at her, startled. "No, I really—you don't have any—"

"Of course, we don't. We're not as *valuable* as you are."

"I–I don't—"

"Are you going to try to say you don't understand?" The shorter, curvier brunette comes up to stand next to the blonde woman, her eyes narrowed at me. "Don't act stupid, little princess. We all know who your father is, just like we all knew who Diego was, before he managed to get ahold of us. We know which cartels to fear."

"My father would never—"

"Sell women? Sure. But he does plenty of other things. My brother died in a drug deal involving some of his men. But you wouldn't know about that, would you? Pretty little princess. Probably a virgin, too. Well, in here, you're cattle, just like the rest of us."

"Leave her alone, Maria." The redhead speaks up from where she's retreated to her cot, her voice tired. "She didn't ask for this any more than we did, and she's not responsible for what her father does."

"Oh, don't let her off the hook that easily. Maybe not–but she's still in a cell of her own, with water, even."

"That won't save her when she's on the auction block, and it won't make it any better."

"No?" Maria rounds on the other woman, her back to the bars. "You mean when everyone bids on her, the virgin cartel princess, so that the ones left to bid on us are just the men who want to spend relative pennies for a woman they can brutalize? She's going to suck up all the air in the room, and we won't have a chance for anyone decent to buy us."

"That's not her fault."

I retreat back towards the cot as they keep bickering, feeling the pit in my stomach deepen. The blonde woman is still watching me from the bars, flickering anger in her eyes.

"The guards will leave her alone, too," she says quietly. "They won't be allowed to touch the virginal Santiago girl, which means they'll turn their attention on us even more. I don't think a single one of us in this cell are virgins, are we? You're definitely not, Maria, after that guard finished with you a few days ago. And we don't have a fancy name to keep us safe."

She sneers at me, her face twisted into an ugly expression. "Don't be in any hurry to get out of that cell, little princess. You're protected until you go up on that auction block, but after that, it's anyone's game."

I stare at her, unable to think of anything to say as the horror of all of it sinks in–not just for me, but for them too. I'm only just now realizing the depths of the depravity that I've been dragged into–that my fears about an arranged marriage were nothing compared to all of the other possibilities out there, all of the ways that powerful men can invent to be cruel to women, and all of the ways that the less powerful ones can choose to take out their frustrations.

I can feel how close I am to breaking down completely. I clench my hands into fists in my lap, trying not to give away how hard I'm shaking. I don't want the others to see how afraid I am. I don't want to cry.

I want to be brave.

Someone will come, I tell myself in the relative silence after the others lose interest and go back to talking quietly among themselves. *My father will find a way to save me. He won't leave me here like this.*

I can't think about the very real possibility that he's dead. That he, my mother, Levin–anyone who I either cared about or who could help me could very well have died in the assault, and that I'm alone now. That no one will come.

If I think about that, I'll lose it. So I sit on the cot, hugging my knees to my chest, and I try to think about anything else. About my sister, about happier days, about how life was before Diego Gonzalez decided that he wanted to use us to gain power.

I don't have any of my books with me, but I have my own imagination. I can use it to go far away from the little cell. So I do, until I hear footsteps coming down the aisle, and my stomach drops again, snatching me back to reality.

They stop in front of my cell. I look up to see Diego standing there, looking at me with a satisfied expression on his face.

"You're the prettiest caged bird I've ever seen," he says with a victorious smile. "Elena Santiago, at my mercy. This is what I should have done with your sister. If I had, maybe none of this would have been necessary. But as much as I would have rather seen her spitting venom at me from behind these bars with her wings clipped, there's a certain pleasure in knowing that it's you."

"Why?" It's the only word I can manage, my mouth forming the sound in a soft breath. I wish I could sound stronger, more determined, *angrier*. But I feel as if I used it all up in the escape. I'd been braver than I ever had in my entire life–and somehow, I'd ended up here anyway.

It doesn't feel fair.

"Why am I glad it's you?" He grins lasciviously. "I'm glad you asked, princess. You see, your sister was defiant. It would have been a pleasure to break her, to hear her beg, when all that fire had finally been put out. But you–"

He steps closer to the bars, licking his lips as he leans in, eyes twinkling with a wicked gleam that makes me feel sick all over again. "You're so very innocent, Elena Santiago. So pure and gentle. I'll have the pleasure of watching that innocence be shattered, of watching you be debased for the pleasure of the man who buys you, of seeing you entirely destroyed. And that, in turn, will destroy your family."

Everything he says makes me feel sick. But I cling to the last words, to the tiny shred of hope that they give me. I don't think that he only means Isabella. And if so, that means my father, at the very least, is still alive.

"Anything is better than marrying you," I hiss, hoping the words sound more convincing than I feel. "I'd rather die than marry you, have your children, act as if I *want* you. Disgusting *pig* of a man."

Diego laughs. "Strong words from a little girl behind bars. But I can assure you, once you experience what's in store for you, you'll understand how very wrong you are. I'll enjoy seeing you come to that realization, in time."

He turns to go, glancing at a guard approaching. "You," he says sharply, gesturing. "Take one of the women who isn't the Santiago girl. Let her see a taste of what's coming for her."

"No!" I jump up, rushing towards the bars as the guard grins, reaching for his keys. "You can't do that! You're selling them too– you can't *hurt* them–"

"Oh, he won't leave any *lasting* marks," Diego says, with that same satisfied smile. "But I can't very well let him teach you this lesson. Your virginity is very important. Very *expensive*. So instead, I'll let you see the consequences of your sharp tongue, exercised on someone with less value. You'll be just a little less innocent when he's finished."

I realize, with stark horror, that Diego is going to watch. He steps back further, the satisfied smirk still on his face as he watches the guard advance on the cell, unlocking the door.

"You." He points at the redhead, who stares at him with wide, terrified eyes, her mouth opening on a plea. As he strides forward to grab her, pushing the other girls out of the way, the blonde looks at me with an expression that clearly says *I told you so*.

It isn't my fault. I know that. I know that Diego is doing this to make the other women hate me, to make me *feel* as if it's my fault, to hurt me in ways that physical violence never could. To scar me in ways that it never could.

But as the guard shoves her against the wall, her face pressed against it as he pushes up the hem of the fragile slip that she's wearing and kicks her legs apart as he fumbles with his zipper, I can't convince myself entirely that it *isn't* my fault. That I should have known how a man like Diego would punish me for my insolence.

"Don't look away," Diego says, his voice closer now as he moves to where he can have the best view. "If you look away, princess, I'll bring in another guard and another, until every woman in this building has had to be the means for you to learn your lesson."

I know when he says that, that I can't look away, no matter how much I want to.

And I know I'll never be able to stop seeing it or stop hearing the sound of her sobs.

I'd never known just how horrible the world could be, until right this moment.

Levin

I've never felt more out of place in my life than I do at this fucking party.

I can blend in well enough with a suit quickly purchased and tailored, expensive enough to pass for one of these self-important billionaires, courtesy of Ricardo. I know the bearing and the behavior—I've spent most of my life around people like this. I've been trained to the point of muscle memory to blend in, to be unseen, to fit in anywhere and with anyone.

But *fuck*, do I feel uncomfortable.

Diego's mansion is far more ostentatious than the Santiago estate. The main gathering point prior to the auction is the central courtyard in the middle of the mansion, with a glass roof domed overhead and a massive fountain in the center, splashing as white-uniformed staff mill around with food and drinks, passing them out to men in suits.

I move through the crowd, taking a glass from a passing tray and sipping idly from it as I listen to the snippets of conversation that I can pick up. I'm aware that there could be information I could pick up here that might be beneficial to the Kings, with so many high-ranking cartel members here, and other associates. So while I wait for the auction to start, I try to do what reconnaissance I can in the meantime. It helps to take the edge off and makes me feel as if I have something to do besides bide my time. But all I can really think about is Elena.

The sense of failure that it's gotten this far burns deep. It's been a long fucking time since I've had nightmares, but the last two nights, I've barely gotten any sleep, caught up in dreams of Lidiya bleeding out in our bed. Elena being dragged away screaming, and the sickening sense of being unable to stop any of it as I watch it happen, frozen in place in the dream, paralyzed.

This is my chance to make that failure right, to save Elena. So even if the means of it makes me uncomfortable–which it does–it doesn't matter.

I have to fix this.

There's not much to hear, as I make my way around the room. Most of the conversation focuses on the auction, on the types of girls the men are hoping Diego has to offer, the things they'll do to them–all conversations that make me sick to my fucking stomach. If I had my way, I'd burn the place down with every one of these fuckers trapped inside.

Unfortunately, that's not in the cards today.

There's one other thing I need to do before the auction starts, and that's look for an escape route. My *plan* is to do this all by the book, to buy Elena and make it appear as if everything is fine, as if I'm just another billionaire with his new acquisition until we can both leave normally. But if things go upside down as they've been wont to do lately, I want to know that we have a way out.

That what happened at the Santiago mansion won't happen again.

Diego's home is well-guarded. I manage to get a decent idea of the layout of the first floor by pretending to get lost looking for a restroom. That quick bit of recon only reinforces my determination to keep this from going badly by any means necessary. If Elena and I have to escape, it won't be easy—and I'm not entirely sure that it will be successful.

I'm in the lion's den now. We only get one shot at this. If we get caught, not only will things be worse for Elena, but I'll be dead. I have no doubt that Diego will make certain of that.

The best plan is the one that Ricardo and I came up with from the start—that I'll sit through the auction, ensure that Elena is "mine" by whatever means necessary, and then play the game until I can leave with my new "purchase" along with the others.

I'd rather fight my way out, if I'm being honest, but that's the option most likely to get me—or both of us—killed. I've learned many times over the years that sometimes the best plan is the quietest one.

A sound from the entrance to the courtyard catches my attention, as the crowd splits apart. It takes me a brief moment to realize what's going on, and then I see four well-armed guards in fatigues walking in, and behind them, a line of women.

"For your viewing pleasure, before the bidding starts in one hour!" A short, rotund man in a black suit speaks from beside the arched entrance. "Look over the merchandise, gentlemen, but don't touch! If you wish to examine any of them more closely, please speak to one of the guards, and they will assist you."

I look for Elena immediately. There are about twenty women in all, a few of them brunette, and I look for her thick dark hair and pretty, heart-shaped face in particular, trying to pick her out.

When I do see her, she's directly in the center of the line. I can see the tight set of her jaw, the way her lips are pressed thinly together as she's guided with the rest to the far end of the courtyard and lined up with the others, as the crowd waits for the signal that they're allowed to approach.

It feels very much like being in the middle of a slavering pack of hunting dogs.

All of the women are wearing the same thing—what looks like an ivory-colored silk slip dress with thin straps and a hemline that barely reaches the tops of their thighs, with lace edging. It looks as if someone took the time to try to style their hair—some differently than others, but other than that, they look clean and bare-faced, standing there looking nervously from side to side as the men start to approach.

I know I can't go directly to Elena without possibly causing some suspicion, regardless of how much I want to. Besides, there's already a line forming to look at her, which makes me instantly concerned. Ricardo gave me access to an absolutely ridiculous amount of money to purchase her, but *all* the men here are rich. I doubt I'll be outbid, but it very well might use up all of her father's liquid resources and then some.

I'm prepared, if need be, to add some of my own to get her out of here. I would have been willing to, no matter what, but seeing the men approaching her only emphasizes the need to make sure that she leaves with me regardless of the cost. The interest in her is overwhelming, exactly as Diego had expected that it would be.

"She looks familiar," I hear one of the men near Elena say as I pretend to look a little more closely at the woman standing in front of me, a pretty redhead who looks past me as if I'm not even there, her expression blank. "It can't be—surely not—"

So Diego is leaving the big reveal for the auction itself, in order to drive up the bidding. He's a shrewd businessman, which will make this more difficult. He's aware of the motivations and tics that his prospective customers have, and he's set this auction up to play to those to the fullest. But I also have some idea of how this game is played.

Viktor never auctioned women like this, in the days when he still participated in the trafficking business. But I saw and heard plenty of his clients, and I also know how they think. The things that they want that make them empty their pockets. I can anticipate some of what Diego is doing, too.

I linger as I walk past each woman in the line, pretending to be looking at each of them with interest as I approach Elena. A tall blonde with sharp features and hazel eyes looks directly at me as I stop in front of her, her lips curving prettily in an attempt at an enticing smile.

"You look handsome," she murmurs. "I'd rather go with you than one of these old pricks. Buy me, and I'll make sure you don't regret it."

"No talking!" A guard from a few feet away from her steps forward, smacking her on the backs of her thighs with a leather strap–not hard enough to mark her, but hard enough to make her jump a little, with a sharp, startled squeal.

I have to bite back my instant reaction. I want to chastise him, to tell him that's not necessary, but it would make me stand out. Not another man here would care about that, and if *I* care, it singles me out–if I show it, at least.

I have to force myself to keep walking. I can't risk Elena's freedom.

She sees me when I approach. For a fraction of a second, her eyes widen in shock and recognition, but her face goes blank so quickly that I doubt anyone else saw. It surprises me, actually, because it's rare for anyone to have such good command of their emotions without training.

I worried that she might give away that she recognized me, but it was impossible not to go up to the line of women–that would have seemed suspicious, too. I'd had to trust that she would understand, that she could manage to play a game that she didn't even know she was in, and she'd pulled it off beautifully.

Once again, as I look at her, I feel that spark of interest, of curiosity. There's more to this girl than I'm aware of; I'm certain of it.

Already in the brief time I've known her, she's managed to startle and impress me more than I would have ever expected.

Her lips press tightly together as I stop in front of her, her gaze canting to one side. I know she's trying to hold back everything she wants to say, the pleas for my help, the questions about why I'm here, about what the plan is. I know she's trying not to look at me so that she won't accidentally let that flash of resignation show again. And I also know that I need to make this as quick as I can, without giving anything away.

I want to give her some hope. I want to give her something to hold onto, through what I know must be the most frightening experience of her life.

"Can you bring her forward?" I motion to the guard standing just behind her. "I'd like to take a closer look."

His face looks absolutely bored as he steps closer, taking her arm and maneuvering her a few steps out of line. I'm not the first one to ask, and everything about the guard's bearing suggests that he's ready for the auction to be finished with so he can get off work and do literally anything else.

It also suggests that he's not paying as much attention as maybe he should be.

I lean forward, looking as if I'm inspecting her more closely–her skin, her hair, trying to get a look down the cleavage of her slip. The conversations around me are growing louder as the excitement in the room increases. I take advantage of that to speak to her in a low voice, so low that I have to hope that she can hear me.

"Just hold on, Elena. I'll have you out of here soon."

She makes no sign whether she heard or not, but I nod to the guard, who tugs her back in line.

I step back, too, and as I do, I find that I have to regain my bearing a little. I hadn't expected to be affected, being so close to her– especially under these circumstances. But the moment I leaned in, I felt her tense, smelled the soft, warm, powdery scent of her skin, and in a split second, I felt a *want* like I hadn't felt in years.

A sharp, visceral bolt of desire that, in the aftermath, makes me feel slightly ashamed. I have no intention of buying her for any reason other than her rescue, but it makes me feel as if I'm no better than the other men here. As if that brief moment of arousal brought me down to their level, regardless of my intentions.

She's beautiful. You can't deny that.

I look at her as she's maneuvered back into line, her inky black hair spilling over her shoulders in sharp contrast to the slick ivory silk clinging to her tanned skin, her face more calm and composed than I would have ever thought she could manage. The other women look as if they're in varying stages of panic, bargaining, or denial. Still, Elena's expression is carefully blank, as if she's transported herself somewhere far away from here.

It's not just her appearance that's stunning. It's everything about her.

I'm going to have a hell of a time outbidding the other men.

I turn away, looking for a waiter with another glass of something alcoholic as I ignore the throbbing in my cock, awakened by that brief moment so close to her. I can feel it pressing uncomfortably against my thigh, half-hard and swollen, and I clench my jaw against another wave of shame that I can be aroused in these circumstances.

It's been a long time since I've lost even the slightest control of my desire. But she does something to me—and it's not something I can entertain.

She's a job. A mission. And right now, if you allow yourself to be distracted, you're going to fail that fucking mission.

"Gentlemen!" Diego's voice comes from the door leading into the courtyard, and a hush falls over the crowd as everyone turns toward where he's standing. The anticipation in the air is thick and sickening, and I grit my teeth as I turn with the rest of them, schooling my face into my best impression of the same eagerness that the rest of the men are exhibiting.

"It's time for the main event—what I know you've all been waiting for." Diego raises his voice with a flourish, and it's clear that he's enjoying the showmanship of it all, the chance to be the center of attention. "If you'll all follow me—"

Diego leads us through the courtyard and the sprawling open space of the first floor, to a huge open room at the back of the mansion that's been set up exactly as if for an auction. Rows of chairs face a stage, with a podium on one side, and spotlights shining down in the center for where the girl of the moment will likely be.

This is it. I don't allow myself to think too much about it as I find my seat, or contemplate all the ways this could go wrong. If I do, it only makes it more likely that it will.

"What are you hoping for?" the man next to me—a tall, slender man with a thick mustache and wearing a tan suit—asks, his tone conspiratorial. "A virgin? Or do you prefer one with a little more experience? I find I like to break them in, myself."

I can feel the small muscle in my jaw leap as I fight to keep my expression relaxed and pleasant. "I don't know that I have a preference," I tell him, hearing the words as if they're coming out of someone else's mouth. "It's more of a thing I just sense in the moment, when I see her. Who the right one is."

"Ah. A spiritual man." The man next to me smirks. "Well, we all have our idiosyncracies, I suppose."

I'm saved from having to respond by another light coming up on the stage, as the same short, rotund man from earlier comes to the podium and clears his throat loudly. "Gentlemen, the auction will begin shortly. If you will all turn your attention to the stage—"

The lights shift to a soft pink, and the first girl is brought out. It's the tall blonde who had suggested that she'd be compliant if I bought her—not that I can blame her, seeing some of the other candidates. Her face has a clear expression of annoyance, as if she knows that by being the first one out, she's the most likely to be purchased by someone who isn't here to spend a lot of money or buy a girl he intends to prize as an expensive commodity. That doesn't bode well for her, and she appears to know it.

The bidding starts, and I begin to calculate this part of the plan in my head.

In order to not seem suspicious, I'll have to bid on girls other than Elena. In order to have enough resources to buy Elena, no matter how high the bidding goes, I can't really afford to win any of the others, despite how much I might like to, in order to be able to let them go back home afterward. So I'll have to carefully balance my bidding, so that I'm always outbid until it comes time for Elena—who will almost certainly be the last one—to be on the stage.

It's a risky plan. It always has been. But it's the one most likely to work. If it doesn't, she'll go with some other man, to be hurt and abused, and it will be my failure that caused it. If the plan doesn't work, I won't get a second chance to save her.

It *has* to work.

Elena

I've never been so afraid in my entire life.

I feel like nothing more than a piece of meat on display, standing in line to wait for the men to come up and inspect me and the other girls. It feels like the most humiliating, debasing experience of my life.

I know it's far from over, too.

I'd known that part was coming. We'd all been woken up early this morning by the guards and marched to a room in the main house, forced to sit and wait as, one by one, the girls were taken out and cleaned up for the auction. Diego had ordered us to be done up with simple hair and no makeup, so the actual process didn't take long. Still, the wait had felt interminable, like waiting for execution.

I'd tried to cling to the hope that there was someone left who could come help me, but it had felt harder and harder by the hour. The worst imaginings were the ones where Diego's men had succeeded in killing everyone that night–Levin, my father's men, my family– and that there would be no one left at all to try to rescue me. No one to try to stop the absolute horror unfolding in front of me.

Whoever buys you will have spent a lot of money, I told myself as I sat in the small, warm room with all the other girls as they were taken out and returned one by one. Each of them came back scrubbed clean, hair shiny, and dressed in a clean ivory silk slip, looking withdrawn and nervous–or defiant, in the case of the blonde girl I'd met when I was brought to the cells. *They'll treat you like an investment. Like an expensive collectible. They won't abuse you.*

It was a very small comfort, though. Not enough to keep my stomach from twisting into knots that I wasn't sure I'd ever be able to untangle, my throat tight with fear. Not all that long ago, an arranged marriage was the worst thing in my future. This is far, far worse. Worse even than Diego.

And there's no way out that I could see, short of a ninth-hour rescue. I couldn't fight. I couldn't run. I tried to think of what Isabella would do, what my brave, stubborn, defiant sister would do in the face of this, and I knew the answer before a few seconds had passed.

She would curse, fight, spit, and kick. She would make herself unsaleable, and she would end up sold off to someone whose only joy would be in breaking her spirit. Just as Diego had tried to do when he'd sent her to the bride-tamer.

The difference is, Isabella had had Niall to go after her. To save her. I'm not sure that I have anyone left at all.

Which means that defiance will only hurt me more in the end.

Just be brave, I told myself when it was my turn. *Don't let them see how afraid you are. How much this hurts and terrifies you.* And I'd managed it, mostly. I'd kept my chin up as the two women assigned to cleaning us up scrubbed me pink and raw in a lukewarm bath, a humiliating process that had them touching me in places that I'd hoped I would only ever wash myself. They washed my hair twice, wringing it dry and then rubbing me down with towels like a horse after a bath, one of them applying moisturizer to my face as the other dried and brushed my hair, running a lightweight oil through it that smelled like flowers and left it thick and shiny.

The silk slip was yanked over my head, my hair was fluffed up once more, and then I was marched back to the room, to sit in silence and try not to think too hard about my fate until all of the girls were finished being prepared.

Then, we were led out to the courtyard.

I grit my teeth, bracing myself for the inspection. It feels like being marched in front of a pack of hungry dogs, except these dogs are dressed in fine bespoke suits and holding glasses of champagne and tequila and scotch that cost thousands of dollars. I'd walked across a marble floor veined with gold barefoot as we were led out to the courtyard, and the ostentatiousness of it all makes me want to vomit. *These men have everything in the world,* I'd thought with disgust as we were lined up. *And this is what they choose to do with it.*

There's a line to inspect me. Men of varying ages, all of them old enough to be my father and some much older, a few of decent enough looks to at least count as tolerable, but I still don't want a single one of them touching me.

"Hands off the merchandise," the guard behind me reminds them, as they look at me with lustful, eager eyes that tell me they're already imagining me stripped naked, bare for their viewing pleasure—and all of the other pleasures they can imagine, too.

As much as I resent being called merchandise, I'm almost grateful for the guard behind me, keeping these men's hands off me for now. I feel very certain that the only thing keeping them from grabbing at me and prying me apart for their inspection is the hulking figure behind me.

Much like José.

My chest cramps with hurt at the reminder of José, who I'd thought of as my protector for so long, a harmless crush, someone who would keep me safe and gently chide my sister and me when we got out of hand. *What kind of world is this that I live in, that can be so cruel to a man that it changes him so much?* The José who had tried to hurt me, and turn me in to Diego as vengeance for his brother, isn't the same man who had guarded me for so much of his life.

For a brief second, as I'm turning my head away from a *much* older man who is requesting that the guard bring me forward and let him get a closer look, I think I hear the sound of a semi-familiar voice. I think I see a semi-familiar *face*–a chiseled, handsome face with sharp blue eyes, short dark hair, a muscled body that I remember thinking about in ways that I knew I shouldn't–

It can't be.

And then he moves past one of the girls a few feet away from me, and I know I'm not imagining things.

Levin.

I feel the look of shock spread over my face in the instant before I manage to shut it down. His eyes meet mine, his face blank except for the barest look of curiosity, and I know what I have to do.

I have to pretend that I don't know him, that I don't know why he's here, even as my entire body starts to buzz with the adrenaline rush of knowing that I at least have a chance at being saved. *He's alive. He's here to help me. That must mean my father is alive, too. He's sent him to finish the job he started.*

It's a hope I wouldn't have dared have a few minutes ago, but now my heart is pounding in my chest. I barely hear the guard telling me to step back into line as the man in front of me finishes inspecting me, my mind racing.

Keep it to yourself. If anyone *suspects, it will all be over. Diego will kill him, and your last hope will be gone.*

Levin is walking towards me, and it's the hardest thing I've ever had to do in my life to look at him with the same bored expression that I've done my best to keep on my face for everyone else. I haven't wanted any of these men to see how afraid I am, how brokenhearted, how lost I feel. I want them to all think that I don't give a single shit about what they're going to do to me. And I think I've done a pretty good job, so far.

But as he stops in front of me, all I want to do is ask if my father sent him, if he's alive, and beg for Levin to get me out of here. I want to know what his plan is and how he intends to save me. I want to know what the chances are that I'm going to walk out of here with him and not with one of these other lecherous pricks.

I press my lips tightly together, biting back all of it, looking away from him. I can't look him in the eye without giving myself away, so instead, I pretend that I can't bear to look at him at all.

Levin beckons to the guard behind me. "Can you bring her forward? I'd like to take a closer look."

The guard takes my arm with the same loose boredom as before, maneuvering me forward so that I'm closer to Levin, presented to him for inspection. I'm only a few inches from touching him, and I can smell the citrus scent of his cologne, feel the heat wafting off of him, the tension in his body. It sends a jolt through me that I don't expect, and I fist my hands at my sides. I want to grab him, cling to him, beg him to take me out of here. But I can't. If I do, it will damn us both.

Levin leans forward as if he's inspecting me more closely, his gaze roving over my face, my cleavage. The room is loud around us, and as he leans very close, as if he's breathing in the scent of my hair, I know he's trying to whisper in my ear. I stiffen, straining to hear him over the noise of the eager buyers all around us.

"Just hold on, Elena. I'll have you out of here soon."

I can't show any sign that I've heard him. I know that. I grit my teeth hard, my entire body rigid, fighting against every instinct I have as Levin nods to the guard, and I'm pulled back into line.

And then he's gone.

I'm trembling all over, from the top of my head to my toes, and I'm grateful that at least that won't be seen as strange. I hadn't wanted to be seen as afraid, but it's almost better now, because I can hide my emotions in that facade of fear.

The last of the men walks away, and the guards start to shuffle us out of the courtyard, just as I hear Diego's voice coming from the archway, announcing to the guests that the auction will begin soon. I feel my stomach cramp again with fear, the unknowing almost painful. *How is Levin going to get me out of here? Is he going to buy me? What if someone outbids him?*

It takes everything in me to stay in the line, to keep walking, to not make a run for it. We're taken back behind the stage that's been set up, the line reshuffled in the order that the girls will be brought out. I'm the very last one in line, which doesn't surprise me. I'd suspected that Diego was going to use me as the capstone of the auction, the prize to be won after all the other girls had been sold off. My capture and sale will be his coup de grâce against the Santiago family.

It also means the wait to find out what my fate will be is going to be interminable.

The blonde girl is the first one out. I can hear the sound of the auctioneer describing her, like an animal being sold at the market, pointing out her virtues and attributes that make her worthy of sale. *Virgin* isn't among the attributes listed, and a wave of chills washes over me at the memory of the show Diego had made the guards put on down in the cells. I have no doubt that she'd been at the mercy of those same guards before.

I can hear the bidding. It's sparse, the price rising before tapering off, and then the auctioneer calls out the final sale. I can hear the footsteps of her being marched off the stage to her new owner as the next girl in line is tugged forward, out from behind the curtain and out to her fate.

I feel faint by the time the girl in front of me is taken out. It feels as if it's dragged on forever. I haven't eaten or drunk anything since this morning, and I hadn't managed much then, as anxious as I was. I'm exhausted from standing, and I'm beginning to wish it would just be over with, regardless of the outcome. I almost feel relief when the guard takes my arm and pulls me forward, marching me up the steps at the back of the stage and out through the curtains towards the spotlight in the center of it.

It's bright. I have to blink to look out at the crowd, and I feel a faint shiver of horror at what I see. The girls who have been sold are out there now, with their new owners—some of them kneeling on the floor, others sitting on laps. It's clear that all of the men are eager to play with their new toys, hands roving over their hair and breasts and thighs, and I swallow back a surge of nausea at the thought that very soon, that will be me.

Unless Levin wins the bid.

"Our last girl for the night is someone very special," the auctioneer begins, but I hardly hear him. I'm looking for Levin in the crowd, desperately searching for his face so that I have something to anchor myself to, that last bit of hope that maybe tonight won't be the horror that I've tried so hard not to imagine. "For your pleasure, Diego Gonzalez has brought you the youngest Santiago daughter! Look how beautiful she is. Twenty years old and still a virgin. The last jewel in the Santiago vault, and one of you fine gentlemen can have her, for a *very* steep price. Imagine, deflowering *her*? What a prize—and worth every bit of money you have left in your pockets, I'm sure—"

The auctioneer's voice trails off in my ears as I find Levin in the crowd, on the right, seated about halfway back. I can see the grim set of his jaw, the way he watches the auctioneer, readying himself as if he's going into a fight. And he is, in a way, I suppose. If I'm bought by someone else, trying to get me back will be much harder— if not impossible.

And by the time he does, it will be too late to keep me from enduring at least some of the awful things in store for me.

I don't listen to the bidding. I hear the starting number, a huge price, and I do my best to tune it out from there. I'll lose my composure if I don't, because I can see how frantic the bidding is already, hands going up, numbers called out as everyone vies for the right to destroy the last remaining daughter of Ricardo Santiago.

All I can do is focus on *him*. On Levin. On bright blue eyes and that face that has looked down at me reassuringly more times than it should have by now, considering how short our acquaintance has been so far. On that hand, raised in the air to call out another bid, that I imagined on me in ways that I shouldn't have thought of. I know he's not here to buy me for himself, and he wouldn't be a man I could respect if he was, but the feeling of safety that he gives me is all tied up in the fantasies I had since meeting him that first day.

The bidding drops to five men, then four, then three. The amount is ridiculously high now, more than I can fathom anyone paying for the "privilege" of taking a girl's virginity. *What is wrong with men?* I think dizzily as I see Levin's teeth clench, and I know he's calculating what resources he has left in his head. I don't doubt that my father is willing to empty every account he has and liquidate every asset in order to get me out of here, but I have no idea what my father's wealth *is*. It's entirely possible that there is someone here with more, someone able to throw more at my feet for the pleasure of ruining me.

Two men. Levin and the very old man who had inspected me so closely in the line, a man old enough to be my grandfather at least, with a lecherous expression on his jowled face as he looks at me from the front row. *No, please. I can't. I can't.*

I feel like I'm going to pass out.

They're still bidding. Back and forth. I can see a red flush creeping up Levin's neck–anger, or stress, maybe. His eyes find mine, and I don't see the same reassurance in them that I did before. I realize, with a flash of terror that chills my blood and makes my knees feel watery, that Levin might not win.

Another bid from Levin. The old man's hand comes up halfway, his eyes raking over me with a sort of nostalgic lust that makes my stomach turn—

—and then his hand drops back into his lap.

The auctioneer calls out the win, a name I don't know. For one dizzying second, I think that somehow the old man has won after all, until I realize that Levin must have used a fake name. I see him standing up, walking past the others in his row, and then towards me, and all of the emotion and exhaustion hits me at once as I realize that he won.

He's going to take me out of here. I'm safe.

My knees buckle, and the last thing I see is the startled expression on his face before the entire room goes black.

Elena

I come to on a couch in what appears to be an informal living room somewhere in the house. My head feels heavy, my eyes a little sticky, and I pry them open as I slowly blink back to consciousness, the events of the day rushing back to me in a whirlwind.

I'm not entirely sure that I didn't imagine it all, until I hear the low sound of Levin's voice, and I turn my head to see him talking to an older man who appears to be a doctor.

"She'll be alright," the doctor says in a low voice. "Just exhaustion and nerves, I think. Not uncommon, these events are a bit-straining, on the girls. But if you're disappointed in your purchase and wish to speak to Diego–"

"No," Levin says, and I can hear the edge in his tone. "I'm not disappointed."

"Very well. When she wakes, she can be readied to join you for the evening. If you wish to rejoin the guests–"

"I'll wait here." There's that same sharp edge, and the man retreats, clearly intimidated by Levin.

"As you wish."

Something flutters in my chest when Levin says that he's not disappointed in me. It's ridiculous, frankly–why should I care whether he's disappointed that I passed out or not? It's not as if I could help it, or even *should* have been able to help it, after what I've been put through today. But it makes me feel comforted, somehow, that he's not upset.

What now?

Levin turns towards me when the door shuts behind the other man, his eyes widening slightly as he sees me. "You're awake," he says, a hint of surprise in his voice as he walks towards the couch where I'm still lying, unsure if I'm ready to sit up or not. "I thought you might be out for a little while still."

"I'm sorry I–"

"No need to be sorry. Today must have been a strain for you." He sits down on the edge of the couch near my legs, gently nudging them aside to make room for himself. His touch is gentle, almost too light for me to feel, but there's a flush of heat that I feel anyway where his fingers brush against my calf.

It's every bit as ridiculous as being glad that he wasn't disappointed in me.

"Are we leaving?" My voice still sounds wobbly, as if I'm trying to speak underwater. "I can get up if we–"

"Not yet." Levin's jaw clenches slightly, and I see a hint of warning in his eyes. "Diego is having a party tonight. All the *honored guests*," he says emphatically, "are staying tonight to enjoy the celebration with their new acquisitions and enjoy the Gonzalez' house's hospitality. As we will also need to do."

The way he phrases it is so careful that I immediately understand what's going on–or at least I think that I do. Diego's guests are staying to enjoy whatever revelry he has planned, and if Levin leaves with me now, it will look suspicious. We won't be able to leave until tomorrow at least–which means continuing to play the game of a rich man and his new purchase.

I'm fairly certain he's also being careful not to say anything in here that might give us away, just in case someone is listening. We have to keep up the ruse until we're well away from Diego's compound and any chance of being caught.

The thought makes my stomach knot all over again. I'm beyond exhausted; everything wrung out of me from the effort of maintaining my composure all day, let alone not giving away that I knew Levin was here and trying to rescue me. But I know I have to get through it.

If I don't, all of this will have been for nothing.

I nod, swallowing hard as I start to slowly push myself up from the couch. Levin instantly leans forward, his arm going around my back to help me. The feeling of that hard, muscled support sends another flush of unexpected heat through me.

"Careful," he murmurs. "Slowly. Someone is going to come help you get ready soon, but there's no rush. We don't want you passing out again."

He's being a little too conciliatory for one of these men, but if someone is listening, it could still be explained away. He's paid a massive sum for me, so it's not beyond reason that he'd treat me with kid gloves, even if I'd bet that same amount of money that none of the other men in that audience would have.

"I just need a second. And then I'll be fine." The words still sound a little shaky, but I *do* feel as if I'm starting to come back to myself, at least a little. "What do you mean, help me get ready?"

Levin shrugs, his arm still pressed against my back, helping me stay upright. I find that I don't really want him to move it. "I suppose they have clothes for the girls to wear to the party tonight. I'm not aware of what that entails. I'm sure it will be–sparse."

There's a note of levity in his voice that I'm fairly sure is forced, but I know it needs to be. He *should* be excited at the idea of seeing me in sparse clothing, after how much he paid for me. *He has to play a role, too,* I remind myself. *Anything he does is to keep us both safe until we can get out of here.*

"I'm good," I tell him after a few more seconds pass. "You can tell whoever is going to–help me that I'm ready."

Levin gives me a momentary, appraising look, but then he nods and stands up, walking over to one side of the room and tapping what looks like a doorbell on the wall. In a matter of seconds, the door opens, and a short, slight-looking woman dressed in the staff uniforms of the household walks in, nodding respectfully to Levin and then crossing directly to me.

"Come along," she tells me, urging me up from the couch. "Time to get you ready for the festivities tonight."

I glance back once at Levin as she ushers me out, suddenly wanting very much to stay with him. He's the only safe thing here, and I catch a glimpse of what looks like a reassuring expression on his face as I'm whisked away. Still, it's not enough to slow the sudden, panicked racing of my heart.

"The worst part is over," the woman says quietly to me, as she walks me down the hall. "You've been bought now, so there's no more wondering."

Is it? The worst part is likely over for *me*, unless we're caught. Levin won't hurt me, and soon I'll be on my way to Boston, away from Diego's clutches and any other man who wants to hurt me on his behalf. But for all the other girls–

I'm pretty sure that the worst is just beginning, for them.

"We'll dress you up pretty, so there's no chance of him being dissatisfied," the woman continues as she leads me down the hall. "I've got just the thing."

It seems somehow more horrifying that there's a room with clothes just waiting for the purchased girls, to show them off after the auction. This entire mansion seems *full* of horrors, and I know I'm going to be spared most of them, so long as Levin and I both play our parts well. It sends another surge of guilt through me, like I'd felt down in the cells. *Why do I deserve to be so lucky?*

My feelings had been hurt that the other girls had been so angry with me, but I can understand it better now. I had a wealthy father to save me, who could buy a man's services and me as well, to get me out of here. I have very little doubt that Levin can pull his part of this ruse off, which means that it's only me who has to manage until we can leave. That's all I have to do, in order to be the lucky one who is whisked away from all of this.

The guilt feels almost as bad as the fear had earlier.

"Here we are!" There's a forced chipperness in the woman's voice as she leads me into a room clearly set up to be some sort of dressing room, with large wardrobes, a long vanity with a mirror, cosmetics and hair products strewn across it, and another long table with shoes and jewelry spread over it. It's yet another ostentatious display of wealth, that Diego has these things here to be thrown away on decorating women that someone else has purchased.

The woman turns to me as I stand, frozen in the center of the room. "Do you want me to pick out what you wear, or would you like to?"

The idea of choice hadn't even entered my mind. I swallow hard, shaking my head. "You choose," I manage, and she clicks her tongue as if she has an opinion about what I've just said, but I'm not sure if it's a good or bad one.

What she pulls out of the wardrobe is lovely, something that I could never have imagined wearing outside of a bedroom with my husband. It's a long Grecian-style dress made of see-through, misty green chiffon, gathered at the waist and falling in pleats in front and behind that will only *just* keep eyes from seeing *every* intimate detail of my naked flesh. It's split up to the waist on either side, leaving me bare from hips to toes, and the neckline of it plunges all the way down to the waist, leaving a deep and wide v of cleavage. The sides are open as well–in fact, the only fastenings on the dress are at the waist and at the shoulders, where the chiffon is gathered in place.

The woman drapes it over a chair, unceremoniously yanking off the ivory silk slip I was wearing. I had on only a thin silk thong beneath it, and she pulls that off, too, discarding both in a bin as she reaches for the chiffon gown. I suspected that I wouldn't be wearing anything underneath it, but I hadn't fully grasped what that meant until the woman puts it over my head, and I see myself in the mirror.

I've never felt so torn about anything. On the one hand, it's stunning. *I* look beautiful in it–the color suits my tanned skin and black hair, and it drapes over my slender curves in a flattering way. But it shows far more than I could *ever* be comfortable with a stranger seeing–and I'm going to have to wear it out into a party full of strangers. The chiffon, draped over my bare breasts and falling pleated between my legs, gives the illusion of hiding my nipples and the bare skin between my thighs until I move, and then anyone watching can see a glimpse of dusky nipples and intimate flesh.

Everyone is going to see me like this. Levin *is going to see me like this.*

The latter thought doesn't upset me as much as it should. But the former is horrifying.

It's not as if I have a choice.

"We'll leave your hair down," the woman decides, *tsk*ing as she makes her way around me, inspecting me. "And just a little makeup. Just something to accentuate. Your hair and face are beautiful already; there's no reason to do very much."

She pushes me down onto a stool, and I sit there, frozen as she fusses around me. She runs some other product through my hair that leaves it smelling like flowers and shining even more than it had already, fluffing it with her fingers, before she brushes a hint of rose-gold eyeshadow and a flick of mascara over my eyes and taps a rosy stain onto my lips. "That's perfect," she says with a satisfied lilt in her voice, before retreating to the table covered in shoes and jewelry.

When she comes back, it's with a pair of nude, strappy heels high enough to keep the dress from dragging too much on the floor–it's a bit long for my slightly-less-than-average height–and rose gold drop earrings set with tiny diamonds. "Just a hint of sparkle," she says, slipping them into my ears. "There. You look like a princess."

I was a princess, or the closest thing to one, I want to bite back. *I still am. I'm still Ricardo Santiago's daughter, and the man who bought me is going to take me home. You're all fools who think you've outsmarted my father, but you're not.*

I keep the words clamped tightly behind my lips, though. For one thing, it would give up the entire ruse. For another, it's not this woman's fault. None of it is. She's doing her job, and if she failed at it, she'd be in her own sort of awful position. I can't be angry at her for trying to maintain some optimism in this house of horrors.

"Thank you," I tell her, a little unevenly, as I stand up. "Should I go back to–him, now?" I don't dare say Levin's false name, for fear I'll fuck it up.

"He'll be waiting downstairs for you. Come along, I'll take you to the staircase, and then I need to go and help the next girl. Most of them are finished up already–we took care of the others while you were recovering."

It's a little embarrassing to know that I was the only one who passed out, but it's not as if I could help it. And I *was* the last one to go out.

She walks me to the edge of the staircase, as promised, and then quickly walks off, towards another room. I'm left standing there, heart in my throat, knowing I need to go down to Levin.

The sooner I do this, the sooner it can all be over.

He's waiting at the bottom of the stairs, still in the same suit as earlier, his jaw set as he looks towards the arched doorway that will undoubtedly lead us to the party in the other room. At the sound of my footsteps, he looks up, and I see an emotion that I've never seen directed at me—at least not until I was kidnapped. It's only on his face for a moment, but it's there—unmistakable and unmissable as he sees me in the sheer chiffon gown, until he wipes it away in an instant.

Lust.

I realize, in the instant before it disappears, that I don't hate it as much as I should.

Elena

"We should go join the others."

Levin's voice is cool, emotionless. There's no hint of what I saw in his face a moment before, not even a little. His hand closes around my upper arm—not too hard, but firmly enough that if anyone is watching, it'll look like a man handling his new possession.

Something about the touch sends another shiver down my spine.

"The party is—not what you might expect," he says slowly as we walk towards the open doorway, his voice very low. "I don't think you need to hide how you might feel about it. I think it will be—expected."

I don't understand what he means at first, or the insinuation that I might not need to hide my emotions, but he will. But then we step through the doorway into the huge room where the party is being held, and I understand immediately.

The room is lit up in a blaze of light from the chandeliers strung along the ceiling. There's a massive fountain in the center, much like the one in the courtyard, with four statues of arched, naked women serving as the centerpiece of it, water spilling from their mouths and carved stone nipples. I've never been inside this room before, so I don't know if that's always the centerpiece. Still, I wouldn't find it at all surprising if it had been brought in, especially for this party, considering what else is going on in the room.

There are tables lined with food at one end of the room, a gilded bar to the right of it with two bartenders serving guests, and more of the staff circulating the room with golden trays filled with champagne glasses and hors d'oeurves. It would appear to be a normal, if ostentatious party, if not for the rest of what I see.

On the velvet couches strewn around the room, I see several of the men from earlier, sitting with their newly purchased acquisitions. The girls are all in various sorts of clothing as skimpy as mine–some are in similar long sheer dresses, others in babydoll nightgowns, and a few are in lacy or strappy lingerie. From looking at them, I can guess that they've likely been dressed according to their new "owners'" preferences, and Levin must not have given them a preference.

Or maybe he did, and she was just pretending to give you a choice.

The thought of Levin choosing something for me to wear to this party should horrify me, but it sends that faint tingle down my spine again instead, a strange feeling that I push away quickly.

It's easy to do, with what's in front of me. It's very clear in a matter of moments that the guests aren't only here to enjoy Diego's expensive alcohol and hospitality–and drugs, too, from the lines on gilded mirrors that I see some of the men snorting, while two others swallow pills handed to them by the girls next to them, chasing the pills down with their liquor of choice.

The party is also, essentially, an orgy.

Some of the men on the couches have their new girls kneeling between their legs, mouths already on their cocks or playing with them. Others are standing while the girls kneel, and a few others have their girls on their laps, legs spread as they play with them. Another man has apparently already decided to share his purchase, as he bounces her on his lap while she leans forwards, giving a blowjob to another man standing in front of her. Three other men are surrounding two of the girls as they're forced to pleasure each other on one of the couches, hands busy on their own cocks as they watch, and yet another of the men has his girl over his knees, her babydoll nightgown pushed up above her bare ass as he lazily spanks her, her reddened eyes tightly squeezed shut.

All of it is overwhelming and terrifying, and any brief arousal I might have felt at the idea of Levin choosing what I'd wear tonight vanishes in an instant, as I'm suddenly surrounded by more lust and sex than I've ever experienced in my life–quite literally from nothing to everything, all at once. I'm in a room full of things I've only ever read about and some that I haven't even imagined. For instance, the girl that I see suddenly pulled up from one of the couches and bent over as the older man who had been playing with her a moment ago suddenly frees his cock and shoves it without preamble into what I'm almost certainly sure is her ass.

I shudder, and I feel Levin pull me closer, his hand still on my arm. We're only a little ways into the room, and it suddenly hits me with an overwhelming, dizzying awareness of what we're going to have to do, if we're going to continue to play this game.

There's not a single man in this room not enjoying his new toy. Levin might be able to find an excuse to stay sober, not to do the drugs being passed around, but he won't be able to get away without touching me at all. If he does, it will be patently obvious that something is off about all of it.

When I look up at him, I see another brief flicker of emotion across his face, one that he quickly tries to hide. But this time, it's not lust.

It's worry.

I'm fairly certain that it's worry for *me*.

He snags a glass of champagne from a passing tray, handing it to me as we approach the bar. "Tequila *añejo*, straight," he tells the bartender. "Best you have."

I take a gulp of the champagne instantly, feeling the nerves coalescing into a ball in my stomach. *If someone has to touch me like–like that tonight, it's better if it's him,* I tell myself. But no one has *ever* touched me intimately, in any way. No one has ever kissed me. The only hands that have ever touched my body like that are my own, lost in fantasies that have never been anything like this.

I don't think I'm an exhibitionist, and the idea of it terrifies me.

"Do you want something to take the edge off?" Levin asks quietly as we step away from the bar, towards one of the unoccupied couches. "Something stronger than that?"

I think he's talking about liquor at first, but then I see his gaze land on one of the staff circling the room with a tray that has small packets of something that's not food or alcohol, and I realize what he means. That it might be easier to bear this if I'm high.

I'm not sure that it would be. I've never had anything in my system stronger than wine in my life, and I don't know what it would feel like. I have no point of reference.

"I don't think this is the time to start experimenting," I whisper, and Levin nods as he pulls me towards the couch. Our conversation has gone unnoticed–everyone is too caught up in their own pleasure–but I know he'll have to join in soon, or those who are finishing up and waiting to recover will start to wonder why he's not enjoying the girl he paid so much to have.

Levin sinks down onto the couch, his drink in one hand as his arm goes around my waist, and he pulls me down onto his lap. I land a little ungracefully on one thigh, one leg draped over his and the other between them, my shoe wedged between his feet as the chiffon of my skirt drapes over his legs, leaving the long tanned line of one of mine bare.

"What are you going to do?" I whisper, taking another gulp of my champagne, as he sips his tequila with the sort of bored laziness that suits the kind of man he's pretending to be. "I know you have to–I just want to be prepared, before you–"

Levin's arm goes around my waist, his fingers brushing against my bare side where the fabric is open. The feeling sends another tingle across my skin and down my spine, an unfamiliar warmth flickering out from where he's touching me. "I'm not going to do more than I absolutely have to," he murmurs, tilting his head so that his lips are very close to my ear. To anyone watching, it would look as if he's beginning to explore his new pet.

"What does that mean?" My breath hitches in my throat. I'm not supposed to be enjoying this. I know I'm not, but his lips are almost brushing the shell of my ear, his breath very warm against it, and *everything* about this is so unfamiliar that it's sending a riot of emotion and sensation through me that I can't begin to understand, made all the more confusing by the fact that I know I'm safe with Levin. If there were anyone who I could trust not to take things further than they need to go, it's him–and that makes it far too easy to let myself start to enjoy the strange new sensations.

"It means I'm going to go very slowly," Levin murmurs. "I don't want to hurt you, Elena, or violate you. I shouldn't be touching you at all, but I think you understand that if I don't, it will draw the wrong kind of attention. So instead, I'm going to act as if I'm drawing this out. Savoring my prize. With any luck, the party will be over, and everyone will be too drunk, high, or have already gone upstairs with their girls to notice that I haven't done much more than touch."

As he speaks, his voice a low, accented rumble in my ear; I can feel the tension in him. He'd done a good job of disguising his accent earlier today to not sound Russian–no doubt a part of his job over the years–but now I can hear it slipping through as he murmurs in my ear. I know that this is getting to him, too. I can feel it in the hardness of the muscled thigh that I'm perched on, how stiffly he's sitting, can see it in the flex of his hand around the tequila glass.

He forces himself to relax, leaning back against the velvet couch as he pulls me closer, adjusting me on his lap. I hear his low grunt as he does so, and I feel something shift beneath me, a throbbing that I realize in a flush of confused heat is his cock getting hard.

Levin might not want to touch me like this, in front of all of these people, but his body has other ideas. And the thought that *I've* made him lose even that small bit of control, that he can't stop himself from getting turned on by having me in his lap, touching me even the small amount that he has so far, sends a prickle of arousal through me that I hadn't expected.

His hand slips over the chiffon, over my bare breast, cupping it. He's taking another sip of his tequila as he does, looking around the room, affecting boredom with all of this. Pretending to be above it, the kind of man who can throw away a huge sum of money so casually on a girl that he's not even frantic to claim the prize he's purchased, just savor it bit by bit. Meanwhile, I can feel myself starting to fray at the edges.

Why does it feel so good? His broad hand cupping my breast feels heated, the warmth of it burning through the chiffon. He just holds me like that for a moment, the weight of his arm across my back as heavy and secure as it had been earlier, my breast against his palm– and then his thumb brushes over my nipple.

I gasp before I can stop to wonder if I should or not. A spark of pleasure shoots through me, my nipple stiffening against his touch, and I feel that throb beneath me again, harder this time, and the pressure of his cock pushing against my ass. He'd been getting an erection before, but now he's stiff, his cock thickening by the moment as his hand momentarily flexes around my breast.

He feels *huge*.

My eyes flutter closed. I don't know what to do. I'm terrified to look at his face. *This is all a game,* I tell myself, swallowing past the lump in my throat as Levin toys with my nipple, rolling it between thumb and forefinger. *None of it means anything.* But it *feels* real. His cock, swollen and hard under my ass, is real. The pleasure sparking over my skin, pleasure I've never felt before, is real.

The wetness I can feel gathering between my heated, flushed thighs is real.

"Your new pet seems to be enjoying herself."

The thick voice coming from in front of me startles me into opening my eyes. A middle-aged man is standing there, eyes glazed from whatever drug he's taken, a glass of dark alcohol in his hand, and his girl–one of the other brunettes–standing just behind him. Her clothing is long gone–such as it was–and she's entirely naked. I can see the glisten of his cum still streaking her flat stomach and upper thighs.

Levin looks at the man with that same bored expression. "I find it's more fun this way," he says lazily, his accent once again gone. He sounds almost American. "Making them beg for it, by the time I'm ready to have them. She'll be so wound up that she'll plead for me to fuck her, instead of screaming and crying. More humiliating in the end, I think."

The man nods, a lopsided smile spreading across his face. "I like the crying," he says thickly, his hand closing around the girl's arm. "Maybe we can let them play together. I'd like that, but I think Rosa here would hate it. A good lesson for her to do as I say."

"I'm enjoying myself as we are, for now," Levin says tightly, and I see his jaw clench. "Maybe later."

I can see the other man's face fall a little, but Levin's voice brooks no argument. I feel my own stomach tighten, wondering if his refusal is going to cause a problem, but the man just shrugs, grabbing the girl he'd called Rosa a little more tightly. "I'll just find someone else for her to play with," he says, slurring a little, and then he moves past us, as Levin's arm tightens around me.

"Will that be suspicious?" I whisper, my voice cracking a bit, and Levin shakes his head.

"As much as I paid for you, they'll expect me to be jealous of you. That man is just so fucked out of his head already that he didn't think of it." Levin shifts, and I can feel that his erection has softened. It makes me feel better, realizing that the encounter turned him off, instead of arousing him like it would have with probably anyone else in here.

I want to ask if we can go upstairs yet, but I already know the answer. The party is just getting into full swing. I know that even the excuse of not wanting to wait to enjoy his prize won't be enough to ease the suspicion of him not enjoying this as much as everyone else is. It's clear that this whole night is a highlight for all the other men, and Levin has to play his part as much as he's able.

So do I—and it's easier than I'd thought it would be. Disturbingly so.

Levin's fingers brush over my nipple again, and I feel my breath catch in my throat. His hand shifts and I feel the touch of it against my bare skin once more, slowly, enough to warn me of what he's about to do before his hand slips *under* the chiffon and his fingers curl around my bare breast.

I moan, a soft, barely audible sound, but I know he hears it from the way I feel his cock jerk beneath me. My face instantly flushes, bright and heated with embarrassment. *What is wrong with me?* I only have a moment to wonder before Levin's fingers slide against my bare, hard nipple, and I feel a jolt of electric pleasure shoot straight down between my thighs.

I feel like I'm going to dissolve. *How is it this good?* He's only touched my breast, and I feel like I'm losing control. *What would more feel like? His tongue—his fingers somewhere else, his—*

I force the thoughts out of my head as Levin lightly pinches my nipple, and I sink my teeth into my lower lip to keep from moaning again. I want more, and it confuses me. *Why do I want this? Why do I want him?*

He's older than me, certainly. Close to twenty years older, if I had to guess. But he's devastatingly handsome, too. I have the urge to reach up and touch his sharp jawline, run my fingers over that smooth skin, and brush my thumb over his full lower lip. As he turns me in his lap, I have the sudden, horrifying urge to lean forward and kiss him, and I only barely manage to stop myself.

"We have to go a little further, to keep up," Levin says quietly. "But I don't want you to have to be more exposed than need be, so we'll do it like this."

He turns me so that I'm straddling his lap, the chiffon draping in front of and behind me so that my legs are bare, and the open part of the dress that shows my back is bare, but nothing else. My breasts and most intimate places are hidden, but as I face him, I realize it's also made me much more vulnerable in other ways.

I'm hovering just above him on my knees, and I can feel the brush of air against the bare flesh between my thighs. I'm mortified to realize how wet I am, and even more so knowing that if I move too much, if I graze against him, he'll eventually know it too.

He won't touch me there. Not unless he has to. It's too far. So just don't sit directly on him, don't make a mess, and he'll never know.

Slowly, Levin's hands smooth up my sides. He's set his glass of tequila aside, and I feel myself shiver as his hands slide over my breasts again, this time atop the chiffon.

I'd never imagined that just having my breasts played with could feel so good. He hasn't touched me anywhere else, and my entire body feels flushed and tight. I'm throbbing between my legs, wet and heated, and I want more. I can't pretend that I don't, even though I don't understand how I can, here, like this, with a man who is pretending to do this in order to get us both out of here alive.

I realize, as he thumbs the chiffon away between my breasts, pushing it to either side so that I'm slowly bared to him without anyone else seeing what he's doing. With me seated on his lap like this, there's no way for any of the other guests to know exactly how far we've gone. He likely wouldn't be expected to take my very expensive virginity so unceremoniously, but it looks like he's toying with the idea, at least. Enjoying me, as he *is* expected to.

All of those thoughts fly out of my head when Levin lowers his mouth to my nipple.

I clutch at his shoulders, gasping. His tongue flicks over the stiffened flesh, sending a river of liquid heat through me. Before I can stop myself, I feel my back arching, sinking down onto his lap before I can remember my resolve, and exactly what he'll know when I get up.

The stiff, smooth fabric of his suit trousers grazes over the sensitive, swollen flesh between my thighs. Worse still, I can feel the hard ridge of his cock pressing against my bare pussy, and it feels even lewder on account of the fact that he's fully, entirely dressed–and I barely am. There's only his trousers between my bare flesh and his naked cock, and I have the sudden, dizzying thought that I wish there wasn't.

My entire body feels as if it's throbbing with need. I feel him flinch as I sink down onto his lap, his hands tightening on my sides. For one brief second, his mouth tightens around my nipple, sucking as his teeth graze against it, and my mouth drops open on a moan louder than before.

"*Fuck*," Levin breathes against my skin, and I know in that instant that I'm getting to him, too. He pulls back, jerking the chiffon back into place, his hand dropping to my thigh and sliding upwards as I feel his chest heave. I know he's struggling to get himself back under control, and I have a wild, entirely inappropriate desire to push, to make him *lose* more of it instead, the way I feel as if I am.

I want more of the strange pleasure swirling in and through and over me. I want to find out what comes next, because my hands on my breasts, my skin, and between my legs have *never* felt like this. I want to grind myself down onto his lap, rub my clit against the friction of his covered cock until I come on his lap, or beg for his fingers to take me there instead.

Dizzily, I turn my head, looking across the room. Most of the men are taking pleasure instead of giving it, but one man has his girl on her back on one of the couches, his head buried between her thighs as he holds her open, his other hand moving feverishly between his own legs as he jerks himself off while he goes down on her. Next to them, another man has the blonde bent over the arm of the couch, fucking her furiously from behind. I can see the jealousy on her face as she looks at the girl in front of her, being brought to a screaming climax by the man's tongue on her clit.

Levin could do that. He could make you come like that. What would it feel like? I can't even imagine it, the kind of pleasure that must be. I feel myself throb at the thought, a fresh wave of arousal coursing through me, and I realize with horror that I'm even wetter than before, that I must be soaking him. I have no idea if he can feel it or not.

His hand is on the top of my thigh, slipping under the chiffon, very near where I want it. But he doesn't move it further, and I know it's a ruse, a ploy to look as if he's touching me more intimately when he's not.

What if he has to ask me to do something to him? Touch his cock, or—or put my mouth on it—

The thought isn't as horrifying as it should be. I feel another pulse of desire at the thought, of Levin taking my hand and pressing it against him, wrapping my fingers around him. *What would his face look like? What noises would he make? Would he come all over my hand? In my mouth?*

There are so many things I know about from my books, in the vague sort of way that I've managed to imagine them, and all of them I've never experienced in reality. Everything about this night is wilder than I could have expected, and it feels like a madhouse, like I'm slowly losing my mind. I've gone from never having so much as been kissed to seeing the lewdest, pornographic displays of sexuality right in front of me, and I don't know how to feel about any of it.

I don't know how to feel about what I'm feeling now.

There's another voice from behind me, a rougher one, and I jerk on Levin's lap, my stomach curdling at the question he asks.

"Well, you're taking your sweet time with her, aren't you? Going to deprive us all of watching you take that virginity you paid so much for?"

It's Diego's voice behind me, and I close my eyes, feeling all the arousal leach out of me in an instant.

I might not be as safe as I thought I was.

Levin

I'm losing my fucking mind. Nowhere, in any of the planning that we'd done, had I expected this to be this goddamn difficult.

I'd expected that they'd put her in something meant to arouse. I'd told myself it would be fine. I'm not the young man I once was, and I'm no fucking virgin. I ought to be able to control myself when confronted with a woman in sparse clothing, no matter how beautiful.

The dress they'd put her in made her look like a princess on her wedding night. Luxurious, elegant, and lewdly sexual all at once, both covering and revealing just enough to drive a man mad with wanting to strip it off and see exactly what's being hinted at underneath. I'd felt a jolt of lust like nothing I'd felt in a long time go through me when I'd seen her, and it had made me feel ashamed, just like in the courtyard.

I'm not here to want her. I'm here to protect her.

Remember what happened the last time you let yourself lust after a woman you were supposed to protect, I'd told myself, that ever-present voice in my head digging in cruelly, reminding me of past failings. It had cooled my lust enough for me to warn her that the party wasn't going to be what she expected.

I hadn't expected it to already be in such full swing, but Diego's guests had wasted absolutely no time. We'd walked into a full fucking orgy, with the men who'd bought girls from the auction today, wasting no time "enjoying" them.

I'd needed a drink as badly as I was certain she did.

I'd also felt guilty about suggesting she take something stronger, some of the pills or other party drugs that I saw circulating–Diego's specialties. I knew they'd be high enough grade that they wouldn't hurt her, and I'd felt desperate to think of some way to make this easier on her.

It had probably been for the best that she'd refused. On the other hand, when I'd pulled her down onto my lap and heard her ask what I was going to do to her, I'd started to wish *I* had something stronger to take the edge off.

I didn't know what the fuck was wrong with me. I've always loved women, always enjoyed sex and novelty, and enjoyed hedonistic pleasures to their fullest, even before I'd ever been in love and long after I'd been certain I never would be again. But I'm old enough not to get instantly hard when a girl sits down on my leg.

Elena had me half-hard the instant her ass hit my thigh.

And after that–

I'd been dancing a fine line. She was willing, up to a point. But everything we were going to do was also because we *had* to, in order to not get caught. It was a blurry line between willingness and coercion, a real grey area that I was hellishly fucking uncomfortable with.

What I hadn't expected was for her to *actually* be willing.

I'm not going to do more than I absolutely have to, I'd told her as I put my arm around her waist, touching her gently where her dress opened to reveal the bare flesh of her side, the slight curve of the side of her breast. When she'd asked what that meant, it had taken everything in me not to say things that I absolutely knew I fucking shouldn't and had no business thinking at all.

It means I'm not going to bite your ear, even though my lips are so close to it. It means I'm not going to slide my hand up between your thighs and show you how it feels to have fingers that aren't yours touch your clit. It means I'm not going to make you come in front of all these people, even though right now I'm having a hard fucking time remembering that any of them are here at all.

Instead, I'd pushed all those inappropriate, lewd fucking thoughts away and told her I'd go slow. That I wouldn't hurt her. And I'd meant it.

I'd never fucking hurt her. I'd never do anything she didn't want.

I tried to control it. I really fucking did. I didn't want to frighten her, or make her feel violated, and I knew damned well that she'd never sat on a man's lap and felt a hard cock pushing up against her ass before. I *knew* that. But it was fucking impossible to wrestle my body into submission. And that was just having her sitting in my lap.

I'd gone slow, both for her sake and mine, as slow as I fucking could without looking suspicious. I'd gone for bored instead, a rich fucking prick who could take his time deflowering his new acquisition because that much money didn't mean shit to him. And *fuck*, had I spent a lot of money getting her.

Ricardo Santiago was going to need a long time to recover from the blow his accounts had been dealt.

I knew I was making her feel things for the first time. Things that she wouldn't have felt until she'd gotten married, had things shaken out the way they were supposed to for her, and maybe not even then. Whatever dried-up old asshole of a man that bargained for her hand in marriage probably wouldn't have made her gasp by brushing a thumb over her nipple, cupping her breast in his hand. *I* was making her feel that way. Teaching her things she'd never experienced before.

I'd been so fucking hard it hurt. I knew she could feel it. I knew it by the way her eyes fluttered closed, the way she swallowed hard as I played with her nipple, drawing out the moment where I'd have to go a little further and realizing with painful arousal that it was turning her on. In this room full of things she'd never seen or experienced before, she was still experiencing arousal for the first time from *me*.

It had turned me on more than it should. Apparently, innocence had a flavor that I enjoyed, and I wasn't sure if I hated myself or not for it. I'd never had a girl so innocent in my arms before. Never fucked a virgin. Never had someone so close to me who knew so little of pleasure.

The man who'd stopped by, offering up his new pet to play with Elena while we watched, had been the only thing stopping me from doing something that would have made me hate myself later.

The sight of his new 'pet' covered in his cum and looking as glazed and miserable as most of the other women in the room, was a sharp and welcome reminder of where the fuck I was and what I was doing. Elena might be more willing than she knew, more receptive to these new pleasures than either of us had expected, but that didn't change the fact that we were at an orgy comprised of bought women and the derelict pieces of shit who'd bought them, and that I shouldn't be enjoying myself at all.

I find it's more fun this way. Making them beg. More humiliating in the end.

Having to say that out loud, with my arm around Elena and my hands on her, had killed what was left of my arousal. Reassuring her that my refusal not to let him enjoy a show with her wouldn't put us in danger had sunk that nail deeper into the coffin of my desire.

If only that had lasted.

Once he'd gone, I had to escalate things, at least a little. But I hadn't expected to hear her moan just from the touch of my hand against her bare breast.

I'd seen her flush, seen how embarrassed she was. I'd seen the way she bit her lower lip as I touched her nipple, toying with it, feeling it stiff and hard and hot under my fingertips.

We had to keep going. Pushing that line. Trying to look as if I were participating in the night's festivities without taking too much of her innocence. But I knew that a part of it was hypocrisy. I'd turned her in my lap not just for her own modesty, but because the idea of anyone else in that room seeing her bare breasts sent a surge of startling, possessive anger through me that I knew I had no fucking business feeling.

I'd had to push the thoughts in my head down, hard, when she'd straddled my lap. I knew she was wearing nothing underneath the dress. I knew she'd be shaved bare. Smooth and warm, and from the noises she'd been making as I touched her, probably wet too. All that was between her and my cock were a couple layers of fabric.

I hated myself for even thinking it. But at my core, I'm a man. A man who has always loved the pleasure of women, and as I slid my hands over the dress covering her breasts again, I'd had to fight away the desire to know what it would feel like to push myself inside of her as deeply as I could go.

The one thing that stopped me, besides the fact that I wouldn't take her in public like this, was the knowledge that she's a virgin.

I'd felt her breathe in as I'd pushed the dress away from her breasts, my hands skimming over her silky skin. But I hadn't expected her reaction to my mouth on her nipple.

I hadn't expected her to grab onto me, to arch and moan, or the way she'd come down into my lap, hips sinking against mine as the heat of her had burned through my suit trousers and into the aching flesh of my cock, it had felt like.

It had felt so fucking good. *Too* fucking good.

She'd moaned again when I'd sucked on her nipple, teeth grazing, and I'd felt myself hanging onto my own personal moral code by a fucking thread.

What is it about her that makes me want her so goddamned much?

It didn't help that the whole fucking room was full of sex, escalating by the minute. The air was thick with it, hot with the scent of bodies and sweat and cum, mingled perfume and cologne, alcohol and smoke, and full of the sounds of it, too–the groans of men and the occasional moan of a woman finding a way to enjoy herself despite the situation. I hated it, all of it, the coercion and the reason all of this was happening at all, but my body reacted to it anyway. I felt it all throbbing just beneath my skin, a need waiting to burst out.

I'm experienced enough with women to know when one is attracted to me. When someone wants me. And I knew what Elena was feeling.

I couldn't let it go too far.

I'd been grappling with how far to let my hand creep up her thigh when Diego's voice had brought all of it to a crashing halt.

"Well, you're taking your sweet time with her, aren't you? Going to deprive us all of watching you take that virginity you paid so much for?"

I know what a fine fucking line I have to tread. The other men here might be so high or drunk or lost in sex that they won't pay too much attention to what I'm doing or not, so long as I'm here and appearing to participate, but Diego won't be so easy to fool. I can tell from his face that he's neither drunk nor high, but what I can't tell, even with all of my training, is whether or not he suspects me of anything.

I also know that there's not a single fucking thing on earth that will convince me to take Elena's virginity like this. I can't have sex with her at all, not and live with myself afterward, but I'd never forgive myself if I let it happen like this, in public, for the pleasure and amusement of these pricks. Whatever the consequences, Diego isn't going to bully me into that.

"I'm going to enjoy that in private, later," I tell him stiffly. "I didn't pay so much for her to rush things."

I can feel how tense Elena is in my arms, her face turned away so that she doesn't have to look at the man who is responsible for her being here at all.

"I would have thought you'd enjoy humiliating her in front of everyone. Forcing the Santiago girl to get her cherry popped in front of all her father's enemies. Maybe even fuck her in the ass, really make sure there's none of that so carefully guarded innocence left."

He grins widely as he speaks, licking his lips as his gaze rakes over her. I'm seized with a sudden, murderous urge to set Elena aside, get up from the couch, and strangle the man until his eyes pop out of his skull.

"That sort of humiliation isn't really what I go in for," I tell him, forcing myself to sound bored, as if this entire conversation is boring me, and not as if I want to kill him in all the slowest possible ways that I know. "I enjoy my pleasure taken more privately. I'm not the same sort of exhibitionist that your other guests are."

Diego's expression doesn't budge. "So why are you here at my party at all?"

There's an edge to his voice that I know means I'm on thin ice. He doesn't necessarily suspect me, not yet, but he's displeased that I'm depriving him of what he'd hoped for from this entire performance– the chance to watch Santiago's daughter cry in front of him while her virginity was violently ripped away. I've made him a very wealthy man, but I suspect he wanted that more than money.

Which just makes me that much more pleased that he won't fucking get it.

"I couldn't ignore your hospitality." I force the most pleasant smile that I can onto my face. "The chance to sit in luxury with a good drink and a beautiful girl on my lap isn't one to be taken lightly. I just prefer to–finish, in private. I want to take my time with her. Make her beg for her own–"

"–violation," Diego finishes, and from the way he says it, I can tell I'm in the clear, that he thinks we've found some common ground, something he can understand. "Well, I'm sorry I won't get the pleasure of watching it. But you paid enough. You take her however you please."

He claps me on the shoulder and walks away.

I *feel* how Elena shudders in my arms as he goes, nearly collapsing against my chest. "How much longer?" she whispers, and I wonder at that moment if all of her reactions, all this time, have just been her playing along for the sake of those around us.

It makes me feel worse to think that might be true. My skin crawls at the idea that she might have hated every moment of it, and I want to pick her up and set her off of my lap. But we're not in the clear yet.

"A little while longer. An hour, maybe, and then everyone will start retiring."

My hand rubs over her thigh as I speak, and I look at my empty tequila glass. "We'll take a break," I tell her. "Get more drinks, and then stall as long as we can."

I see a hint of relief on her face. Gently, I help her up, but the moment she's standing on her own two feet again, I see her gaze flick downwards, and her cheeks burn so red that they look as if they might combust.

All it takes is one glance at the front of my trousers, soaked with her arousal, to see why she's so embarrassed.

"Oh god." Her hand covers her mouth, and she looks away. I can see the hint of humiliated tears in her eyes, and I pull her closer, not wanting anyone else to see.

"There's nothing to be ashamed of," I tell her quietly as I lead her towards the bar, unwilling to leave her alone in a room full of lust-addled men. "It's a natural reaction, Elena."

"Here? To *this*?" Her voice is a panicked squeak. "I thought you wouldn't know–"

"Oh, Elena." I motion to the bartender, who remembers what I'd ordered before and starts to pour, pushing another glass of champagne toward her. "I knew. I could hear you. Feel it. I know what it feels like when a woman is turned on."

Her face turns even redder, if that were possible, and I see what almost looks like a flicker of hurt in her eyes. I'm not sure why–the idea that I've been with other women shouldn't bother her. It's not as if anything between us is real, and besides–*surely she knows I'm nearly twenty years her senior?* She doesn't need to know I've fucked my way across every country I've ever set foot in, but she can't imagine that I'm as virginal as she is.

"It's nothing to be embarrassed about," I repeat, gently, as I take my drink and steer her back towards another empty couch. "But if it makes you feel better, we'll do this a little differently."

I sit her down next to me, her legs over my lap, the drape of her dress hiding the mess that she'd made of the front of my trousers. I slide my free hand up under her skirt, caressing her inner thigh, but to anyone looking, I might just as well be fingering her.

From the look on Elena's face, they'd be well within their right to assume that. Her free hand grips the edge of the velvet sofa as her lips part slightly at the feeling of my fingers brushing against the soft skin of her upper thigh, just inside of it, trailing down to her knee and back up again. To me, it's a fairly innocent caress, but her expression looks as if I might as well have reached between her thighs.

I need to get her upstairs soon, before one of us combusts.

Fortunately, within the next hour, as I'd predicted, the party starts to wind down. The more elderly of the guests fold first, taking their new 'purchases' upstairs as they get too drunk or exhausted to keep partying with the younger associates of Diego's. But one by one, all of them start to peel away, heading off to either sleep off their substances or keep fucking in private.

When only a few are left, I take that as my cue, and help Elena up off the couch.

"We're going up?" she asks, her voice trembling a little, and I nod.

"We have to stay here tonight," I tell her quietly as I put an arm around her waist, fingers possessively pressed against her hipbone as I lead her towards the doorway. "It's expected, or I'd take you out of here right now. But we'll be behind a locked door, and I won't leave you alone. Tomorrow, we'll be out of here for good."

She nods as we reach the stairs, headed up to the room I was shown earlier would be ours for the evening. It's a two-room suite, with a huge bedroom and an attached separate sitting area with couches and a fireplace, and an attached bathroom as large as the sitting area.

I'm not unaccustomed to luxury, having spent plenty of time in five-star accommodations throughout my life and in Viktor's home, but Diego's mansion borders on obscene.

The moment we're alone, the door securely locked behind us, I press my finger to her lips as I look at her. It looks like a caress to anyone watching, but she takes it for the meaning it is, giving me an almost imperceptible nod.

Once again, I'm wholly impressed by how quickly she catches on.

I make my way around the room, looking for any hint of microphones, small cameras, or any other way that the room might be bugged. It takes longer than I'd like, but once the first pass is complete in every room, and I find nothing, I make a second round with a small, palm-sized device that will make sure of it.

The room is empty. No one will see or hear us, and I feel some of the tension finally leach out of me as I turn to her, finally able to speak plainly for the first time since I'd arrived here.

"Diego will expect that I'm going to take your virginity tonight," I tell her gently. "The kind of man I'm pretending to be wouldn't wait any longer."

A sudden, terrified expression flashes across her face. I realize too late that she's misinterpreted what I've said–that she thinks I'm implying that I *will* have to take her virginity tonight, not that we'll have to fake it. But before I can explain to her what I meant, she lurches forward suddenly, her hands grabbing at the front of my shirt as she pushes herself up on her toes and presses her mouth hard against mine.

It's a clumsy, forceful kiss, lips and teeth shoved against mine, but I can't fault her for it. I can feel the fear trembling through every inch of her body. And yet, even so, as she arches against me with her hands in my shirt, her tongue teasing the edge of my lip as she kisses me with the sort of furious inexperience that has never turned me on in my life.

And yet, I feel a wave of almost dizzying arousal as her mouth crushes against mine, my cock surging against my fly, straining with need as my hands close on her waist for one brief moment of weakness in which I envision everything I could do to her. Everything I could teach her in that huge bed only steps away from us.

No one to see. No one to hear. Only the two of us, and the rest of the night to enjoy it. I can feel the nervous desire in her too–but I remember the look of fear on her face, and my hands tighten on her waist as I gently set her back away from me as I break the kiss and step back too.

That's not what I'm here for. And no matter what my mind tries to come up with, I can't rationalize it.

"That's not what I meant," I tell her gently. "I meant that we'll have to fake blood on the sheets, so that there's no suspicion raised before we can put a good distance between ourselves and this place. That's all. I'm not going to have sex with you tonight, Elena. I'm not even going to sleep in the bed with you, so there's no chance of temptation."

To my utter surprise, I don't see relief on her face. Instead, a look of hurt settles there, and I can see her almost draw in on herself, her lips pressing together as she looks up at me, her arms wrapping around her waist.

"Is it because of me?" she asks, her voice taking on that slight tremor again. "Because the kiss was too clumsy? I can try it again. I just–I've never kissed anyone before. Or been kissed."

A wave of guilt that threatens to drown me washes over me, saturating me in it. *Her first fucking kiss, you asshole. You should have caught her before she did it.* That's *going to be her first kiss forever. And you were stupid enough not to see it coming.*

I know that the next thought that enters my mind isn't one I should have. I *know* it's not going to help matters. I know I'm rationalizing things that can't be.

But god help me, I can't stop the words that come out of my mouth.

"We'll try it again, then."

I can't let that be her first kiss. That's all. Who knows who will be next? She deserves to have it be good, after everything that's happened to her. One good first kiss.

I step closer to her. In the cool silence of the room, I can smell the sweet floral scent coming off of her, mingled with the warm, soft scent of her skin. It makes my mouth go dry, my chest ache as I reach for her waist with one hand again, gentler this time, pulling her up against me.

Her body goes soft against mine, pressed against me, her breasts brushing against my chest, hips to hips, thighs to thighs. My cock throbs, straining, and I wonder all over again how I can be so fucking aroused by a woman that I've barely touched. Barely kissed. I haven't felt this way since—

Don't you dare fucking think of that. Not now. Not fucking now.

I slide my hand along the side of her jaw, my thumb brushing over her lower lip, her cheekbone, my hand curling around to the back of her neck. Her hair falls like silk through my fingers, and in the silence of the room, punctuated only by her quick breaths and mine, I swear I can hear the sound of my own heartbeat.

Or hers.

I see her eyes widen as I bend my head and hear the quick hitch of her breath. I feel her hands brush against my sides, circling around to press against my back, holding me closer as my lips brush against hers. A better first kiss, to wipe away the last one.

Soft, at first. Her bottom lip, full and soft, pressed between mine. My nose brushing against hers. Gentle, urging a little, but not too much. Letting her feel the warmth of my breath against her sensitive mouth, my hand holding the back of her neck, her waist, keeping her close. Keeping her safe.

I feel her shudder, feel her gasp. Her lips part under mine, the cue to deepen the kiss. To brush my lips over hers again before I press harder, firmer, my tongue sliding over that plush lower lip, pushing inside. Tasting her, champagne still bright on her tongue, and oh *fuck*, she tastes like fucking heaven.

I want to taste the rest of her. I want to fucking drown in her, until my blood is fizzing with her, until I find out every fucking moan and cry that she can make, exactly the way she moans at that moment, the soft sound on the verge of driving me mad as she arches into the kiss, her tongue sliding along mine, soft and quick and eager. I know in that instant that she'd let me take this as far as I would let it go.

It's up to me to stop. To do what's right. To keep myself from sinking into her, into the sweet eagerness of her kiss, because if there's one thing that my godforsaken life has taught me, it's that all a man like me can do to a woman like Elena Santiago is ruin her.

You ruined one woman's life by wanting her. By loving her. Don't fucking do it again.

That reminder does it. I pull away, breaking the kiss, tearing myself away from her through sheer force of will as I step back, teeth gritted against the desire burning through my veins, threatening to reduce me to nothing.

"I hope that was better," I tell her, and I mean every fucking word of it. But I can't look at her a second longer, can't stay in the room a second longer, or I'll do every fucking thing that I want to do to her, and then we'll both be lost.

So instead, I turn on my heel, ignoring the look on her face as I bolt into the bathroom and slam the door behind me.

Elena

I've never been so confused and wildly aroused all at once in my life.

What the fuck was that kiss?

I raise my fingers to my lips, hand shaking, as he storms away. *I hope that was better,* he'd said.

It had been. So much better than my own clumsy, embarrassing attempt at kissing him. I'd been so humiliated, especially when compounded by the fact that I'd misunderstood him. I'd thought he'd meant that we'd have to sleep together tonight, in order to avoid getting caught. It had been my way of trying to make him feel better about it, not so much as if he were forcing me.

I feel very sure, at this point, that Levin would never force me into anything. Which has had a strange, roundabout way of making me want him more.

And then he kissed me–like *that*. A second try. A better first kiss, I suppose he'd been thinking. But *why*, if that was all he was going to do?

I stand there, frozen, my lips still tingling from his kiss as confusion overwhelms me, staring in the direction he'd gone when he'd stormed into the bathroom.

What do I actually want from him?

Rationally, I know it doesn't make sense for me to want him to be my first at all, and *especially* not in these circumstances. Not only is he a fairly decent bit older than I am, but he's also in charge of getting me to safety. He's supposed to be my *bodyguard*, not my lover. If I were going to want anyone of my own choice, I should want someone closer to my age, more like me, more like the person I was raised to be. Not a dangerous older man with an uncertain past and a violent edge to him, tasked with doing anything necessary to keep me safe and get me to my sister in Boston.

Shouldn't I?

I especially shouldn't want him now, like this, in Diego Gonzalez' mansion, surrounded by bedrooms in which a few dozen other men are enjoying women coerced into being with them. I shouldn't even be able to be aroused in these circumstances. And yet–

In here, especially, it feels as if the rest of the world is gone. As if there's only this room, and me, and Levin.

And my mouth is still burning from the kiss.

All I know of love and sex, I know from my books. From romance novels that paint scenarios every bit as dangerous and fraught as this one. I know that's a part of it, that I'm romanticizing all of this, romanticizing *him*, and yet as I slip into bed, still tangled up in the chiffon dress, my body still throbs with an arousal that I can't fight.

I feel like I'm buzzing with it, coming out of my skin. I can feel my heartbeat, my pulse throbbing in my throat, and I lie there motionless for a few seconds, wondering if he's going to come out of the bathroom.

The light stays on under the door, but it doesn't open.

My hand slides down under the blankets I'd tugged up over myself.

I need something. I need release. I push the chiffon aside, finding the bare skin underneath, my teeth sinking into my lower lip against a gasp when my fingers slip between my swollen, sensitive folds. My fingertip grazes against my clit, sliding through heated arousal, and I have to fight not to moan as my head falls back.

I'd wondered if he was going to do this, all night. If he'd slide his hand a little higher, and touch me here, where I'd been aching all evening. I press my finger down, a little harder, moving it back and forth, in small circles, chasing the relief I need so desperately.

What if he's doing the same thing?

The image in my head is instantaneous, the thought of Levin standing in the bathroom, hand clutched around his cock as he strokes feverishly, imagining me. I think of the arousal I left on his trousers earlier, and I feel a flush of desire instead of shame, wondering if he was turned on by it. If he liked that he'd made me so wet.

The way he'd kissed me a little while ago suggests that he did.

I fight back another moan as I rub my finger over my clit, imagining that it's his fingers instead. Better yet, his *tongue*. I imagine it, as wet and hot as I am right now, sliding over my aching flesh, and I want so badly to know how it would feel. I want to know what it feels like for him to make me come with his tongue, his fingers, his–

My other hand slides down, fingertips parting my folds, and I imagine him seeing me like this, legs spread, my dress tangled around me, head thrown back in pleasure. I imagine him groaning softly, leaning forward, his cock rock-hard as he looked at me, and whispered how beautiful he thought I was. I slide my fingers around my entrance and imagine that it's his thick cock, nudging up against me, on the verge of sliding inside. On the verge of teaching me what it would feel like, for the very first time.

I don't go quite as far as pushing my fingers inside myself. I've never done that before. But I tease myself, there at the very brink, imagining his cock as I circle my clit faster, my breath coming in short, quick bursts as I think of him in the other room, hand gripping the edge of the sink as he strokes his cock, driving himself towards the same release that I so desperately need.

It might really be what he's doing, and that only fuels my arousal. My back arches, hips grinding upwards into my hand, seeking more of the pleasure as I let my knees fall to either side, rubbing quick and fast. I want more, I *need* more, and I slip the very tips of my two fingers inside of myself, just a little, imagining that it's his cock nudging inside of me.

Just a little, I hear in my head, as if it's his voice. *Just let me feel you a little bit, princess. You're so hot and wet and tight, and my cock aches for you. Just a little. I won't come. I promise I won't.*

I imagine myself letting him. I remember how thick he felt when I sat in his lap, how huge, and I scissor my two fingers just inside of myself, imagining him stretching me open with just the swollen tip, nudging inside, promising me he'd keep control. Watching as I stroke my clit for him, his hand moving up and down his shaft, as I watch, too, just the head of his cock sliding in all that heated arousal that he'd created, taking just a little of his pleasure.

I won't come, he'd promise me, but I'd see how difficult it is from the set of his jaw, from how tense he'd be. *Just a little bit*, he'd say, but I'd see how much he wants to keep going, to push the rest of that huge cock inside of me, opening me up, taking me for his own.

I'm getting close; I can feel it. My clit throbs under my fingertips, and I imagine feeling his cock throb inside of me, just the barest inch, as he touches himself too. I imagine those blue eyes fixed on mine, hungry and needing more, and I imagine him losing control, his hand stuttering on his cock as I clench around him, pulling out of me just in time to not come inside of me but not before he comes *on* me—

That's what sends me over the edge. The thought of Levin losing control, his cock throbbing in his hand as his cum covers me, coating my thighs and clit and dripping down my pussy as I come for him, too, that's all it takes to make my entire body seize with pleasure, clenching around my fingertips as I turn my face into the pillow to muffle the sounds, fingers flying over my clit as I come apart at the seams.

It's better than any orgasm I've ever given myself before. I've been teased all night, shown sensations I'd never felt before. Now I finally get the relief I need, arousal dripping over my fingers as I come and come, muscles tight and body shaking with the spasms as I bite the pillow, shuddering through each wracking burst of my climax.

I forget that Levin could come out of the bathroom and catch me at any moment. I forget everything except the pleasure that I want to keep going on forever, the way it feels, the way my entire body seizes with it, until at last, I'm limp and gasping on the bed, flushed and hot and still shivering with the aftershocks of my violent release.

A few moments later, I hear the door to the bathroom click open, and my face heats all over again.

Could he hear me? Was he waiting for me to be finished? Is that why he took so long?

The idea that he wasn't pleasuring himself, but fully aware that I was and waiting so as not to embarrass me, is more humiliating than I could possibly have anticipated. I shove my dress back into place as much as I can, tugging the covers up and trying to look as if I'm on the verge of falling asleep when he comes out, but I can't discern from the look on his face whether he knows or not.

If anything, he looks as exhausted as I feel. He circles around to my side of the bed, jaw set in a way that's beginning to be familiar to me as he looks down at me with some trepidation.

"Lay still," he says calmly. "And I'll fake the blood on the sheets."

Levin

When I stalk into the bathroom, I'm so aroused that I can't think straight.

I had to get away from her, put some space between us, or I would have done something that she would have regretted later. How could she not?

I've introduced her to things that she's never felt before tonight, and she's confused and curious. I can understand that. But it's my responsibility to make sure it doesn't go further than necessary, and I know that too.

I was brought here to keep her safe, not corrupt her. And I know all too well how even the beginning of something like this can complicate things beyond repair.

I can't quell my arousal, though. My cock is so hard it aches, straining against the fly of my trousers. I grip the edge of the counter as I glare at myself in the mirror, trying to wrestle myself into submission, gritting my teeth against the waves of throbbing lust.

In the end, there's really only one way to deal with it.

I undo my belt, thumbing the button open with a near-frantic desperation as I yank the zipper down and reach for my cock. It slips out instantly, hot and straining against my palm, and I hiss through my teeth as I wrap my hand around myself, desperate for the release I've needed all night.

Don't think about her. Think about anything else.

I fucking try. I try to think of other women I've taken to bed, particularly hot porn I've watched, women I've lusted after but not managed to seal the deal with, *anything* other than the gorgeous woman in the room on the other side of that door, because as far as I'm concerned, fantasizing about her while I stroke my cock is just as bad as walking in there and acting on the urge to fuck her until she screams my name.

Don't think about her squirming on your lap. Don't think about that little gasp she made when you touched her breast, or the way she moaned when you brushed your fingers over her nipple. Definitely, don't think about how she was so wet that she covered you in it, soaked through your fucking pants, that the scent of her pussy is probably on your cock right now. Don't think about the way she tasted when you kissed her, the way she wanted it, how soft she was, how fucking good it felt–

"Fuck!" My hand seizes around my cock, the word hissed out through gritted teeth, as I try to be quiet. I don't want her to realize what I'm doing on the other side of the door. I don't want to disgust or frighten her, but then I go still for a moment as I hear what sounds like a small, shuddering gasp from the other room.

Oh, holy fuck.

The tidal wave of lust that crashes into me when I realize what she's doing is almost unbearable. I can picture it so fucking clearly, her lying on that bed with her hand between her legs, her fingers sliding through all that slick heat as she finds her small throbbing clit and starts to stroke it–

What if she's thinking about me, too? What if she knows what I'm doing? What if she's fantasizing about the same thing?

It doesn't make a damn bit of difference, and I know that. I can't touch her. I can't go any further than we did tonight, and what we did tonight can't happen ever again. But my cock is harder than I ever thought possible at the realization that she's on the other side of that door, touching herself the same way I am, *wanting* the same way that I am.

I grip the edge of the counter so hard that my knuckles turn white, my hand moving feverishly along her cock as I give up trying not to imagine her. I can *see* what she must look like, the way her legs would fall open at the touch, can hear the small gasps and moans she's undoubtedly making right now, those full lips parted as she rubs–

I want to know how she touches herself, with one finger or two, the motions she likes, what makes her gasp, what makes her hips jerk, and her back arch. My hand spasms around my cock as I imagine how she must taste, the way she'd cry out at the feeling of my tongue sliding through all of that hot wetness, curling around her clit, *sucking*. I wouldn't even need to fuck her to be satisfied, just taste her, just find out what it's like to have her come on my tongue, riding my face as she cries out her pleasure, nails digging into my scalp.

Fuck, fuck, fuck.

I truly don't know what's come over me. I've always enjoyed experienced women, women who didn't get attached, women who knew what they were doing in bed. Even the only woman I'd ever fallen in love with had been experienced in bed. I've never been aroused by innocence or naivete, especially when it comes to sex. But something about the soft, aroused wonder in Elena's face as I'd touched her in ways that she never had been before drove me insane tonight.

It's *still* driving me insane.

I'm so fucking close. My balls are tight and aching, my cock throbbing in my hand, and I can hear the rustling from the other room, the sounds of her quickened breathing. I wonder if she *knows* I can hear her—I don't think that she does. I think she's trying to be quiet, trying not to be heard, and that somehow turns me on even more.

It feels lewd, illicit, *taboo* to be doing this, each of us masturbating on the other side of a door, wanting the other, touching ourselves to keep from doing the thing that we know we shouldn't. It's the hottest fucking masturbation session of my life–and also the guiltiest, because I know I shouldn't be thinking of her like this.

She's a job. A mission. A responsibility.

It should help, but it doesn't. Everything has narrowed down to the throbbing, straining flesh in my hand, to my tightened balls desperate for release, a release that I'd give just about anything at this moment to have inside of her.

Anything except my self-respect, apparently.

Those lips. She'd be just as clumsy at giving a blowjob as she was at kissing, probably, but I can't imagine right now that it would fucking matter. I'd teach her how to do it, just how I enjoy having my cock licked and sucked. I'd be slow and patient and tell her what felt good and what didn't, telling her what a good fucking girl she was when she learned, when she wrapped those perfect lips around my cock and made me come, and then swallowed it all–

Fuck!

My cock throbs in my fist as I angle it towards the sink, feeling that familiar tingle, the tightness before my release, on the very brink of it. I run my tongue over my lower lip, tasting the remnants of that champagne kiss on my mouth. Just as I'm on the edge, I hear a faint shuddering moan from the other room, and I know she's coming too.

I clench my teeth so hard it hurts as my cock explodes, painting the ceramic in front of me with my cum, thick spurts of it as my hand jerks along my swollen length. All I can think of is her; all I can *see* is her, thighs clamped around her hand and face turned into the pillow as she shudders through her orgasm, and that image sends another violent burst of pleasure through me as I fight back a deep groan that I know, if I let it out, would sound like her name.

I stand there for a long moment, one hand still wrapped around my pulsing cock and the other gripping the edge of the sink, head bowed as I try to catch my breath. I'm not sure I've ever come so hard from jerking off, and I'm still half-erect, my cock considering a second round as I reluctantly let go of it and tuck myself away, turning on the sink to clean up.

There are other things that need to be dealt with tonight. Other problems to solve, and my lust is no longer the most pressing one.

I step out of the bathroom just in time to see her guiltily readjusting her dress and squirming further beneath the covers, and I feel another throb at the knowledge of what she was just doing, what she's trying to cover up.

Her fingers are probably still wet. They probably still taste like her.

I grit my teeth, forcing back the thought as I circle around the bed, coming to stand next to her. "Lay still," I tell her gently. "And I'll fake the blood on the sheets."

Elena's eyes go very wide, and I realize in an instant how that must have sounded.

"I'm not going to hurt you." I shake my head. "I would never hurt you, Elena. Just pull back the covers, and we'll have this sorted in a few minutes."

There's a knife in my bag. I hear the rustling of the covers as I take it out, and turn to see that she's thrown them back, her dress tugged to one side but still covering her–barely–as she spreads her legs open. I'm fucking grateful that she figured it out, because I'm not sure how I would have managed to ask her to do so.

Spread your legs for me would be a dangerous thing for me to say to her right now.

She watches in what looks to be horrified fascination as I draw the blade down my upper arm, where the cut can be concealed by my clothes tomorrow, until the blood wells up. I transfer the knife to my other hand, reaching up and smearing my fingers across the wound, and then I reach out, wiping it on the sheets between her thighs. I repeat it once more, until there's enough of a stain to look convincing, but not so much that it looks fake.

"There." I look at her, watching her face relax slightly. "It's done. You can stay in the bed, I'll sleep on the sofa in the other room."

"Won't they think that's strange?" Elena asks, her teeth worrying at her lower lip. "I don't know how anyone would find out, but if they do–you sleeping in the other room–"

It sounds very much like she wants me to stay in bed with her, and for a moment, I'm tempted to give her what I think she's asking for. I think she wants the comfort of not being alone, not sex.

But I'm not altogether sure that I can sleep in bed with her, and not be tempted beyond my self-control.

"I don't know that they'd find me not sleeping next to a girl I bought all that strange. Maybe that I gave you the bed and took the couch. But no one is going to find out anyway, so it doesn't matter." I step back, rallying my control. "I'll be in just the other room, Elena. If you need me, call out, or come wake me up. But wake me up from a distance," I add, thinking of how I'm likely to react if she jerks me out of a deep sleep close to me. "My training makes me–jumpy, if someone wakes me while I'm asleep."

Her eyes widen again, and I know she must have questions after that comment. But she doesn't ask them. She just nods, burrowing deeper into the bed. "Goodnight," she says finally, after a long moment.

Fuck, I want to stay with her. It's been a long time since I've passed a night with someone else in my bed for the whole night, since I've woken up with another body curled close to mine. The thought of it sends a sweeping ache through me that I'm usually able to keep at bay, one I haven't felt in so long that I'd almost forgotten it.

Which is precisely why I can't sleep next to her.

"Goodnight," I tell her, reaching out to switch off the light next to the bed.

I catch just a glimpse of the disappointment on her face before I turn away.

Elena

Despite everything, I actually feel as if I got a full night's sleep–the first since I'd been kidnapped. It's a sleep free of dreams, too, which is a relief after so many nights full of nightmares in the cells. I'd been afraid of more of them, but I slept deep and dreamless, and when I wake to the sun streaming through the window, I see a tray of covered food sitting at the end of the bed. Through the arched doorway that leads to the other room, I can see Levin sitting up on the couch, his back to me, bent over what's probably his own breakfast.

"How long do we have before we leave?" I ask as I sit up, and he turns sharply, looking at me from over the back of the sofa. There's stubble on his face, and it only serves to make him more handsome, throwing into focus the sharp line of his jaw. I feel a shiver run through me as I remember last night, and I have to tamp down the sudden wash of arousal that threatens to make a flush creep up my neck.

"We should leave soon," Levin says, standing up and crossing to the doorway. He's changed clothes, into dark blue chinos cuffed at the ankle above his boots and a charcoal button-up rolled up to his elbows. He looks fucking gorgeous, and I feel my stomach tighten at the thought of all the things he could do to me in this bed, right now, if we weren't in a hurry.

If he hadn't made it very clear that he doesn't plan to do those things at all, beyond what's necessary to keep up our ruse.

"Do I have time to shower? Are there even other clothes in here?" I look around the room, and Levin smirks.

"I was told that typically the buyers bring a change of clothes for the girls they buy, to leave with them the next day. So I brought something for you from home." He crosses to the leather duffel bag sitting by the dresser, crouching down to unzip it. I see the muscled flex of his thighs and ass as he does, and my mouth goes slightly dry.

Get a grip, Elena. He's not going to fuck you.

He stands up, handing me what he'd brought—a pair of dark blue jeans and a silky black sleeveless shirt. "These are yours, right?"

I nod. "They are. Thank you. Do I have time to shower?" I desperately want to clean off all of yesterday. I can still smell all the flowery oil they put in my hair, and it reminds me of the whole horrifying ordeal.

"If you're quick. Eat something, too," Levin says, nodding at the tray. "I don't think you ate much at all yesterday."

I hadn't; he's right about that. I still can't summon much of an appetite, my stomach twisted in knots at the thought of how close we are to getting out of here, but I know I need to eat. It won't do anyone any good if I pass out again as we're trying to leave.

"I'll be in the other room," Levin says finally, backing away from the bed a little awkwardly. "If you need me."

His eyes flick over me once, briefly, and then he pivots sharply and walks off.

He heard you last night. He must have. A shiver that's half embarrassment, half arousal runs down my spine as I take the lid off of the tray, picking up a piece of toast with jam. I won't be able to eat much, but I can probably manage this.

One piece of toast and a few bites of eggs later, I get out of bed. I can't get the dress off fast enough, and I glance towards the other room as I pull it over my head, half-hoping that Levin might glance back and get a glimpse of me naked–purely by accident, of course. But he stays with his back steadfastly to me–almost certainly because he knows that I'm getting undressed.

Does he want me, or not? And if he does, why is he being so difficult about it?

Last night, downstairs, I'd understood. He hadn't wanted me to feel coerced. And I'd been a little bit afraid when I'd thought that he'd meant, once upstairs, that he would *have* to take my virginity for us to succeed at our plan. But once I'd known that wasn't what he meant–

I'd been a little disappointed. I hadn't wanted to be forced into it out of circumstance–but once it was no longer anyone else's choice but mine and his, I'd found myself wishing it might happen. And then when he'd kissed me–

How could someone kiss like that and not want to keep going?

Except he had, if he'd been pleasuring himself in the bathroom, the way I suspect he had. He'd wanted me, and he'd walked away.

And why not? You're his job, not his girlfriend. Not even a one-night-stand. He might be attracted to you, but he's probably separating business from pleasure. You need to get over it.

I let out a sigh as I turn on the shower. It's not as if I'll be around him much longer, anyway. Once we're away from Diego's compound, we'll head straight to the hangar to get on a plane to Boston. One flight, and I'll be in the States, and headed for my sister's house, where she lives with Niall. Levin will no longer be a part of my life.

Which is for the best.

There are two options for me, once I'm in Boston. The one I expect is that I'll wait until the issue of the Gonzalez cartel is resolved and it's safe for me to come home. At which point, my father will arrange a marriage for me as he always would have done if Diego had not become a problem. The other is that I'll stay in Boston with my sister and start a new life. Go to college. Date, like any other girl. But I'll only ever be with part of my family, in a place that's not really my home.

If you come back here, do you really think your father will be able to make a match for you? After you were auctioned? No one will believe you're still a virgin. You'll be over twenty, and your virginity doubtful. Not a prize for any other family.

I hate the voice whispering in my head, but I know it's not wrong. I scrub at my skin angrily, tears welling up in my eyes at the realization that even if I do come back home, things will never be the way they once would have been. And if I stay in Boston, everything will be different, too.

It's not that I wanted to marry someone I didn't know, almost certainly wouldn't want, and probably wouldn't love. But I hadn't been angry or resentful about it the way Isabella had. It was how things were. And it would have pleased my parents. Kept me near my family. Ensured a future that felt good and familiar.

I've spent hours and hours reading about love and adventure in books. But imagining it happening in reality is a terrifying prospect that I'm not sure I'm ready to face.

A knock comes at the door, startling me. "Elena? We need to go soon." Levin's voice comes through, a hint of urgency in it. "I don't want to wait much longer."

Fear prickles down my spine as I wonder if he has a reason for his hurry, beyond simply wanting to be gone, and I turn off the water. "Five minutes!" I call out, toweling off quickly as I reach for the clothes. There are panties and a bra tucked into the shirt, and I feel my cheeks flush all over again at the idea of my panties in Levin's things.

It feels good to be wearing my own clothes again. I run a comb through my hair and step out into the bedroom, and see Levin waiting with an urgent expression on his face.

"Is everything alright?" I can feel knots of anxiety clenching in my stomach. "What's wrong?"

"Nothing yet," Levin says tersely. "But the rest of the mansion is starting to wake up, and I'd like to go before too many others are milling around. I'd especially prefer not to talk to Diego again, if at all possible." He glances at me. "Try to look as if you had a-long night."

One that you didn't particularly enjoy. I catch the subtext of what he's saying without him having to elaborate, and nod. "Let's go, then."

His bag is already zipped up and by the door. He reaches for it, then hesitates, holding it out to me. "I'd probably have you carry this," he says, somewhat reluctantly, as if he doesn't like saying it. "It'll leave my hands free, anyway."

I start to ask *for what*, and then I see his shirt shift at the back, and the slight outline of something tucked there. I know without asking what it is.

It makes me feel better, actually, knowing he's armed.

I can hear the buzz of the house waking up as we head for the stairs. There are already some guests milling around downstairs, the girls close to them, looking exhausted. One of them, a brunette whose name I don't remember, has bruises on her chin and throat. I have to look away, feeling an aching guilt clutch at my chest.

I'm going to safety. She will probably never feel safe again.

It doesn't seem fair.

I wish I could ask Levin to save them all, but I know he can't. More than that, from what I know of him so far, I think he would want to.

I think it's probably eating him up inside, too, that he can't. And I know it would be unfair to hurt him by asking for something that he knows he can't do.

We're almost to the door when a voice behind us says, with perfect clarity and surprise, "Levin Volkov?"

I feel Levin stiffen next to me, going absolutely still for a second. His hand closes around my arm, and I think for a moment that we're just going to keep walking. That he's going to ignore it, and we're going to get out of here.

"Levin!" The voice comes again, and I see Levin's jaw clench.

"You've got the wrong person," he says quietly, and that's when I hear the last voice in the world that I ever want to hear again.

"That's certainly not the name you gave me," Diego says, his voice carrying sharp and harsh over the light din of conversation in the room. "But I'd be very interested in knowing what Levin Volkov is doing here, especially with Ricardo Santiago's daughter."

Levin turns around, slowly, his jaw clenched. "I don't know what this person is thinking, but–"

The man who first spoke isn't someone I saw yesterday. I see the girl standing next to him and remember, faintly, that someone had bought her at the auction for a man who had put his bids in remotely. *He must have come to pick her up today,* I realize, and I feel as if I might pass out all over again at the realization that we've come so close to getting away.

If I hadn't showered, if we'd left earlier–

"I'm sure it's you. We worked together, in Munich. Remember–"

"Well, I think this is a conversation worth having elsewhere," Diego says, stepping forward. "Gentlemen–"

"I have places to be," Levin says sharply. "And no time to deal with nonsense like this. I'll be leaving now–"

"No, you won't," Diego snaps. "This can be settled, but I'm not going to let you leave with Elena Santiago to take her back to her father, if you are Volkov. My guards will watch her until we're finished with our conversation."

I see the moment Levin's face hardens, when he realizes there's no way out of this. It's the moment that two of Diego's men step toward him, and three more towards me, and his hand moves so fast that, for an instant, it's nothing but a blur.

"Don't fucking move," he snarls, the gun pointed directly at Diego. "Elena, get outside."

"Don't let her go!" Diego snaps, and Levin's finger twitches against the trigger.

"Grab her, and I shoot. You can have your men kill me, but you'll be dead before I hit the floor. If you know my name, then you know who I am, and you know that's the truth. So back the fuck up and get your men off of her." He doesn't flinch, his gaze fixed on Diego's face. "Elena, *go!*"

I don't hesitate. I believe him. I don't know what he means about who he is, exactly, but he survived the attack on my home, and he made it here to buy me from the auction, and right now, there's no one else in the world I'm more likely to trust with my life.

So I turn and run for the door, certain that at any moment I'll feel hands grabbing me, dragging me backward.

But they don't. I burst out into the courtyard, only to see more of Diego's men around the waiting cars, looking at me with instant suspicion. And why wouldn't they? It looks, for all intents and purposes, as if one of the auctioned girls is making a run for it, and I suppose, in a way, I am.

"To your right! The motorcycle. Go, Elena!"

I hear Levin's voice behind me, and then a gunshot, and another, as I make a run for it, darting towards the motorcycle that I see parked near the end of where the cars are waiting. I hear footsteps behind me, and I hope to god they're Levin's as I rush towards the waiting bike.

"Get on behind me!" Levin is on the bike in an instant, starting it as he turns sharply, shooting to my right. A bullet whizzes past me, and I scream as he grabs my arm, helping me up onto the back of the bike.

"Hold onto my waist and don't let go!" he shouts, and then the engine is roaring, and he throws it into gear.

I've never been on a motorcycle before. I cling to Levin's waist for dear life, exactly as he'd said, my cheek pressed to his back as he speeds across the compound, dust flying in a thick, choking cloud around us. I hear Diego shouting from somewhere and hear more gunshots, but the dust helps make us a harder target to hit as Levin speeds toward the compound gates.

They're starting to close. He hits the gas, holding on with one hand as he aims at the guards closing the gate with the other. Two shots, and they're both dead, dropping into the dirt as we fly through the closing gap, and I hear the sound of it shutting behind us.

"We're not home free yet!" Levin shouts above the engine. "Keep your head down! They'll send someone after us."

It becomes evident just how right he is in a matter of minutes. We haven't even reached the main road before I hear the roar of engines behind us. I twist my head around to see two cars and three motorcycles coming down the road behind us, dust swirling around them.

"There's too many!" I yell at Levin, panic filling my voice, and I feel the rumble of his laughter as, somehow, he pushes the bike even faster.

"I've had worse odds!" he shouts, and then he leans forward too, and I'm lost in the mingled terror and thrill as he goes sideways onto the main road, driving the motorcycle forward at top speed in an effort to keep out of range of Diego's men following us.

How is this happening? This was never supposed to be my life. I feel like I must have died in the attack. Everything over the past few days, everything happening now, is some sort of strange, fevered, last-minute activity of my brain, making up an adventure that could never happen in real life.

Until more shots come whizzing past us, and I'm suddenly very convinced all over again that this is, in fact, real.

"Can you go faster?" I shout at Levin, but I don't think he can hear me. I'm also not sure that he *can*. The motorcycle is flying at a speed that I find absolutely terrifying, and I'm certain at any moment that we might go down. If we do, I know we won't survive it. I can imagine what will happen if my skin hits the asphalt at this speed, and it's too horrifying to contemplate for very long.

They're gaining on us. I can hear the sounds getting closer, the bullets coming faster, and I press my face against Levin's back, waiting for the moment when I feel the impact of one hitting me. He's weaving on the bike, moving back and forth, and as the road turns into a curve, he tilts it so far to one side that I think I'm going to throw up from how close the road is to us.

But it's worth it because, in my periphery, I see two of the other motorcycles spin out as they try to take the tight turn, crashing to the asphalt as the cars and the remaining bike try to avoid it.

Another rattle of gunfire, and I close my eyes tightly, clinging to Levin. I try to focus on anything other than what's happening, the fear chilling me to the bone, the very real possibility that I could die at any second. I focus on the way his shirt feels under my cheek, the scent of his skin and his cologne, the burn of the wind whipping across my face. Anything not to think about how close we are to absolute obliteration.

"I'm going to try to lose them!" Levin shouts, his voice barely making it to my ears as the wind whips it past. As I see a canyon coming into view next to us, he suddenly veers off of the road, flying down the rocky dirt.

I'm sure that we're going to crash. I stifle a scream as the motorcycle sways, and I hear the roar of the one remaining bike from Diego's coming after us, and the sound of more gunshots, and I feel faint from terror.

This isn't how I imagined this morning going at all.

We're almost at the end of the canyon when I hear Levin shout, "Lean *down*, Elena!"

I obey him almost automatically, my body moving before I even realize I've told it to, and I lean to one side as he twists, shooting over the top of my head. Once, twice, three times, and I hear the screech of the motorcycle behind us and the crash as it hits, and I'm sure that whoever was on it won't be following us any longer.

"You're doing great!" he shouts. "Hold on a little bit longer, and we'll be able to stop!"

A little bit longer ends up feeling like an hour. I'm tense the entire time, waiting to hear the cars behind us again, clinging to Levin with a death grip. When we turn down the main road of the first town we see coming out of the canyon, Levin slows the motorcycle, and I let go of his waist the slightest bit, trying to catch my breath.

"Are we okay to stop?" I ask as he pulls into a spot behind a bar, killing the engine.

"Not for long." He wipes the back of his hand across his forehead. "We can't stop anywhere for the night. We need to get to the airplane hangar. I want to wait a little bit, though, see if we've lost them."

"And if we didn't?"

"Then it's going to be a hell of a ride to that plane."

My stomach tightens with anxiety at that. I sit there, frozen on the back of the bike, feeling entirely lost. None of this is anything I know what to do about, and I'm just relying on Levin to get me where I need to go to be safe, and doing what he tells me to do. It makes me feel helpless, and I don't like that.

"Shit," he says suddenly, revving the bike again, and I open my mouth to ask him *what* in the second before I see the two cars that were following us pull into either end of the back alley we're parked in, blocking us almost completely off.

"Give it up, Volkov!" one of the men shouts as he gets out of the car, gun aimed at Levin. "Get her," he adds, pointing at me, and two of the men move forward.

"Don't even fucking think about it!" Levin snaps, his weapon aimed as he slams another cartridge into it. For a brief second, I think that he's got it handled–and then I feel hands on me from behind, dragging me off of the motorcycle.

The men from the other car snuck up on me, while Levin was distracted.

I scream as they start to haul me backward, and Levin whips around, off of the bike in an instant as he opens fire on the men holding me. I hear gunshots from the direction of the other car, hear them pinging off of Levin's motorcycle, and I hear him swear as he shoots at the men trying to get me back to the car.

The one to my left drops, and I feel a spray of blood across my arm and chest. Another from the right, and then the one holding me jerks backward suddenly, going limp as he drops me. Levin's arm is around me before I can hit the pavement.

"Let's go," he hisses, his gun still aimed in front of us as he ducks us behind a row of tires, pulling me back towards the now-empty car. The other men are still coming towards us, looking for where Levin has hidden us, and I know we have only seconds to get into the other car.

"Go, go!" Levin shouts it as he yanks the door open, pushing me over the driver's seat and into the other side as I crouch down, covering my head as I hear the other men open fire again. Levin curses next to me, turning the key into the ignition as he throws the car in reverse, and I hear the squealing of tires as he pulls out.

"They're going to be coming after us," he growls. "Fucking assholes, ruining my *fucking* bike–stay low, Elena. Better chance of nothing hitting you that way."

He pulls onto the road with another squeal of tires, and I can hear the other car behind us, gunshots still going off. I have no idea how far we are from the hangar, and I'm afraid to ask. I can feel myself starting to shake as I look down at the blood covering my arms, and I clench my hands into fists, willing myself not to have a panic attack. To hold it together until it's safe to fall apart.

That might not be until we get to Boston, the way things have been going.

"We're almost there," Levin tells me, his foot sinking down on the gas. "When I tell you to run for the plane, Elena, run. Don't look back, don't wait for me. I'll be behind you, I promise, but fucking run. Okay?"

I swallow hard, nodding. "Okay," I whisper, and he nods.

"Almost there."

I feel the car skid sideways as we pull into the gate. Levin turns the steering wheel sharply, slamming on the brakes as I see the plane waiting yards away, and he nods at me as he turns the car so that my side is facing the plane.

"*Now*, Elena!"

The car hasn't completely come to a stop, but I'd promised to do as he said. I fling open the door, the car slowing, and roll out onto the tarmac as Levin keeps going, scrambling to my feet. I hear more tires squealing, more gunshots, and look up to see Levin out of the car, too, firing at the other men as he starts to run toward me.

"Go!" he shouts, and I bolt for the plane.

I'm certain, with every step, that it's my last. I can hear the blood pounding in my ears and feel my heartbeat more clearly than I ever have. *I've got to get on the plane,* I think over and over, with each smack of my shoes against the tarmac, until I'm at the steps and rushing up them, hoping against hope that Levin is behind me.

I trip and fall as I reach the aisle, bruising my knee, but I don't care. I'm on board, and I gasp for air, still feeling faint at the sight of so much blood on my arms.

I almost scream when hands reach for me from behind, helping me up to my feet.

"It's me," Levin says calmly, and before I can stop myself, I turn in his arms, flinging mine around his neck.

He holds me for a split second, and I can feel his chest heaving against mine, his muscled arms wrapped around me, and I've never felt safer in my entire life. And then he steps back, holding me at arm's length as he looks me up and down as the plane starts taxiing down the runway.

"Are you alright?" he asks, his voice thick with worry. "Is all the blood someone else's?"

I nod, feeling as if I'm not quite sure if I can speak. "I think so," I manage. "Nothing really hurts, other than my knee where I tripped—"

Levin's hands slide down my sides, over my arms, his eyes flicking over me with a sudden intensity that catches me off guard, his blue eyes fixed on mine. "You're sure? Nothing hit you? You're okay?"

Suddenly, his hands on me feel like more than just hands checking for wounds. I'm intensely aware of how close I am to him, of the way he's looking at me, the flicker of something like fear in his eyes.

"I'm fine," I manage. "I just need to clean up, that's all. I'm not a huge fan of being covered in someone else's blood."

"There should be a bathroom near the back of the plane." Levin swallows hard, nodding at me. "Go ahead. I'll be right here when you get back."

For some reason, I feel loathe to walk away from him, even for a minute. There's a look on his face that I can't quite decipher, as if he's remembering some old pain, and I have a sudden deep urge to know what it is. To understand why he's looking at me as if he's seeing something that's been torn away from him.

But I also want to get cleaned up. And something tells me that even if I ask, he's not going to say.

So instead, I turn and walk away, leaving him as he sinks down into one of the seats, his hand pressed to his mouth as I leave.

Levin

She's fine. It's not the same thing. Not at all.

I still can't stop the frantic racing of my heart, or forget the way it had felt as if it'd stopped for a moment when I saw how covered in blood she was.

Blood, everywhere. Gallons of it, drenching white sheets, spilling out of her. More blood than a body so petite should be able to hold. Sunlight, glinting off shattered glass, a diamond ring. A wound so gaping it could never be closed.

It never *has* been closed. I can feel it in my chest now, the memory as sharp and cutting as those shards of glass, even all these years later.

The only woman I ever loved. The woman I failed to protect.

The woman who died, because I asked her to stay with me. Because I was too fucking weak to keep walking through life alone, once I knew she existed in it.

Elena is fine, I tell myself again, as I watch her walk away. There's no hitch in her gait, nothing that makes it seem as if anything is wrong with her at all. It's all the blood from the men I killed, not hers.

But I still feel as if I did something wrong. As if it's my fault that man recognized me, when I'd had no idea he would be there. He hadn't been on Diego's guest list because he'd bid in remotely. I couldn't have known.

It feels like my fault anyway. My fault that she was in danger. My fault that she had to see the things she saw today.

Maybe it's time to hang it up, Volkov. Maybe this isn't the life for you anymore.

I tell myself that it doesn't matter. That we'll be in Boston before too long, and I'll deliver Elena to her sister, and that will be the end of it. I probably won't ever see her again. I'll go back to New York, back to training Viktor's next crop of assassins for the Syndicate, and all of this will be in the past.

It won't be the best job I've ever done, but it'll be done, at least. Elena will be safe, and the deal with the Santiago cartel will hold.

I feel fairly secure in that, until the moment I feel the heavy press of a gun against the back of my head.

I don't have to look to know that's what it is. It's not the first time it's happened. If I survive this one, it won't be the last, most likely, considering how my life has gone. But the question is, *why the fuck is anyone on this plane who would put a gun to my head?*

"Up, Volkov," a thick, accented voice says. "Up, and we'll talk before we kill you."

Two men push past the one behind me, headed towards the back of the plane. Headed, undoubtedly, towards the bathroom where Elena is cleaning up. The thought incenses me, burning through me with a ferocity that I haven't felt in a long fucking time, and I feel myself tense, ready to make a move when I have a chance.

The plane was meant to be the safe point. Once we were here, nothing else was supposed to be able to go wrong. But something has gone very fucking wrong.

Elena's scream from the bathroom gives me the moment I need. The man holding the gun to my head flinches, ever so slightly, and I duck, rolling to one side out of the seat. He doesn't fire, as I'd expected he wouldn't. A gunshot going off in an airplane is no small matter, and he won't shoot unless he absolutely has to.

What he *does* do is also exactly what I'd expected. He comes at me with a knife, and I'm ready for him.

Elena screams again, and I look up to see the two men wrestling with her, also armed with knives. She's bucking in their grasp, fighting, and I see them trying to cuff her as I attempt to get the man trying to stab me into a leglock, twisting away from the stabbing blade.

I've spent years training in as many martial arts as I could. I'm good at this kind of fighting, but the man is more wiry than I am, and it makes him a difficult opponent. The blade grazes my arm, reopening the wound from last night, and I hiss through my teeth as I manage to grab him and fling him onto his back.

"Levin!" Elena shrieks my name as I see them getting cuffs onto her, shoving her into one of the seats as the other two men advance on me. "Levin, watch out!"

One of them flings a knife toward me, and I barely dodge it, the point sinking into the aisle an inch from my face. I let out an angry snarl, grabbing it as I wrench towards the man I have down, driving it into his throat and yanking it out again as blood sprays across me and the seats surrounding me.

One down, two to go.

A two-on-one fight isn't great at any time, but it's much worse in the cramped quarters of an airplane. One of the men manages to throw me back into the wall, coming at me like a barreling giant as he drives a knife toward my face. I grab his wrist just in time, grateful only for the fact that his bulk is making it hard for his friend to get to me as we wrestle for control of the knife, just in time for another to come flying towards my face and bury itself in the seat inches from me.

"Crack a fucking window with that, and we all die," I growl, shoving the man backward who is almost on top of me, his guard broken by the knife that almost hit him, too. I drive my hand into his throat, slamming the side of it against his windpipe, getting in the strike twice before I manage to wrest the knife out of his hand and slash the serrated edge across his throat, sending another arterial spray across the plane as I turn to face the last of the three men.

"Maybe try fighting hand to hand, instead of throwing from a distance," I hiss at him. "Like a fucking man."

And then I'm on him. His knife hits my thigh on the outside, stabbing and nearly sinking deep enough to cause real damage, but I hit the side of his hand with mine, sending him screeching backward as I cut it open. I jerk his knife out of my leg, one in each hand, as I advance on him, feeling particularly without mercy as I hear Elena's muffled sob from the back of the plane.

"I'm not in any fucking mood," I growl, kicking out one foot and tripping the man, knocking him into a row of seats. "So tell me what the fuck is going on, and we'll decide if you die slow or fast."

"It doesn't matter," he sneers at me. "You can kill me, but it won't change anything. You're fucked. Both of you are."

"I don't like fucking riddles." I drive my knee into his balls, pinning him to the seat as I push the knife blade into the side of his throat. "I'm getting real good at opening throats today, son. It's not an easy thing to do. Requires a sharp blade, which you boys seem to have plenty of. Like you knew how you wanted to die."

"You're a fucking idiot," the man hisses. "Never even considered that maybe Diego got to your pilot first. That maybe he paid him more. That maybe you were never going to fucking Boston."

One blade still against his throat, I reach down with my other hand, pressing the second knife into his groin. "Start fucking talking. Where is the plane going?"

The man hesitates for one more second, before I push the point harder, and his face goes chalk white.

"South America," he manages, his voice suddenly choked with fear. "Diego has a buyer for her there. Someone who will make sure she regrets the day her daddy ever crossed the Gonzalez cartel. That's where the plane is going. And you can't stop it now. When it lands, there will be enough men there with guns to make sure you're as dead as you can possibly be. And she'll never go anywhere else again."

The last words end on a gurgle as I slash the blade across his neck, the hot spray of blood coating my hands as I drive it into him, wanting him to feel it. I want him to hurt, because it's the only outlet I have right now for the rage that feels as if it's set my blood to boiling.

Elena's cuffs are plastic, the zip-tie kind. I cut her hands free, careful to slice through them slowly, and she winces as they fall away, looking at me, with a small, frightened smile on her face.

"Now you're the one who needs to clean up," she whispers.

"Elena—" I'm not sure what to tell her. I need to get into that cockpit, and I'm almost certain it's going to be locked. We're in danger still, more danger than we've ever been, and I don't know how to break it to her.

"I heard them," she whispers. Her eyes are round and frightened, but her voice is only shaking a little, her chin tilting up as she looks at me. "I trust you. We'll be safe, won't we?"

I don't know what to tell her. I'm not sure that we will be, that I can fix this.

But I have to try.

"Wait here," I tell her firmly. "I'm going to try to get into the cockpit. Just don't move, okay? Put on your seatbelt, and stay here. Promise me."

Elena swallows hard, but nods, sliding into the seat that I point to and fastening her seatbelt. "Right here," she says, forcing a small smile onto her face, and at that moment, I want to fucking kiss her.

She's terrified, I can tell. But she's also braver than I could have ever expected.

Which is good, because she's going to need to be, if we're going to survive this.

"I'll be back."

I hope to god, as I turn away, that that's actually a promise I can keep.

I stride towards the cockpit, knife still gripped in one hand. If the plane gets to where it's meant to be going, the odds that I can get us both out of this are much slimmer. Possibly none.

I need that pilot to turn this plane around.

It's no surprise, when I reach for the door handle and try to turn it, that it doesn't budge. I would have actually bet money, if I'd thought I needed to, that it would be locked.

I still need to get it open.

Quickly, I shove the knife into my belt as I fish out the small leather pouch I keep in my back pocket, unzipping it quickly. I've had to pick locks on a time crunch before, but this is particularly urgent. I fight the urge to glance back over my shoulder and check on Elena as I crouch down, slipping the pick in as I tilt it carefully to one side.

For a moment, I'm not sure if it's going to give. I grit my teeth, forcing myself to go slow, not to cause too much noise or break the pick. I don't think the pilot can hear much, but I don't want him to know I'm about to come in if I can help it.

Another few seconds, and I feel it give. The moment it pops, I reach for the handle, opening it slowly as I set the pouch aside and pull the knife out of my belt.

Carefully, I slip through the door into the cockpit. There's a moment where the pilot doesn't hear me or see me in his periphery, and the moment he does, flinching to one side, I'm behind him with the point of the knife pressed into his neck.

"Don't move," I warn him, reaching for the headphones he's wearing and tugging them off.

"Hey! Get your hands off of me! Who the hell do you think you are—"

"Levin Volkov," I tell him tightly, the point of the knife still pressed just below his jaw. "Former Russian assassin and now Elena Santiago's bodyguard, so if you know what's good for you, you'll do whatever it is you need to do in order to point this plane in the direction of Boston, Massachusetts, and not where it's going now."

"I can't do that." There's a thread of fear in the pilot's voice, but it's steadier than I would have thought, which is impressive for a man flying a plane with a knife against his throat. "I've been paid to take the girl where this plane is going."

"Last I heard, you were paid to take her to Boston."

His jaw clenches, and I see him swallow hard, his Adam's apple bobbing against the point of the knife. "Someone else paid more."

"Is that someone else named Diego Gonzalez?"

"I've got nothing else to say to you." Another hard swallow and I can tell just how afraid the man really is. "This plane is going where it's going."

"I'm afraid I can't allow that." I push the knife in a little harder, the point piercing the skin enough for a trickle of blood to slide down his throat. "Change the flight course, or I'm going to kill you. Those are the only options."

"What the hell do you think you're going to do without a pilot?" It's a last-minute show of bravado, and he knows it as well as I do. "You're gonna fly this thing?"

"I can try. I've got some flight training. Not as much as you, but I'll take my chances with that over the half an army of armed men that I was told would be waiting for me on the tarmac in South America. So turn the plane around, or—"

I dig the knife in a little deeper, twisting it. "I'm not as big of a fan of killing as a lot of the men I've worked with. But I have no trouble with it if need be. So make up your mind before I make it for you."

"You killing me is better than what the Gonzalez cartel would do to me if I turn this plane around. So—"

The man moves faster than I thought he could. He twists around in the seat, grabbing for my hand holding the knife, and I react on instinct, pushing it hard against his throat. I feel the pop of flesh as it digs in, the tearing of skin, and I hear the pilot's howl of pain, but he doesn't stop right away.

He lunges towards me, still grappling for the knife, and as I grab for his other arm to try and get control, his hand swings wide and hits the steering.

The plane shifts, nose going down, and I faintly hear Elena's shriek from far away as I grab the pilot in a headlock, twisting him around and shoving him back towards the seat.

"Get the nose up! Now! Get this plane back in the sky and towards Boston."

"No." His voice is choked with pain, blood dripping down his neck and over my hands, but he struggles, still trying to get out of my grasp. "I'd rather die here than let the cartel take me apart bit by bit."

"You're going to get your fucking wish."

The pilot tries to get out of my grasp again, hands flailing for the controls as he drags us both a few steps closer, no doubt in an effort to go ahead and send us all down to our deaths. I wrench him to one side, yanking the knife out with one hand and pressing my forearm to his throat as blood gushes out over my arm, strangling him as he bleeds out.

I have seconds to get us back on track. I throw the pilot's body to one side, seeing him still twitching out of the corner of my eye as I sit down, reaching for the controls.

I hadn't been lying when I said I had some flight training, but I know by the sinking feeling in my gut that it's not enough. I might have been able to fly us out of this if the pilot hadn't sent us into a nosedive, maybe gotten us back on track to Boston, maybe even gotten us there safely if I was very careful and remembered it all. But as I try to drag the plane back up, wrestling with it, I know I can't stop this.

We're going to crash in the water. When I see that, I know it's the only chance we might survive. There's no keeping the plane from crashing, but if I can mitigate it somewhat, we might not die.

It's the best I can do.

I wish I could tell Elena what's happening, tell her to hang on, tell her that I'm going to do my best to keep us in one piece. I could do it over the PA system, if I had time, but I can't spare a hand or a moment, even though it makes me feel like shit to know how terrified she must be right now, not knowing what's going on.

All I can focus on is the possibility, however slight, that I can keep us both alive. That once the plane is in the water, I can get us both out of it and to some kind of safety until I can figure out what comes next. The odds won't be good, even once we're out of the plane, but I've spent my whole life living by the idea that so long as I'm actually alive, everything else can be solved.

Well, just about everything. Some things can't ever be fixed. But I'm still alive anyway.

We're about to test just how true that is.

The plane is going down, faster now, as I try to haul the nose up enough to keep us from breaking apart instantly. I brace myself for the crash, knuckles white, and I hope against hope that when it's all over, Elena and I will both still be breathing.

I'd love to see you again, Lidiya. But I have to hope that it's not today.

She, and Elena, are the last thoughts in my mind as the plane hits the water.

Elena

The plane is sinking.

I feel woozy as I blink, looking around in a daze. The impact of it hitting the water threw me to one side, wrenching me against the seatbelt, and I can feel that something is hurt. Bruised, definitely; much worse, probably. The pain arcs through me, hot and throbbing, and I can see that the plane is starting to fill with water through my glassy vision.

"Help!" My voice is raspy, choked with fear. "Help me! Levin! Help!"

I'm not sure if it's loud enough for anyone to hear. I'm not sure if he's even still alive.

It's as if I start moving outside of myself, my body's will to survive taking over. My hands fumble at the seatbelt, yanking at it, seeing the rapidly rising water as the plane sinks further, knowing that I have seconds. A minute or two, if I'm lucky.

I'm not even sure how I made it this far.

I push at the clasp of the seatbelt, yank at it, and jerk as hard as my numb hands possibly can, but it won't come free. *It's jammed*, I think somewhere dimly in my head, and the fear that washes over me after that is so cold and overwhelming that it freezes me in place. I can feel my teeth chattering, my body shaking, and everything hurts.

I've been afraid of dying before, but it's never felt so immediate. I've come closer to it than ever before in the past several days, but there was always so much happening, everything too fast to really contemplate the reality of it. Now it's here, staring me in the face as I'm trapped, and I can't pretend that it's not coming for me.

I'll never see my family again. My sister. Their faces swim in my head, a torrent of memories that should be comforting but only serve to make my chest clench with terrified hurt–the strength of my father's arms around me, the vanilla tobacco scent of his shirt, my sister's laugh and the swing of her dark hair. The scent of our gardens at home, warm dust and flowers, and all the things I'll never see again.

And then, irrational and yet still there anyway–

I wish I'd gotten Levin to sleep with me.

I'm going to die a fucking virgin.

It seems horrendously unfair, all things considered.

The water is rising. My legs, my hands, my chin. Freezing. I gasp in the deepest breath I can, just before it touches my lips, but I know I won't be able to hold it for long. I was never good at that.

I hold my breath for as long as I can, the water closing over my head, squeezing my eyes tightly shut. My lungs are burning, my hands still ineffectually yanking at the jammed seatbelt–and then I feel other hands close over mine.

When my eyes fly open, I see Levin in front of me.

He pushes my hands aside, and I see, blurrily, a knife in one of his. He saws at the seatbelt, slicing through it raggedly, and then his arm slides around me as he pulls me free, dragging me through the water towards the broken-off back of the plane.

I'm out of air. My lungs are screaming for it. *Hang on. A little longer, and you'll have it. Just hang on—*

I'm not sure I'll ever know how I manage it. Through sheer force of will, I keep my lips clamped shut as Levin swims us toward the surface. I hear his voice as we break above the water, and I gasp for air like a newborn baby, as if I've never taken a breath before in my life.

"Hang on!" Levin shouts, his arm wrapped around my waist. "I'm going to try to get us to shore. Just hold on to me, Elena!"

I cough, still seizing for air. "I'll try," I manage, my voice cracking, and I'm not sure he hears me. But it doesn't matter.

It feels like a dream—or a nightmare. All around us, the water is on fire from the spilled oil, burning like some terrifying hellscape that Levin pulls us through, swimming one-armed as he holds on to me. There's floating wreckage from the plane, and Levin drags me towards a piece of the wing that's bobbing atop the water, guiding me to it.

"Hold on to this," he rasps. "I'm going to push it as we swim. If you can help swim, that's better, but if you can't, just hold on. We won't make it to shore if I have to do it with one arm and this bag."

"What bag?" I croak, but once again, it's too quiet for him to hear me. I grab onto the wing as he starts to swim again, pushing us towards a shoreline that I can't make out.

I want to pass out. The pain is growing, much worse than before, and I think something must have cut me, because the salt feels like fire on my skin. But if I do, I know I won't make it.

"Just a little further!" Levin calls out near my ear, and I'm pretty sure he's lying, but I know he's trying to be encouraging. I don't see a beach, a shoreline, or anything but dark water all around us. It feels like floating in a void, and I want desperately to close my eyes, but I force them open, stinging from the salt water.

And then I feel it. Sand, under my feet, my knees, the rest of me as I collapse forward, and Levin drags me the rest of the way, detaching me from the plane wing as he carries me further up the beach, stumbling. It's then that I realize he must be hurt and exhausted, too, although I have no idea how badly.

He lays me down on my side on the sand as I cough up more water, his hand pushing my wet hair away from my face. "You're safe now," he murmurs. "We're out of the water. You're safe. I've got you."

I've got you. That's what I need to hear. My eyes close, my entire body going limp as it accepts that we are, at least right now, not going to die.

And then everything goes black.

—

For what feels like a long time, I'm not sure what's a dream and what's reality. I feel myself being picked up, moved, and laid on a blanket. I see, dimly, Levin's face hovering over me, feel his hands on me, and the thought passes through my head that I wish I were conscious enough to enjoy it.

"Rest," I hear him murmur, his voice roughly accented, his hand brushing away my now-dry hair. And then later, "*fuck*, you're running a fever. There's nothing here for that. *Shit.*"

There's a litany of alternating commands and pleas that break through the pain and heat that throb through me, anytime that I'm awake. *Drink. Eat. Rest. Don't die. Don't fucking die.*

I think I hear him say more words to me while I'm sick on the beach than I have the entire time I've known him so far. As if, by speaking to me, he can keep me here. One sentence I hear again and again, and it makes me wonder what he means by it.

"I can't fail again. This can't happen again."

I don't remember anything after that, for a long time.

When I finally do wake up, *really* wake up, I see him crouched on the sand in front of a pile of kindling stacked in a sandy pit that he's dug out. There's a blanket wrapped around me as well as the one I'm lying on, and I push myself up slowly, feeling everything in me protest as I try to sit up.

He turns around instantly, the second he hears me move, dropping what he'd been using to start a fire. "Elena." The sound of relief in his voice is palpable. "You're awake."

"I think you could call it that." My voice sounds hoarse and rusty, and I cough, feeling the scrape of pain in my throat. "I'm not sure I like the way *awake* feels right now."

"I don't blame you." Levin balances his hands on his knees, looking at me narrowly, as if he's trying to decide just how bad of shape I'm still in. "I wasn't sure if you *would* wake up, for a while there."

It's not a surprise, exactly, but hearing it said so baldly feels like a shock. I swallow hard, pulling the blanket more tightly around myself. "What happened?"

Levin presses his lips together, letting out a long breath through his nose. "Let me get the fire started, and get us both something to eat, and I'll tell you."

I sit there, watching as he finishes kindling the fire, slowly getting it started until it's a small, bright, crackling flame leaping in the darkness of the night. He helps me move closer so that I can get warm, and then hands me what looks like a military ration packet.

"This is dinner," he says apologetically. "It's not great, but it'll keep you full and alive. You need as many calories as you can get–I couldn't get you to eat much while you were out."

He pauses for a moment, ripping open his own package of food as he glances over at me.

"The plane went down. You know that." He rubs a hand over his mouth, the tray of food balancing in his lap. "I tried to keep us up, after I killed the pilot. But it was too late. All I could do was try to mitigate the crash."

"I guess it worked." I pick at a few pieces of trail mix, knowing I need to eat, but it feels like my throat is closing over. "We're alive."

"Yeah, we are." Levin shoves his fork into what looks like some form of gluey concoction that I think is *trying* to approximate lasagna, or ziti, but isn't really succeeding. His voice is full of a forced optimism that makes my stomach clench.

"How long was I out?" The question sticks in my throat along with the food.

"About two days."

"And you've been–"

"Trying to keep you alive." He takes another bite of the food, wincing, and sets it down.

"You ran a hell of a fever. I have some medical things–" he nods towards a bag sitting in the sand a few paces off, "but nothing for that. It was touch and go for a little bit. Not to scare you," he adds apologetically.

"No, I'd rather you be honest." I force down another bite of food, but I'm not sure how much more I'll be able to manage before it starts coming back up. "What else is in the bag?"

"Some survival things. It's all I was able to grab off of the plane before I had to get you and get us out of the wreckage. I had a hard enough time getting to you." Levin pauses momentarily, as if he's considering how much to tell me.

"I want to know," I tell him, but even as the words come out, I'm not entirely sure they're true. The expression on his face looks as if he's trying to keep from telling me just how bad things are, and failing.

"There's not much in there," he tells me finally. "There were a couple of blankets, which you've got right now, some of these MRE-type rations, bottled water, a first-aid kit. I used a lot of that to patch up your injuries and mine." He turns, showing me a roughly-stitched gash on his arm. "Luckily, you seemed to have more bumps and bruises than wounds. There was just one deep cut on your side and some superficial scratches."

I wince. "Did you have to stitch—"

Levin nods, his mouth twisting down in a regretful expression. "I'd avoid looking at it for now," he says gently. "It's not the prettiest job. It will probably scar."

I feel a pulse of hurt in my chest, a lump rising in my throat, but I shove it down as hard as I can. *Don't be foolish*, I tell myself firmly, forcing a small, wan smile onto my face. "It's just a scar," I tell him as bravely as I can manage. "Better that than dead."

"That's true." Levin gives me an appreciative look. "You've been tough through all of this, Elena Santiago. I'm impressed."

Hearing him say that sends an unexpected flush of heat through me, and I feel my cheeks turn pink, making me hope that the firelight isn't bright enough for him to see it. "Where did you learn to do all of this?" I ask, reaching for the MRE to try and force a little more down.

Levin hesitates again, and I can see his expression turn guarded. "Now," he says carefully, as if he's thinking about each word before he chooses it, "I work for a man named Viktor Andreyev, based out of New York. He's the *pakhan* of the Bratva there. But before that—"

It's clear that he's unsure how much he should say. "Just tell me," I say quietly, looking at him from across the fire. "I can handle it. I'm a cartel boss's daughter. And I think we're past keeping secrets at this point."

He smiles grimly. "Alright. That's fair, I suppose. But I don't know that you're going to enjoy being on this island with me, once you know."

Levin

"Only one way to find out."

The way she says it is with a kind of bold-faced optimism that makes me wonder how a girl who seems so much scrappier than she looks ever managed to reconcile the type of life that her parents had planned out for her. She doesn't have the same defiant fire that her sister has, but she's brave in a way that continuously surprises me. I've only ever known one other woman with that kind of sweet stalwartness.

I just can't quite believe that she'll look at me with that same sort of trust once she knows the truth.

"I used to work out of Moscow," I tell her, hands balanced on my knees as I turn towards her. Her face is half-illuminated in the firelight, her black hair tossed over one shoulder, and it's been a long time since I've seen someone so beautiful. Even as exhausted as she clearly is after the crash, her face a little more hollowed and ashen from the fever and two days without much to eat or drink, she's still stunningly lovely.

"And this was for someone other than Viktor?" Elena asks, poking at the food with her fork. I want to tell her again to eat, but it's hard to push when I know just how bad it tastes. Even I'm having a hard time stomaching it, and it's far from the first time I've had to live off rations like this for a little while.

I nod. "I worked for an underground organization called the Syndicate."

"That sounds dangerous." She tilts her head sideways, looking at me.

"It was." I sit back in the sand, watching her expression. "As an assassin-for-hire, mostly. A spy, sometimes. Sometimes a little of both."

I wait for her face to change, for there to be fear or horror or anger, for her to put distance between us, literally or figuratively. But she doesn't move; if anything, there's only curiosity in her gaze.

"How long?" she asks, and I blink at her.

"Since I was sixteen, essentially. I was a grunt until my father died, and then they started training me to take his place. The training was–punishing. But it was all I knew."

"And you left? It doesn't sound like it's the kind of thing you can leave easily."

I can't help the small snort that escapes. She's more right than she knows, but I'm not about to tell her the worst parts of it. "It wasn't easy," I tell her honestly. "But it was what I needed to do at the time. I couldn't stay after–"

Elena looks at me curiously as I break off, but I'm not sure how much to say. I want to tell her enough that she'll feel that I'm not hiding things from her unnecessarily, but there are things that I can't talk about. Things that I don't *want* to talk about.

"I was married, once," I tell her shortly. "I'm a widower now. And things changed for me, after that."

The silence that hangs between us for a moment is thick and heavy. I see a look of shock on her face for a brief second, and then it fades into something softer and sadder.

"I'm sorry," she says, her voice very quiet. "Was it–recent?"

I shake my head. "No. About twelve or so years ago, now."

She hesitates, her teeth sinking into her lower lip, and I can tell she's trying to decide whether or not to say something.

"Go ahead," I tell her. "You can ask whatever you want to. I won't be upset."

"Was that–" her teeth sink further into her lower lip. "Is that why you didn't sleep with me? That night at Diego's?"

Is that really what she thinks? I shake my head quickly, emphatically. "No. I've been with other women since she died. Twelve years is a long time."

"Then why–"

"My job is to protect you," I tell her firmly. "To keep you safe, not use you for my own pleasure. The only reason I touched you at all during that party was because it was necessary to keep you safe, Elena. That's where it ends."

I see her chin jut out a little, a stubborn set to her jaw, and I can almost *hear* what she's thinking.

"You didn't have to kiss me in the bedroom to keep me safe," she says, confirming exactly that.

"That was–"

"Don't say it." Her teeth sink into her lip again. I can't help but wish she'd stop–the last thing I need is to look at her mouth, that full, soft lower lip, while she talks about my kissing her and reminds me just how good it felt. "I don't want to hear you say it was a mistake."

"I won't say it, then."

There's another long, heavy moment of silence, and Elena abandons the rest of the food, pulling her knees up to her chest as she wraps her arms around them. "Is that what you do with other women, then? Use them 'for your pleasure'?"

I can't help but wince at the way she says it. I don't entirely know how the conversation ended up on this track. Talking to Elena about sex and pleasure and what I do with other women on this deserted beach is a dangerous path to go down, and I know it.

She needs to understand that I'm not the kind of man she needs to get involved with. That wanting me leads her down that same dangerous path, and it only ends one way.

"In a sense," I admit. "But I've always made sure that the women I'm with want me. I'm clear that it's a one-night thing, and I make sure they're fine with that, so much as I'm able. I know it's shallow, in a way, but–" I shrug, giving her a lopsided smile. "I'm not the kind of man who can exist in a life of celibacy, like some men I know. And even the most celibate man I knew, a former priest, ended up finding a woman who wore him down eventually. But the least I can do is not fall in love again."

The moment I say it and see the expression on her face, I know I've said too much–opened up too much. I know she doesn't fully understand, and I can't make her without telling her so much more than I want to talk about.

I should have said less.

"I'm sorry," I tell her abruptly, turning to poke at the fire and build it up a little more. "I've told you more than I needed to."

"No, I–" She hesitates. "I'm glad I know. I'm sorry you–that you had to go through that."

"It's nothing that others haven't gone through, too. You've been separated from your sister."

"At least she's still alive." Elena purses her lips, leaning forward so that her chin is on her knees. "It must have been lonely, all this time."

"I've gotten used to it." The words come out shorter than I mean for them to, bitten off. "Why don't you tell me a little about yourself, Elena? I feel like I've been doing all the talking."

She takes a deep breath, tilting her head to one side. "I don't think there's all that much that's interesting. I've spent my whole life cooped up in that house. Only allowed to leave with a bunch of security guards and at least one of my parents, usually to go out shopping or to church or something like that. The rest of the time–stuck at home. A hothouse flower, a caged bird–whatever allegory you want to come up with applies."

"So, what did you like to do while you were stuck at home?" I glance over at her. "You must have had some kind of hobby."

"Reading." She looks at me almost defiantly, as if she expects me to have a negative opinion about it. "That's what I spent most of my time doing. Or walking around the garden with Isabella. She and I spent a lot of time together. She was always more adventurous than I was–I just went on adventures in my head. More of a reader than a doer. Although now–" she smiles wryly, a slight curve of her mouth. "I guess I got more of an actual adventure than I bargained for."

"It does seem like it." I can't find it within myself to tell her just how dire the situation still is, not tonight, at least. "What kind of books did you like to read?"

She purses her lips, and I can tell she's debating whether to tell me the truth or not. "Romance novels," she says finally, with that same defiant note in her voice. I struggle to hold back a laugh–not because I think less of her for it, but because she so clearly expects me to.

"Well, there's nothing wrong with that," I tell her, a small smile playing at the corner of my lips. "Sounds like as good a way as any to pass the time."

Elena narrows her eyes at me a little, as if she's not sure whether she believes me or not. I just shrug, reaching for our trays of food to clean up, but privately I can't help but think that it was wise for me to stop when I did, back at Diego's. I'd known that she was sheltered, of course—any girl of her background would be—but from what she's said, even more so than I'd thought. And while I don't think any less of her for her choice of hobbies, I know that a girl as naive as her, with all her ideas about love and romance and sex coming from between the pages of a book, could be led down a road that would end in heartbreak if the other person weren't conscientious about it.

Which means I need to be the conscientious one. She's not someone I can indulge my desire for, and that shouldn't change.

No matter how difficult it might get.

Elena

I know Levin expected me to be shocked or scared by the revelation of what he used to do. I think it was meant to put me off, to make me want to put a clear distance between us. But if anything, it just made me more curious about him.

Nothing he's done so far has given me any reason to think that I should be afraid of him. He's protected me even beyond the letter of what my father paid him to do, gotten me out of that plane when it could have killed him. I don't know what we're going to do now, but I feel instinctively as if I can trust him to figure it out. He'll get us out of here. I just have to be patient, and he'll figure it out.

"We should get some rest," Levin says, once he's tossed the empty trays into the fire. "I know you've been doing a lot of sleeping lately–or at least something like it–but more rest can only do you good. And I can't say I've gotten much the last two days."

It's obvious that he hasn't, looking at him. There are bags under his eyes, which look a little more hollow than before, a tiredness at the edges of his face that I recognize. Even so, he still looks incredibly handsome. To me, it just adds to the rugged look that he seems to have cultivated, the stubble on his jaw a little thicker, the sharp lines of his face a little more pronounced.

"Elena." His voice is gentle, but my cheeks flush at the idea that he's caught me staring. "Do you need help with…anything?"

I know what he's asking, and I blush deeper at the idea of needing to be helped to wherever will serve as a restroom out here. "I think I can make it," I tell him firmly, the words sticking in my throat as I shrug off the blanket and stand up.

Thankfully, he doesn't argue. "Don't go too far into the trees. There are snakes out there, among other things."

A shudder goes down my spine at the thought of snakes, not to mention what "other things" he might be referring to. I have no intention of going any further than I need to for a bit of privacy.

When I come back down the beach, feeling every muscle and joint in my body protesting from both the deep bruises caused by the crash and two days of lying still, Levin is arranging the two blankets into a makeshift bed on the sand. He gestures to it when I'm within hearing distance.

"Made up the bed for you." There's a hint of wry humor in his voice. "Not the most comfortable, I'm afraid."

"Where are you going to sleep?" I look at him curiously.

"Over there." He nods to the sand on the other side of the fire. "Not the worst place I've slept, if I'm being honest."

I blink at him. "You can't sleep on the sand. Just sleep on the blankets with me. It's probably not much better, but—"

"No." His voice is firm as he backs away from the makeshift bed. "I'll be fine, Elena."

"Levin." I mimic his intonation on my name, and I see him wince a little. "Just come sleep on the 'bed.' There's no reason for you to be uncomfortable—"

"There is," he says, just as firmly as before. "Let's not waste time we could be sleeping, arguing."

He turns away, walking to the other side of the fire as he lays down on the sand, facing away from me, clearly indicating that the conversation is over. Something about it pisses me off, but I don't have the energy to argue with him—not now, anyway. I can still feel the exhaustion and pain from the crash and the fever dragging at me. I pull back the top blanket, wriggling under it as I try to get comfortable on the one underneath it.

The night is colder than I'd expected, and there's a sharp breeze coming off of the water. I huddle under the blanket, not wanting to let Levin know how cold I am, but after a little while, I hear his voice drifting over toward me.

"Are you alright? I can hear your teeth chattering from over here."

"I'm fine," I murmur, but after a moment, I let out a sigh, tucking the blanket tighter under my chin. "It's cold."

"It'll be hot as hell tomorrow, but it gets chilly at night. I'm sorry. There's not anything other than those two blankets." There's an apologetic note in his voice, and I can tell he feels bad about it. I know I shouldn't say what I'm thinking, but I can't seem to help myself.

"You could come over here and share the blankets. Then we'd both be warmer."

There's a long moment of silence, and I think he's going to tell me no. I know he must be cold too, but he seems to be determined to keep a physical distance at the very least. And then, just when I'm beginning to resign myself to being cold for the rest of the night, I hear the sound of him getting up.

"Just to stay warm." Levin crouches down next to me, sliding under the blanket as I move over to make room for him, rolling over to face away from him. I know if I face him, I'll be far too tempted to try to get another kiss.

The blanket is too small for there to be any real distance between us. I can feel the muscled bulk of his body behind mine, the tension in him as he tries not to press up against me, but there's not really anywhere for either of us to go. His arm is lying on his side, trying not to touch me, but after a moment, I feel him shift, and his arm moves over my waist. He's not holding me, not exactly, but his arm curls over me, and the heavy weight of it makes me feel safer than I have in a long time.

I shouldn't feel that way. We're on a deserted beach god only knows where, and I have no idea what the plan is for rescue or how we're going to get out of here. Levin hasn't told me how bad of a situation we're in, exactly, but I'm getting an idea.

At this moment, though, all I can think about is how good it feels to have someone close like this, curled around me, the size of him enveloping me, a strong arm holding me. I've never slept in a bed with anyone, never had a man so close to me. It feels good–even better than I'd imagined it would.

It's harder to fall asleep than it was before–not because I'm cold any longer, but because I don't want it to end. I can feel him breathing, slow and steady, and then I feel something else, too.

Something presses against the curve of my ass, hard and thick, and a jolt goes through me as I realize he's getting hard from being so close to me. I'd felt it before, when I was on his lap at the party, but now we're all alone, very far away from anyone who could see or hear. Alone on a beach, under a starlit sky, and it feels more romantic than it should.

I want to squirm against him. I want to feel him get harder, find out what it's like to get him even more aroused than he already is. The sense of power that it gives me is intoxicating, knowing that he's getting turned on by *me*, just from lying next to me.

It takes everything in me not to move, lying very still. But I feel his breathing change, and he shifts away from me a little, clearing his throat.

"I'm sorry," he says, his voice slightly hoarse. "It's not on purpose."

Slowly, I crane my head a little, looking at him backward over my shoulder. My back arches a little as I do, my ass brushing up against him, and I feel him stiffen all over. "I think it's a compliment," I tell him teasingly, and I can almost hear his teeth grinding. "You hinted earlier that what happened back in Mexico was a mistake, but you must want to. I can feel it, Levin."

My voice is breathier than I mean for it to be, but I can't help it. There's a tightness coiling in my stomach, heat blooming over my skin at the feeling of him so close and so turned on, and I want to keep going. I want him to cup my face with his hand and kiss me, pull me harder against him, grinding against me until neither of us can take it any longer. There are a dozen half-formed fantasies in my head, and I want all of them to come true.

"This has nothing to do with that, Elena," he says gruffly, and I twist a little more towards him, laughing softly.

"It's pretty obvious." I don't know why I'm still whispering–there's no one to hear us–but the moment feels too intimate to speak more loudly than that. "I can feel it–"

"You're very innocent," he says quietly, and I can tell that he's trying to be kind, but the way he says it sends a small jolt of hurt through me. I don't want him to think of me as childish or innocent, or naive. I want him to see me the way I see myself–as someone capable, smart, who knows what she wants, if she were given the chance for it. And it feels like, right now, I've been given an opportunity to have it.

To enjoy something I never would have gotten to, otherwise.

Surely *something* good has to come out of all of this?

"Sometimes it just happens," he says, his hand resting on my hip, as if to hold me a little bit away from him, and in place so that I can't squirm against him. "It doesn't have to mean anything, Elena."

I know I should let it go. I should pretend that it's not happening, close my eyes, and try to sleep. But my entire body feels as if I'm vibrating with how close he is to me, my heart pounding in my chest, my skin as hot and flushed as if I were on fire. I'm not cold any longer, not with him so close to me. I can't even remember what it felt like to be cold.

I twist under his arm, rolling towards him before he can stop me, so that we're suddenly face to face, so close that my nose is almost brushing his, my legs bumping up against him. If I moved a tiny bit closer, I'd feel his erection pushing against my stomach, and it's all I can do not to move that fraction of an inch. My hands are between us, and I start to reach out to touch him, but he stops me before I can. His hand grabs both of mine, holding them still, as he looks down at me. I can just barely see his expression, silhouetted in the moonlight.

"What would you do if I told you I wanted it too?" I whisper, and I feel him breathe in deeply, as if he's trying to control himself.

He wants me. I know he does. I can feel it in every straining line of his body, in the way his hand is wrapped around mine, keeping me from getting any closer. I can feel it in the hitch of his breath, see it in the set of his jaw.

"I would tell you," he says, very slowly and carefully, "that it doesn't matter. Because this is not going to happen, Elena."

I tilt my chin up, almost daring him to kiss me. I can see the glint of his pale blue eyes, and for a brief second, I think he might do it.

And then he shakes his head, slowly, and reaches for me. My heart skips a beat in my chest as I tense, anticipating him pulling me closer, the slide of his fingers through my hair, the warmth of his body flush against mine.

His hands close over my shoulder and my waist, and he turns me over, gently but firmly, so that I'm facing away from him again. I can feel that he's lying on the very edge of the blanket, leaving a sliver of space between us.

"Go to sleep, Elena."

My entire body feels as if it's faintly pulsing, thrumming with desire. I never knew it was possible to ache like this, to feel my heartbeat beating through my veins, to feel hollow when I don't even know what it's like to be filled up. I feel as if my skin is too tight, my lungs too small, as if I can't breathe deeply enough. I want him, and I know that I never knew what it felt like to want anything before this.

I know he's not going to give in. Not tonight—maybe not ever. I close my eyes, willing myself to sleep. I'm exhausted, and I can feel it starting to creep in, my body relaxing by degrees despite the steady throbbing just beneath my skin.

When I do fall asleep, all I dream about is him.

The hand on my waist, sliding lower, dipping below the edge of my shirt, brushing against the taut flesh there. Hesitating, unsure whether to go up or down—and then his fingers move upwards, sliding against my breasts, cupping, teasing, finding my nipples, and tweaking them between his fingertips. I arch against him, pushing them into his hands, wanting more.

I feel his breath on the back of my neck, the hard press of him against the curve of my ass, his other hand running through my hair, making a gentle fist in the soft strands as he tugs my head back. His lips run along my throat, brushing lightly, his tongue drifting down the line of it all the way to the hollow at the base, kissing me there lightly as his hand moves lower. It drifts back down my stomach, to the very edge of my jeans, tracing a line just under the waist as his hand moves closer to where I need it so badly—

I'm aching, throbbing, so wet that I can feel it. I gasp as he flicks the button of my jeans open, drawing down the zipper, wiggling them lower down my hips as his lips caress the edge of my collarbone, sending shivers over my skin again and again.

I arch my hips up, wanting more. I want him to touch me in all the places I've never been touched before, to give me everything I need. I want to learn how it feels, and I want to learn him too, if he'd just let me—

He's so close. His fingers brush over my smooth flesh, so close to where I need his touch the most, and I let out a low, soft moan, pleading without words for more.

I can feel how hard he is. How much he wants it, too. His hips grind against my ass, a groan vibrating against my skin, and I don't know why he won't give in, why he won't just—

And then there's nothing, every sensation is gone, and I hear a helpless moan come from my own lips as I twist around to see—

I jerk awake in the darkness, shivering again, my body throbbing with that same aching need that I'd felt in the dream. I can feel how wet I am, my thighs sticky with it, and my fist closes in the blanket as I twist around to see that Levin is gone, the space next to me empty.

My heart stutters in my chest for a different reason as I sit up, holding the blanket against me as I look around for him. The fire is just embers now in the makeshift pit, and it's still fully dark, the moon half-hidden behind clouds now. I feel a jolt of fear as I look, my mouth going dry at the sudden reality of being all alone—and then I see his shadow further down the beach, standing with his back to me.

I know I should leave him alone. He got up for a reason, and I know deep down that he did it with the assumption that I'd be asleep and wouldn't know. But curiosity overtakes me, once again.

I want to know what's going on in his head. He's a confusing, mysterious man, and instead of putting me off, it just makes me want him that much more. It feels like an unbearable curiosity, a need to get him to open up, to show me what's behind all of the walls that he's so constantly putting up.

Before I can talk myself out of it, I push the blanket back, getting up and walking barefoot through the sand toward where he's standing. I try to be as quiet as I can, not wanting him to hear me before I can see what he's doing. Whatever it is, he's so engrossed that he doesn't move, not until I'm almost right behind him and I whisper his name.

"Levin?"

Levin

I wake from a dream that I know I had no business having. But so close to her, it was impossible not to.

In the dream, she'd been just as willing as she was waking, but in the dream there was no reason for me to stop. When she turned towards me, chin tilted up as if daring me not to kiss her, there was nothing stopping me from grabbing that delicate chin in my fingers, holding her face very still as my lips came down on hers, tasting their sweetness again. I drew that full, soft lower lip between mine, my tongue running over the edge of it, and in my dream, I tasted the champagne on her mouth again.

There was no reason not to keep going. It wasn't real. I could slide my hand upwards and cup her soft breast in my palm again without guilt, feeling her nipple stiffen under my fingertips, give in to the delicious throb in my cock that urged me forward as I broke the kiss to run my lips down her throat. She was so soft and warm, and I pulled her in closer, grinding against her lower belly as I pushed her shirt up, baring that perfect, tanned flesh under the moonlight.

Her moan was the sweetest thing I'd ever heard. In the dream, her clothes were gone in an instant and mine too, leaving her bare and arching underneath me, her thighs parted so that it was effortless to slip between them, my cock brushing against her wet, hot entrance.

I wanted her so fucking badly. I wanted to taste her, feel her, drive her wild with lust until I heard every sweet sound that she could make. I dipped my fingers between her thighs as I dragged my tongue along the hollow of her throat, feeling her clench and tighten around them, wetter than anything I'd ever felt. So wet, so needy, and all for me.

Please, she gasped in the dream. *Please, I need you. I want you. Please.*

I'm no stranger to women begging for more. I've always fancied myself a good lover, always tried hard to please the women I've been with. But this felt different. This felt like it mattered.

Somewhere in the back of my head, I knew I shouldn't. I felt her hips arch upwards, rubbing against my fingers, saw her perfect lips part on another plea for my throbbing cock, and I knew how easy it would be to give her exactly what she wanted. One sharp twist of my hips, and I'd be buried inside of her, in fucking heaven.

It was just a dream, after all. There was no harm in it. Just a dream—

But my guilty fucking conscience woke me up.

I wake up harder than I can remember having been in years, my cock like an iron rod against my thigh, trapped in a tangle of boxers and jeans that's hellishly uncomfortable. My entire body feels as if it's too tight, as if I could come out of my skin at a touch. I'm fairly sure I was a few moments away from coming in my sleep—something that I *definitely* haven't done in years.

What the fuck is wrong with me?

I need to get some space.

Elena is, blessedly, asleep. I can feel the soft rise and fall of her breathing next to me, her hair fallen a little over her face, her hands bunched up in the blanket in front of her. Asleep, she looks sweet and peaceful, and I don't want to wake her. I *especially* don't want to wake her in the state I'm in, because my self-control is already hanging by the barest of threads.

So I get up, as slowly and carefully as I can, gently tucking the edge of the blanket in around her to hopefully keep her from getting chilled until I come back. *If I wake her up when I come back,* I tell myself, *I'll just say I went to relieve myself.*

It's not entirely a lie. Just–a different kind of relief than she'd likely interpret it as.

I make my way a decent distance down the beach, not so far that I can't still see her shape by the fire or hear her if she shouted for me, but far enough for some privacy. My cock is aching with the need for relief, straining against my fly until I feel certain that it's possible it might break through.

Hurriedly, I thumb open the button of my jeans, yanking down my zipper. There's no taking my time with this–it's a need right now, rather than a pleasurable way to pass a half hour. My cock is barely out before I wrap my fist around it, biting back a groan as I start to stroke, my hand sliding urgently up and down the taut length.

It won't take long, I know that. The tip is already slick with pre-cum, dripping into the sand as I roll my palm over the sensitive, swollen flesh and let out a hiss of pleasure through my teeth, lubing the rest of my shaft with it. My hand flexes around my cock as it throbs, and my hips jerk forward, fucking my fist as urgently as if I were where I really want to be right now.

It's not good enough. It's never fucking good enough, but it feels particularly lacking right now. *It's all you get,* I tell myself firmly, sliding my palm over the sensitive tip again, squeezing as I slide my hand down to the base, trying my damndest not to imagine that it's Elena's wet heat that I'm buried inside. It feels like a monumental effort.

Another jolt of pleasure arcs through me, my balls drawing up tight at the base of my cock, and I know I'm so fucking close. I slide my other hand into my boxers to cup them, rolling them lightly in my palm, trying to think about anything other than teaching Elena how I like my balls played with while she wraps those perfect lips around my cock, or how they'd feel slapping against her clit as I fucked her from behind–

You're going to fucking hell, Volkov. You already knew that, but it bears repeating right now.

"Levin?"

I almost jump clear out of my skin. I let go of my cock as if it's on fire, moving to shove my stubborn erection back into my jeans–a useless effort, as hard as I am right now–but it's too late, anyway. Elena is circling around me, curious as a cat–and as fucking lightfooted as one, too. I hadn't heard her come up, not so much as the slightest footstep.

Or I was just so fucking distracted by jerking my cock that a meteor could have landed, and I wouldn't have heard it.

"Yes?" My throat sounds as if it's closed up, the word coming out half-strangled as I try to turn away from her to keep her from seeing my cock and what I've been doing.

Again, a useless effort. Her gaze latches on immediately, and I see a glint in them that tells me she's far more interested than she should be.

"Do you want help with that?"

Her voice has that soft, breathy tone that I've noticed it takes on when she's aroused. It's a detail about her that I shouldn't know, that I feel guilty for knowing, but my cock just won't get the fucking memo that I'm not supposed to be turned on by any of this. The sound of those few words breathed out like that in a soft whisper, sends a jolt of lust through me that threatens to tip me over the edge.

"You should be asleep." It's not even close to being an answer to her question, but I can't bring myself to lie to her. I also can't bring myself to say *yes, I want you to wrap those long, pretty fingers around my cock and do what I was just doing, but with your hand. I want you on your knees, while I teach you to suck a cock for the first time in your life, and I hate myself for being turned on by that, but* fuck *if the idea of it doesn't make me nearly come every time it pops into my head.*

"That's not an answer."

I turn away from her, finally managing to get my erection back into my pants, painful as it is. "Elena—"

"I wondered if that's what you were doing. That night at Diego's, when you went to the bathroom and stayed in there after you kissed me. I thought you might be—" she pauses, as if trying to decide how to phrase it. "Pleasuring yourself."

"That's one term for it." Again, the words come out strangled. I feel as if my brain is half-dead from lust, as if I'm struggling to think through a fog. "You should go back to bed, Elena."

"I'd rather be out here with you."

"Elena!" I turn sharply towards her as I manage to zip up my jeans, and she flinches back.

I force myself to soften my expression and my voice, not wanting to frighten her. I never, ever want to frighten her. But *fuck*, if I don't need her to understand that she's toying with things she can't possibly fathom the seriousness of.

"Even if we were going to do anything—which we're *not*," I add firmly, "this isn't the time, Elena. You need rest. This morning, you were burning up with a fever. I wouldn't be any kind of man I could respect if I so much as kissed you right now. Go back to bed."

I know I'm dancing a fine line. She could—and I have a feeling she might—take what I just said as a tacit suggestion that I might change my mind in the future. But she's being stubborn as hell, and I need her to walk away before I lose what little control I have left.

"Are you going to come to bed too?"

Why does just hearing that make my chest feel like it's going to crack wide open?

"I'll be right here, where I can see and hear you if something happens. I need some time, Elena. I'll come back before you wake up."

She hesitates, and for a moment, I think she's going to keep arguing. But then she nods, slowly, and turns to walk back down the beach.

I let out a slow sigh of relief as I watch her retreat. I can tell she's still frustrated with me from the set of her shoulders and the way her fists clench and unclench as she walks away, but she's just going to have to be frustrated.

I want to go back with her. I want to hold her in my arms and fall asleep with the soft weight of her curled against me. I want a dozen other things that I don't dare think about, or I'll follow her back to bed and give her everything that she keeps begging for and more. I'll do things that will make it hard to live with myself later.

Why the fuck is she getting to me like this? After all the women, all these years—

That's not something I can spend too much time thinking about, either.

I sink down into the sand as I watch her walk away, sitting there overlooking the water. The tightness in my chest doesn't ease, not even when I glance over a little while later and see her curled on the blanket again, asleep from what I can tell. She looks peaceful once more, and I rub a hand over my face, feeling an exhaustion that sinks all the way down to my bones.

I miss you. My lips form the words, silently, spoken to someone who is no longer here to hear them. I can see her in my head, closer than she's been in a long time—all long blonde hair and bright blue eyes, that attitude that both infuriated me and made me fall in love with her radiating out from her delicate face.

I never knew, before Lidiya, what it felt like to be in love. I never thought I would know. I had given it up as something that would never be a part of my life. To have experienced it and then have it so cruelly ripped away is something that I never want to feel again.

There's something about Elena that pulls me in, that distracts me in a way that I haven't been in years. Not just a feeling of protectiveness towards her, or even the desire that I keep trying to pretend that I don't feel, but a curiosity about her that I know I shouldn't indulge. I'd thought I was past the point of feeling something like that–especially when it comes to someone so naive– but I can feel the first twinges of it. I know the kind of danger it would put us both in. More than that, I know the ways it could hurt her.

The ways *I* could hurt her.

Elena is very different from Lidiya, in so many ways. But there are things about them that I see in common–the tenacity, the bravery, the fire that Elena has. It's a quieter kind of fire, one that comes out when she's challenged or threatened, and all of those things are so very similar to the things that made me fall in love before, all those years ago.

If I'm not careful, if I let her too close, I could end up making the same mistakes again–this time with someone too young, too innocent for the damage that my past and my future could do to her.

And I'm responsible for her. I can't forget that.

I can't fail her. I can't fail to protect her the way I did Lidiya.

Just the thought of going back to sleep next to her brings my desire raging back, my half-hard cock pressing painfully against my jeans as I grit my teeth. It's going to be a long night if I don't manage to take the edge off.

Glancing back once more at Elena to make sure she's still sleeping, I shift so that my back is to her, my hand slipping into my jeans. I have to bite back a groan the moment my hand wraps around myself, my oversensitized cock throbbing against my hand instantly after having had to stop before.

I shouldn't think of her. I close my eyes, trying to think of anything else, like I had back at Diego's. But just like then, it feels impossible. Then it had been the thought of her in the bed on the other side of the door, her hand between her thighs. Now it's the all-too-close memory of her body so close to mine, her nose almost brushing mine, her breath warm against my cheek. It would have been so easy to have her. She fucking *wanted* it.

It's entirely on me to keep this from going too far, and right now, the thread of my self-control feels on the verge of snapping.

My hand tightens around my cock as I stroke faster, giving myself over to the fantasy, if only so I can finish this. I'm so fucking close, and I imagine her arching back against me, her leg hooked over mine, the heat of her as I slide into her from behind with my hand on her hip, pulling her into me.

God, it would be so fucking good.

I can almost hear the sound of her moans as I thrust into her, filling her up, my hand sliding around her hip to slip between her slick folds, rubbing her clit until she spasms and cries out, coming hard on my cock.

That's what tips me over the edge, a groan slipping through my clenched teeth as I lean forward on my knees, my hips thrusting as I fuck my fist the way I wish I were fucking Elena right now, eyes closed as I envision the dark spill of her hair over my chest as I let myself fantasize for just one second that I'm coming inside of her instead of over the sandy beach.

Fuck. I sag forward as the last shudders of pleasure ripple through me, my cock throbbing one last time as the last of my cum spills out onto the sand. Then I feel my body go lax, the guilt following immediately on the heels of pleasure.

I've got to stop letting myself think of her like that.

It's a slippery fucking slope, and I know it. Letting myself imagine it is a path to being unable to stop myself from finding out the reality, and I've been around long enough to know that.

At least now I should be able to sleep next to her without an erection so hard it hurts. How I'll feel when I wake up in the morning is anyone's guess.

I tell myself when I go back to the blankets and lay down next to her, curling myself around her back as I tug the top blanket over us both, that I'm sleeping next to her to keep her warm and safe.

That it has nothing to do with wanting to have her in my arms.

But as I close my eyes, feeling the warmth of her sinking into me, feeling her squirm back a little in her sleep to be closer, I know I'm going to sleep better than I have in years.

Elena

I wake up alone on the rumpled blanket, much to my disappointment.

Levin is on the other side of the makeshift fire pit, rummaging through the bag of supplies. I sit up, letting the blanket drop away. The sun is up, and like Levin had warned me, it's already getting hot.

At the sound of me sitting up, he twists around, glancing over toward me. "How did you sleep?" he asks, pulling out two more of the MRE pouches. "How are you feeling?"

"Sore. Like I slept on the ground." I give him a wry half-smile. "First time for everything, I guess."

I see him flinch at that, and I realize what I said a moment too late. "I think the plane crash probably didn't help either."

My side twinges at that, as if the reminder made the stitched-up wound on my side ache, and I reach for the hem of my shirt, tugging it up a little on the side.

"Elena–" Levin warns, but it's too late.

The gash runs from the bottom of my ribs down to my hip. The stitches are better than I might have expected, but I can see from the swollen edges of it that Levin was right–it will scar. And it won't be pretty.

"I'm sorry." There's a regretful look on his face. "Not really a skill they teach us. More about stopping a man–or yourself–from bleeding out rather than making it look pretty."

"It doesn't look so bad." I peer at the closed gash again. It's ugly, there's no doubt about it, but the stitches are straighter than I might have otherwise expected.

Levin chuckles. "You don't have to lie to me."

"I mean–I think someone else might have done a worse job. Not a doctor," I add, a small smile twitching at the corners of my lips. "A doctor might have kept it from scarring. But someone else like you."

His eyes widen slightly, and then he laughs. A real laugh, not the dry chuckle I've heard from him before. He rubs one hand across his mouth, shoulders shaking until he's finally able to stop, and then he shakes his head.

"You continuously surprise me, Elena Santiago."

The compliment sends a flush of warmth through me, but I try not to show it, hoping that my cheeks aren't turning as pink as I feel like they are. "Why? Because I'm not in tears that I'm going to have a scar?"

Levin shrugs. "Plenty of people would be."

"Plenty of girls, you mean."

He shakes his head. "I've known a decent few men that would be upset about a scar like that. Especially if it fucked up their handsome faces. On the side– maybe not so much."

"A scar on the side isn't so bad?"

Levin chuckles again. "Women like the war stories."

"Oh?" I cock my head at him. "How many 'war stories' do you have?"

His mouth twitches. "Plenty. Too many to count at this point."

"At least none of them are on your face."

Levin turns a little towards me, tapping the side of his jaw. "There's one here. I just usually keep some stubble, cover it up a little. Nothing that can't be disguised, thankfully."

"And where else?"

The silence is instant. Levin's mouth tightens, and I know I've pushed a little too far.

"Well, I'm not looking to impress any women," I tell him lightly, trying to shift the tone of the conversation back to levity. "So I guess I'm out of luck."

"You never know," Levin smirks. "Some men like a tough woman. Actually, any man who doesn't isn't a man worth his salt, in my opinion."

"Are there a lot of men like that in Boston?"

He lets out a breath, standing up, and walking over to me to hand me one of the MRE packets. "Are you thinking you'll stay in Boston, then?"

I hesitate, not quite sure what the answer is to that. "I don't know," I tell him finally, honestly. "I haven't thought that far ahead. But I'm not sure how I could go back home. My father won't be able to make any kind of marriage arrangement for me now that I would want–not that I necessarily would have loved who I would have ended up with before, but there would have been more value in it–if that makes sense."

Levin lets out a long breath, raising an eyebrow as he sits back in the sand and opens his 'breakfast.' "In terms of the kind of world I know your family exists in, yeah, it makes sense," he says finally. "But in terms of thinking of you as someone whose only value lies in what kind of marriage you can make, or how 'pure' the man who agrees to marry you thinks you are—" he shakes his head, the last part coming out laced with distaste. "I can't really make that make sense in my mind, even though I know it's the way things are. Or—" he shrugs one shoulder. "Even if I can make sense of it, I can't agree with it."

I look at him in surprise. I hadn't really wondered what his thoughts were about it, but hearing them feels different than I'd thought it would. "Do you think I should stay in Boston?" I ask suddenly, poking at the food he handed me, and Levin frowns.

He's quiet for a moment, and I can't help thinking how handsome he is. His jaw is tensed, making the sharp lines of his face stand out even more, and his blue eyes stand out against the dark of his hair and stubble in a way that makes my heart stutter a little in my chest.

He hadn't said anything about last night, and I'm certainly not going to unless he does. But I can think of so many things that I wish we'd done together—and so many that I still want to.

"That's not something I'm qualified to give my opinion on," he says finally, shoveling a bite into his mouth. "Your decisions are yours to make, Elena."

I laugh at that. I can't help it. "My decisions have *never* been mine to make," I tell him flatly. "Not ever. They've always been someone else's. I don't necessarily think that's going to change just because I'm in a different country or city."

"Who do you think is going to make those choices for you in Boston? Your sister? Her husband?" Levin looks at me curiously. "I know Niall; he *definitely* isn't going to tell you how to live your life."

"I'm sure my father will have some kind of influence." I give him a small, rueful smile. "But first, we have to get there. What kind of chance do we have at that?"

Levin looks at me, a startled look on his face as he sets his food down for a moment. "You sound pretty chipper for a question like that." He presses his lips together, cocking his head slightly as he watches me. "I thought you'd be in a worse mood, considering our circumstances."

And considering how frustrated you left me last night, I want to say, but I don't. I'm not even sure what to say at first, and I muscle down a few more bites of the food, feeling a knot of anxiety forming in my stomach. "It's not going to be fixed by crying about it," I tell him finally. "Just like the scar."

Levin breathes in slowly, and I can see him hesitating, see the wheels turning in his head about how much to tell me. "Elena–"

"Just tell me the truth." I set the tray of food down. "Just be honest with me? In the last week, I've seen my house set on fire, been shot at, and seen men killed. I've been kept in a cell and auctioned off to the highest bidder–and that didn't feel good, even if the highest bidder was you. I–" I swallow hard, shaking my head. "I survived a car chase and a plane crash and ended up on this beach–and I'm pretty sure there's more to come before I'm safe and sound in Boston. I don't want to be treated like I'm fragile. I think I've proved so far that I'm not."

Both of Levin's eyebrows go up at that, and he nods slowly, a small smile twitching at the corners of his mouth. "I think you're right about that, Elena. I just don't like having to say the kind of news that I have for you."

I feel my stomach drop. "So it is bad."

He nods slowly. "I'd hoped there would be a radio in that bag we could use to get help. It's part of the reason I grabbed it, besides the hope for food and water. Usually, there's some kind of waterproof pouch for something like that, for exactly this reason. But not this time."

I'd wanted the truth, and I still do. But hearing it is beginning to send a cold chill through my veins. "It doesn't work?"

Levin shakes his head. "Not after how wet it got. And I don't know that I can fix it. That's not something I know how to do."

"How else do we get out of here?" I ask, hearing the words come out a little more breathlessly than I'd meant for them to. I clasp my hands together, shoving them against my lap to try to stop them from shaking.

Levin lets out a long breath. "I'm not sure that we do, Elena," he says finally. "If there is a way, I'll find it. But you asked me to be honest, so I am. I don't know if there's a way out of this."

A few beats of silence pass as I try to make sense of it, as I try to breathe past the lump in my throat, as I try to think of what to say. Finally, I manage to force the words out.

"Have you ever been in a situation like this before?"

Levin looks at me curiously. "Stranded on a beach? No, I don't think—"

"Where you thought you were going to die." I blurt it out, the last word coming out almost as a gasp, and I wish I could bite it back. I don't want him to realize just how afraid I am.

Levin's face softens, and after a moment, he nods. "Yes," he says finally. "I have."

"Tell me about it?"

His eyes widen slightly. "I don't know if that's helpful, Elena—"

"You got out of those situations, or you wouldn't be here now." I swallow hard, past that growing lump in my throat that I desperately don't want to turn into tears. "So tell me. Please."

Levin sighs, frowning. "Well, honestly—there's been a lot of them. We'd be here for a while."

I laugh, a sharp burst of sound that fills the space between us. "I think we have some of that now."

He nods, a rueful twitch at the corner of his mouth. "Well, you might be right about that." He leans forward, arms balanced on his knees as he looks at me. "I told you I worked as an assassin, Elena. Being in danger of dying was just a Tuesday afternoon for me."

"What was the scariest one? The closest call."

Levin tilts his head slightly, as if he's trying to recall. "There was a sniper," he says finally. "Sent by someone I was after to kill me. She was the best of the best. We're on good terms now, actually. She's the only other one I know who left the Syndicate and is still living. She'd already left by then–her story is what made me think I could get out, actually. She was working freelance, and turned out it was on the opposite side of me. I spent three days holed up in a hotel room, lights off, waiting for the moment when I'd slip up and give her that sliver that she needed to put a bullet right here." He taps his forehead. "One shot was all she needed, and we both knew it."

"How did you get out of that?" I realize I'm leaning forward, caught up in wondering he'd managed to outsmart someone who sounds so dangerous. "Did you get the drop on her or something?"

Levin laughs. "Not even close. My boss assumed after three days that I needed backup. He sent someone else to take care of the target. Once he was dead and she wasn't getting the paycheck she was promised, she had no reason to kill me. She went off to shake down some of his associates for what she could get out of them, and I went back to my boss." He winces. "I took a good beating for that one."

I stare at him. "A *beating*? Are you serious?"

"It could have been worse," he tells me, shrugging. "And no, Elena, I'm not going to describe to you what I mean by that. Some things a man really doesn't want to relive. But I screwed up that job, and there was a price to pay for that. Better than the bullet through the head Valeria wanted to give me."

"That was her name? Valeria?"

Levin nods. "Nicknamed the Widow Maker. Best sniper in–well, I'm not sure I've met a better one, actually. And not a woman you want to be on any side of. If you're on her good side, she'll use you for something. If you're on her bad side–you'll be dead before you probably even know it."

"She sounds like an interesting person."

"That's one way to put it." Levin chuckles. "There's plenty of stories like that, though. Not quite as close of a call, but still closer than I would have liked. There's always someone who wants a man who was in the line of work I was in dead. Probably a few left still– especially after getting tangled up with Diego like this."

"I'm sorry." I look at him, feeling suddenly guilty. "I didn't mean–"

"I'm not saying this is your fault," Levin says firmly. "It's not, Elena. I took the job. I'm just saying–the cartels aren't something to fuck with, and I've done a decent bit of that since I got here. I'm sure the list of enemies I have is likely a bit longer now, that's all." He glances ruefully toward me. "Not that that's going to matter, if we don't get off this beach."

The silence hangs heavily between us for a long moment, the reality of what's happening slowly sinking in. *We really might die.* It rolls around in my head, over and over, until I can feel a slight, shivery panic starting to run through my blood.

I don't want to feel like that. I don't want to spend my last days having a panic attack on a beach in the middle of nowhere. I don't want to spend it terrified and shaking and crying until the inevitable finally catches up with us. And I can only think of one thing to do about that in the moment.

I stand up suddenly, tipping the tray of food into the sand as I reach for the hem of my shirt, stripping it off over my head. It's not in the best shape–torn in a couple of spots from the crash, the side of it stiff from dried blood, and I toss it onto the sand, reaching for the button of my jeans.

"What are you doing, Elena?" Levin's voice turns gruff, and he stands up slowly, dusting sand off his thighs.

"Well, since we're probably going to die anyway, we should probably enjoy our forced beach vacation, don't you think?" I shove my jeans down my hips, kicking them off into the sand next to my shirt. "I've never *been* on a beach vacation. No time like the present, right?"

"Elena!" Levin says my name sharply as I unhook my bra, tossing it defiantly onto the growing pile of my clothes. I see his jaw tense as he struggles not to look down, to keep his eyes on my face, and I hook my thumbs in the side of my panties, shoving them down my hips, too, until I'm completely bare under the sun.

"You can look if you want," I tell him thickly, feeling my heart racing in my chest. There's a wild, daring feeling fizzing in my veins, a feeling that nothing matters now that we're potentially so close to the end. I'd never been the kind of girl who stripped naked in front of a man, who went skinny dipping in broad daylight, who did anything other than what she was told to do–but why not start now? I might never get the chance to start again.

The muscle in Levin's jaw leaps again, and I can see the struggle on his face. I can see that he *wants* to look, no matter how hard he's trying not to.

"You can do *whatever* you want," I say slowly, backing away from the pile of my clothes, towards the edge of the water. "But I'm going to go swimming. You should come with me. What else are we going to do?"

Levin's mouth opens, but before he can say anything, I turn away from him. I can feel his eyes on me as I walk, and then start to run, down the beach.

All the way into the chilly, sparkling blue water.

Levin

I know better than to do what she wants me to.

Nothing good will come from being that close to her, not even clothed, and *definitely* not while she's naked. It had taken everything in me to keep my eyes on her face when she'd started stripping off her clothes all the way down to her skin. When she'd turned and run down the beach, I hadn't been able to stop myself from seeing the perfect, stunning view of Elena Santiago's ass as she went straight for the water.

I'm hard already, just from her taking her clothes off in front of me. That defiant attitude that she'd had, that insistence on finding some measure of enjoyment in all of this, not to mention the fact that I know this is *exactly* the reaction she wants from me, all add up to a painful erection once again testing the limits of the zipper holding my jeans together. And if I strip down to my underwear and go into the water with her–

I know better than to test my limits like that.

And yet I find myself following her down the beach.

"Elena!" I call after her, but she ignores me, running straight to the edge of the water and then into it. "Elena, be careful—"

"Of what?" she yells back, turning to face me as she backs into the water. She gives me a full, achingly gorgeous view of her bare breasts and everything below them, tan and perfect under the bright sun. "Having some fun?"

I open my mouth to tell her to come back, that she's being naive and foolish, that this is a serious situation—but I can't seem to force any of the words out. I'm not sure that I've ever known anyone so capable of being optimistic in the face of this much danger, and her positivity is infectious. I can feel it getting under my skin, making me want to give in to what she wants.

A little bit of it, at least.

What would it hurt? I ask myself as I follow her down the beach. *What am I going to change, by making her get out of the water and just sit on that beach? What does going for a swim hurt? It's not as if I'm going to fix the fucking radio.*

For her sake, I'd tried to make it sound as if there were a possibility. I'm not going to fix the fucking radio, and I know it. Our chances are so slim that they're not worth speaking about, and I don't want to tell Elena that, not so plainly. I'd been as honest with her as I could stomach.

"Come on! It's only a little cold!" she calls out, up to her chest in the water now, just her slim tanned shoulders and arms above it. I can see the water beading on her skin, glinting in the sunlight, and an ache spreads through me that I can't entirely put a name to.

I want her. I want more than just to fuck her like all the other women who've passed through my bed in the last decade. I want to lay her down and show her all the different ways I can make her feel pleasure, touch her in all the ways that no one else has done before. I want to teach her all of it, and learn everything about her—all the secret spots on her body, all the sounds she'll make when she comes, and everything else in between. I want to make her feel so fucking good that no one else can ever compare to it.

More than anything else, I know that's not fair, because whatever we did together, it wouldn't be able to last. And I'd ruin her for anyone else, any of those boys she might find in Boston that might actually be able to make her happy.

Worse still, I *want* to ruin her for any other man. And that makes me feel like the kind of man I've never thought I was.

I walk up to the very edge of the water, letting it wash over my bare toes as Elena frolics a yard or so away from me, running her hands through the crystal water before reaching up, trailing her fingers through her thick black hair, the tops of her breasts rising above the water as she does so. I can feel my mouth go dry at the sight, my body tensing with the urge to go to her, and I know better than to walk into that water.

"Levin!" She calls out my name again, brighter and happier than anyone should ever sound under these circumstances, and I find myself reaching down to strip my shirt off over my head before I can stop myself.

She goes very still in the water, staring at me as I toss it onto the sand.

What the fuck are you doing? I can hear the thought shouting at me from the inside of my head. Still, my hands are at the belt of my jeans, undoing them, pushing them down so there's only the thin fabric of my boxers keeping my hard cock from springing out, and it's too close for comfort.

"I knew you'd come around!" Her hands are cupped around her mouth, her breasts vanish from view under the water again, and I know I still have a chance to put my clothes back on and go back up the beach. "Come on! It's fun!"

I keep the side of my hand against my cock, relying on the shock of the chilly water to make my erection go down before Elena can realize how turned on I am. I step into the water, walking towards her as it splashes up around my calves, and despite myself, I have to admit that it does feel good. Refreshing, especially considering I haven't had a shower in longer than I normally would.

And cold enough to do something about my arousal before I get to her.

"I've never gone swimming like this." Elena spins around in the water, going up on her toes as she runs her arms through it. "It's beautiful out here."

"Elena—"

"Don't say it." She turns back to face me, her mouth suddenly thinner than before, her lips pressed together. "I don't want to hear how serious it is, Levin. Not right now. You already told me the truth. Now I just want to enjoy this despite how bad it is, okay?"

There's a small tremble to her chin that stops me from saying anything else. She tips that chin up, swallowing hard, and then her lips spread upwards in a smile as she reaches out, splashing a wave of water toward me.

It flies directly in my face, showering me in cold droplets, and I feel an instant burst of annoyance, an urge to reach out, grab her by the shoulders and shake some sense back into her.

And then I hear her laugh, and the annoyance starts to melt away.

"Splash me back!" she calls out, swimming around me and sending another wave towards me. "If you can get me!"

Don't let your guard down. If you allow yourself to relax, if you let yourself stop watching what you say and do, you're going to slip up. You know it.

Another splash, and she swims back, giggling as she smooths her hands over her dark hair, gleaming like a raven's wing in the sunlight.

I can't remember the last time I really let loose. Getting drunk in a series of bars and letting down a string of women whose names I don't remember doesn't count; I know that. I can't remember the last time I felt happy, that's for sure—not *really* happy. Not the kind of happiness I see on Elena's face, a smile spreading across it like sunshine.

My hand skims across the water, splashing her back, the water raining over her in a sparkling wave. It splashes over her hair, slicking it back, and she laughs out loud, shaking her head.

It sounds like music.

When she swims towards me, her tan skin gleaming under the water, I reach for her. It's supposed to be to stop her, to push her away. She swims right up in front of me, and I grab her slender waist, a jolt going through me at the feeling of her soft skin under my hands. I want to pull her close instead, to feel her bare and smooth against me, and I hesitate for the brief second that it takes for her to take advantage of my indecision.

Her hands land on my shoulders, gripping them as she pulls herself through the water, all the way up against me as her legs go around my hips. I *feel* her soft gasp more than I hear it as she locks her ankles behind me, her breasts pressed against my chest, her lips a breath away from mine.

"If we're going to die anyway," she whispers, tilting her head slightly as her wet, dark hair falls forward, "why shouldn't we?"

And then her mouth is on mine.

It's not as clumsy as the first kiss. It's as if she did her best to remember everything about the kiss I gave her in that bedroom, and thought about how she'd do her part differently if she got another chance. Her lips brush over mine, lightly at first. Then her tongue flicks out against my lower lip as if she wants to taste me, sliding lightly over the curve of it as she arches against me.

I should stop her. I need to stop her. My hands tighten on her waist, and it's meant to be to push her away, but somehow I end up pulling her closer. The feeling of her breasts pressed against me, soft and plush, is intoxicating. Even in the chilly water, she feels exceedingly warm, and I can imagine just how much warmer she must be between her thighs.

And then she shifts against me, her legs tightening around my hips, and I can feel that heat pressed against my cock through the fabric of my boxers, drenched and sticking to me in the water.

It makes me feel as if I'm going to lose my mind.

She deepens the kiss, her hands against my chest, fingernails scratching against my skin as her teeth scrape lightly against my lower lip, her tongue soothing away the sting. It slides into my mouth, tangling with mine, and she gasps again, lightly, her back arching.

I shouldn't run my hands from her waist up her back, up to the sharp blades of her shoulders, feeling the smooth lines of her body under my hands. I want to learn every inch of it, run my hands back down and squeeze her full ass in my palms, pull her harder against my now-throbbing cock.

I'm hard as hell, and I know she can feel it. Her hips roll against me, and she gasps again, moaning softly as her hands slide up to cup my face, nails scratching around to the back of my head as she kisses me harder still.

I know what she wants. I try to say her name in a way that means *we should stop*, but it comes out a mumbled groan against her lips, a sound that I can tell only inflames her more.

Her hand slides down my chest, trailing over my abs, over the wet fabric of my boxers. Mine can't move fast enough to stop her as she slips her hand inside, her fingers closing around my cock, and for a brief second, I think I've found heaven.

And then I realize what she's doing, as her hand strokes down the length of it to my swollen tip, and it jolts me out of the moment.

"Fuck, Elena!" I break the kiss, twisting my head away as I grip her waist, disengaging her from mine and setting her a few inches away as I back up, fumbling with my cock to get it back into my boxers. "We can't do this. I shouldn't have let it get this far."

Her teeth sink into her lower lip, and for a second, I think I see her eyes mist over, before she swallows hard and tips her chin up, turning away with her arms wrapped over her chest.

"Can you grab me a blanket?" she asks finally, her shoulders curved slightly inward as she faces away. "It's going to be cold when I get out of the water."

I want to go to her. I want to wrap my arms around her, turn her around, and kiss her senseless, if only to see the smile on her face again. I can imagine how it would feel for that smile to spread across her mouth while she kisses me, the way she would gasp and moan, the way she would arch into me. The sweet way her body would open up for me, willing and eager, giving me everything I'm aching for.

Instead, I force myself to turn away and walk out of the water, back up towards the beach and the blanket that she asked for.

Away from what I want, in that moment, more than anything else in the world.

Elena

I don't want Levin to see how disappointed I am. I stay turned away from him as he strides through the water back up to the shore, my arms wrapped across my chest, as if he hasn't already seen it all. I feel like I want to curl into myself, embarrassed and unsure of how I've fallen short again, but I also don't want to go back and undo it.

Kissing him feels better than anything I ever imagined–and I've imagined plenty of times what it would feel like to kiss someone, touch someone, do *all* of the things I've never gotten to do. Someone that I picked, that I *wanted* to seduce.

I've read stacks of romance novels, picturing the hero in my head, imagining myself in the place of all the heroines. I've imagined the moment where the man can't stop himself any longer, where his desire takes over, where he just can't take how much he needs the heroine.

I thought that's where Levin and I were. I felt how hard he was, the way he held me tighter, his tongue tangled with mine, and I thought we crossed that line. I thought when I touched him, he'd give in.

A shiver runs down my spine at the memory of feeling him, hot and hard and throbbing in my hand. He felt so big, even more so than when I'd been in his lap at the party, and it scared me a little, but it didn't stop me from wanting him.

It didn't matter, because he pushed me away anyway.

"Elena!" He calls my name from the shoreline, and I glance over my shoulder to see him holding one of the blankets. I swallow hard, keeping my arms wrapped around myself as I start to walk through the water up to the shore, unable to look him in the eye. *If we're going to die anyway, what does it matter?* I feel silly saying it now, overdramatic, but it was how I felt.

I still feel that way. Why bother with pretending that we don't want each other? Why bother worrying about what's going to happen later, if there isn't going to *be* a later?

Clearly, he doesn't see it that way, though.

I can see him averting his eyes as he holds the blanket out to me as I step out of the water. "Here," he says stiffly, and I take the blanket from him, wrapping it around myself as I walk past him.

"Thanks," I mumble, walking quickly through the sand back up to where I left my clothes. The reckless fun of the day is gone, but I can still do something useful–which, in this case, will be washing my clothes and leaving them out to dry, so I don't feel quite as disgusting.

I also want to put some space between Levin and me for a little while.

I thought I'd be better at seducing someone, if I had the chance.

I never thought I would have the opportunity, really. I always assumed I'd be married off to someone I didn't choose, someone that my father arranged a marriage with, and that the best I could hope for was maybe two out of three of not old, ugly, or mean–but probably not all of those. I never saw myself in a position to seduce someone that I actually *wanted*, not really.

Now I have the most gorgeous man I've ever seen in my life protecting me, and I want him. The things that we did at the party should have frightened me, I think, but all it did was make me want to know more–to *feel* more. I want to find out all the mysterious things that I don't know about, all the things I never thought I would have the chance to try with someone who made me *actually* want to do them with him. It feels like I have the kind of fantasy I never thought I would get to experience at my fingertips–and it's just out of reach.

I don't want to die without knowing what it's like.

Levin, unsurprisingly, keeps his distance from me throughout the rest of the day. I keep the blanket tucked around me like a beach towel as I wash my clothes in the salt water and lay them out to dry, studiously not looking at him as I drape them over rocks.

"The salt is going to leave those stiff as boards," Levin notes from where he's sitting on a boulder near our makeshift camp, fiddling with the damaged radio. "They won't be very comfortable."

"Better than blood-soaked and filthy from sweat," I retort, still not looking at him. "I was thinking of cutting the jeans shorter, actually. If I could borrow your knife–"

I hear him get up, crossing the sand to me as he holds it out, pressing the handle into my palm. "Careful," is all he says before retreating back up the beach.

Gritting my teeth, I slice off the fabric slightly above the knee on both sides, jerking the blade across it a little harder than necessary. I toss the leftover material aside, leaving the now-shorts to finish drying as I stalk back to the campsite and give Levin his knife back.

I've never wished so much for something to do. Even back at home, on afternoons when I was meant to stay in my room because my father had visitors that he didn't want to see me or Isabella, I had my books to keep me busy, or the gardens to sneak out into. Now there's nothing but the day stretching on, and the newly strained tension between Levin and I to try to ignore.

As soon as my clothes are dry, I snatch them and walk off a little ways down the beach to get dressed, half-hoping that Levin won't be able to resist sneaking a glimpse as I tug on my newly cut-off shorts and slip the blouse over my head.

The clothes *are* stiff, just like he said they would be, but it's still better than the shirt being half-soaked in blood. The cut on my side stings from the salt water earlier, and I wince as I shrug into the shirt, feeling the tug on the stitches. I hadn't noticed earlier when we were swimming–I'd been enjoying myself too much–but now I can feel the soreness creeping in.

I go for a walk down the beach anyway, mostly to avoid the awkwardness with Levin while he tries to work on the radio. When I come back, it's nearly twilight, and he's starting a fire with a fresh bunch of kindling, two of the MRE pouches ready and waiting for our dinner.

"There you are," he says, sitting back on his heels as he watches the twigs catch fire. "I've been slaving over a hot stove for dinner," he adds, nudging one of the pouches towards me with a smile that tells me that he's trying to smooth things over.

I reach for the packet of food, resolving to let it go for now. Nothing is going to be made better by the two of us fighting–I know that. If there *is* a way off of this beach, we'll have to find a way to work together to figure it out–or at the very least, we'll need to be getting along.

"I want to hear more about what you used to do," I tell him as I poke at the food, forcing it down bite by bite. "You don't have to tell me any of the really gory stuff if you don't want to. Just–I don't know. Something adventurous."

Levin chuckles from where he's sitting by the fire. "There's a lot of stories like that," he says, taking another bite of his own 'dinner.' "You'll have to be a little more specific."

"How many countries have you been to? All of them?" I cross my legs, leaning forward as I muscle down another bite, too, reaching for the bottle of water sitting between us. "Or just most?"

"Most," Levin says, taking the water bottle when I'm finished with it. "I've been to just about every continent, though. Nothing in Antarctica–the penguins don't put out contracts on folks often." He grins at me, and I feel my mouth twitching in response, a smile spreading across my face in spite of myself.

"What was your favorite country?"

"Hmm." Levin considers, taking another bite and setting the tray aside. "Russia was home, so that's pretty far up the list, even if there were a lot of mixed good and bad things that happened there. France is beautiful. I particularly liked going to Japan, too, but I didn't end up there often. Their own organizations tended to snuff things out before we got to it."

"Not a fan of Mexico?" I tease him, and I see his jaw tense.

"It's nice enough," he says, his voice more clipped than before, and I know I've pushed him a little too far once again.

"Did you ever go anywhere just on vacation?" I ask curiously. "Just for fun, not for–business?"

He laughs quietly, his face softening again, just a little. "Not often," he says ruefully. "I used to not have the time. The Syndicate didn't like us wandering off too far. And then–"

His voice trails off again as he goes quiet, and I sit there, watching him on the other side of the firelight. *There's so much I don't know about him.* So many times that I seem to trip over a topic that makes him shut down, and I suspect it has to do with his late wife.

Everything about him intrigues me, makes me want him more–to know him, not just physically, but who he is, too. He's older than me, but in a way that makes him seem worldly and sexy, that draws me in instead of repelling me.

He's the only man I've ever met who makes me feel like this.

"It's been a long day," Levin says finally, when we've finished eating. "We should both try to get some sleep."

I nod, smoothing out the blanket that we used as a makeshift bed last night and laying the one that I used earlier–dried now–atop it. I glance over at him, and I can see his hesitation. I know he's thinking of sleeping on the other side of the fire, in the sand again, instead of being so close to me.

"Keep me warm?" I ask softly, and I see the momentary tension in his jaw before he nods.

He joins me on the blanket, tugging the top one over both of us. I can feel the inch of space he's left between us as if it were a gulf, pointedly keeping us from touching as much as he's able to, as if he's not sure what will happen if he so much as brushes against me.

Ironically, that makes it even harder to stifle the desire simmering through my veins. I'm hyper-aware of him lying behind me, the warm scent of his skin lingering on the blanket, the memory of how good he felt last night curled up close to me. I want him in a way that I've never wanted anything, and I can feel it almost vibrating through me, until I have to clench my hands in fists against my chest to keep from reaching for him.

"Elena?" Levin's voice carries towards me through the darkness, a low murmur. "You're fidgeting."

I can hear the question in his voice, and it makes me want to laugh. I sink my teeth into my lower lip, not wanting to answer, but a moment later, I hear him again.

"Are you alright?"

I let out a sharp breath, feeling frustration well up in my chest. "You can't honestly act like you don't know why." I swallow hard, tensing next to him, wanting to touch him so badly it almost hurts. "I know that you know."

"We shouldn't talk about it." His voice is low and quiet, as if there were anyone out here to hear us. "Just go to sleep, Elena."

"So you do know." I roll over suddenly to face him, frustration pulsing through me until I feel like I could explode with it. "After what we did at the party, I don't know why it matters so much. We could just—"

I hear him let out a sharp, short sigh. "That was to keep you safe, Elena. That's the *only* reason that happened at the party. I didn't have any other choice."

"And if you had?" I don't think he can see the expression on my face, even in the moonlight, but I glare at him anyway. "You're telling me you wouldn't have done *anything*?"

There's a moment of heavy silence, and Levin lets out a long breath. "I'd like to think that I wouldn't have," he says finally. "Honestly, Elena? I can't say for sure. But I can keep it from going too far now."

I move a little closer on the blanket, my heart pounding in my chest. "You said you wanted to take care of me," I whisper. "I have something that I need you to take care of."

Slowly, I reach up for his hand, intertwining my fingers with his as I bring it lower, down to the edge of my shirt, and then lower still, in between my thighs. "I want to find out what it feels like," I murmur, sliding my hand over his until it's pressed squarely where I need his touch the most. "I've only ever made myself come. I want to find out what it feels like for someone else to do it. Someone that I really want."

I *feel* the shudder that goes through him. His head tips back, and in the faint moonlight, I can see his jaw clench. I feel his hand flex against me, briefly cupping between my thighs as he lets out a deep, shaky sigh, and I can feel him relenting.

He looks at me, his gaze fixed on mine, and there's something resolute in his eyes.

"Just this, Elena," he says quietly. "I'll show you. I'll make you come, and you'll enjoy every second of it." There's a low, husky promise in his voice that sends a shudder of anticipation through me, pulsing down between my thighs where his hand still rests. "But *only* that. No sex. Alright?"

I nod, breathless at the thought of him touching me. "Yes," I whisper, looking at him as my teeth sink into my lower lip, my body tense and trembling. "Please—"

"Don't worry," he murmurs, his hand sliding up to flick open the button of my shorts, deftly sliding the zipper down as his fingers slip inside. "I'll make you come, *ptitsa*. Just like you asked me to. But slowly. The way *I* want to make you come."

A jolt of lust sparks through me as I feel his fingers slide over my bare flesh, still on the outside, not dipping between my folds. My hips jerk forward instantly, arching into his hand. Levin chuckles lightly, his hand cupping me again as he reaches for my shorts with his other hand, tugging them down.

"So eager," he murmurs, his voice deeper, thick with desire. "Slow, I said, *ptitsa*. Let me make it feel as good for you as I can."

I swallow hard, one hand resting against his chest as he gently rubs his fingers back and forth, stroking the outside of my pussy softly, teasing me until I can feel my breath catching in my throat. Then, right as I'm on the verge of begging him once more to do *something*, two fingers dip between my folds, brushing against my clit.

I suck in a breath, gasping as an electric burst of pleasure washes over me, sharp and unexpected. "Levin—"

"I'm just getting started," he murmurs, his fingertip just grazing my clit. "Slow, Elena. I want you to feel all of it. I want it to feel better than anything ever has."

His free hand reaches for my chin, tipping my face up so that his lips graze over mine as lightly as his fingers are working lower down, a teasing, soft touch that has me breathless in an instant, trembling.

"Does that feel good, *ptitsa*?" he asks softly, his lips brushing over the edge of my jaw as his fingers press a little more firmly, rolling against my clit in quick, short strokes that leave me open-mouthed, a helpless moan spilling from my lips as my hand tightens in his shirt and I arch towards him.

I can't speak. All I can do is nod as his lips slide down my throat, his teeth lightly grazing my skin as his fingers move just a little faster, testing rhythms to see what makes me gasp and cry out. It feels as if everything does, each variation better than the last. All I can do is moan as I writhe against him, feeling the pleasure build in a sweet, delicious crescendo that has me begging with the only word I can think of–his name.

"Slowly, Elena," he murmurs. "Enjoy it. Don't rush."

I don't *want* to rush, because I have no idea if this will ever happen again. This might be the only time he touches me like this, and I want to savor it, *remember* it. I lean into him, my mouth pressed to his collarbone as I grip the front of his shirt, hips grinding against his hand as he settles into a firm rhythm, his fingers sliding over my clit in the same motion, again and again.

It feels so fucking good. *Too* good. I want more. I want *everything*, all of him, and it's everything I can do not to beg for it as I feel my pleasure reaching its crest, so close to the edge, and I know I'm about to go over.

"I–" I gasp against his skin, my entire body starting to tremble. "I'm going to–"

"I know, *ptitsa*," Levin murmurs. "Good girl. Come for me, Elena."

That shatters me. I cry out, my moan rising in pitch as my entire body seizes, hips arching into him as I come harder than I ever have in my life. I've never felt so much all at once. I know I'm impossibly wet, drenching his hand as the orgasm ripples through me in seemingly endless waves, over and over, until I don't know if it will ever end–and I don't ever want it to.

I expect him to stop, but he doesn't. His mouth presses against my throat, sucking lightly as his fingers slide lower, circling and teasing my entrance as I collapse against him, still shivering with pleasure.

"Show me if you can come for me again," he whispers in my ear. All I can manage is another helpless moan as I nod, my forehead pressed to his shoulder as his fingers slowly tease me back from the ebb of pleasure.

I want him to slide his fingers inside of me. I grind against his hand, trying to find the angle that will give me what I need, feeling hollow and aching to be filled up. He deftly keeps his fingers on the outside of me despite my best efforts, only teasing until he slides them up again, through the slick arousal left from my orgasm, up to my still-throbbing clit.

When his fingertips brush against my over-sensitive flesh, I cry out, shuddering against him as he deftly finds that gentle rhythm again, easing me into the slow arc of pleasure once more.

"Levin, please—" I manage to breathe the words between gasps, feeling as if there's nothing beyond the steady thrum of sensation rippling through me from what his fingers are doing. "Please, I want—"

"Shh," he murmurs, his fingers speeding up just a little, circling where I need them the most. "I know what you need. Just a little more, and you can come for me again, little bird."

I let out a sob of pleasure as his fingers stroke directly over my clit again, moaning his name, wanting more and knowing that this is as far as he's going to go. *Greedy*, a small voice whispers in my head as Levin pushes me to the brink of a second orgasm, my thighs trembling around his hand as I writhe against him. *Isn't this enough?*

It doesn't feel like enough. It doesn't feel like it could *ever* be enough. I'm acutely aware of where I am, on a blanket on an abandoned beach beneath the stars, clinging to the most gorgeous man I've ever seen as he makes me come for him without asking for anything in return. It's wild and romantic and beyond anything I'd ever thought would ever happen to me, and I want to keep going. I want to take this all the way to the conclusion, all the way until I find out what I've been missing out on all this time.

"That's right," he whispers against my ear as I start to shudder again, the pleasure rising until all it can do is crash over me yet again. "Come for me again, Elena."

My body obeys, hips thrusting as I ride his hand to the inevitable climax, my head falling back as I cry out, a high-pitched sound that's something like his name. I don't ever want it to end; the feeling carrying me higher than I ever imagined. I press my mouth against his shoulder, my back arched as I try to pull him closer, to get as close to him as I can possibly be.

"Come for me," he murmurs as I do exactly that, his fingers never stopping. "That's right. Such a good girl, *ptitsa*."

I'm gasping, small, sobbing breaths when I go lax against him, still trembling from the force of the second climax. I feel his hand slip away from me, and I want to grab his wrist and pull it back, for him to never, ever stop. The idea that I might never feel him do that again is unthinkable.

But I also want to do something for him.

I can feel him pressed against my thigh, as close as we are. He's incredibly hard, stiff, and straining against the fabric of his jeans, and I'm overwhelmed with the desire to touch and explore him, to find out how I can make *him* come as hard as he just did for me.

Levin rolls onto his back on the blanket, jaw clenched as he sucks in a deep breath, and I can tell that he's fighting for control. I push myself up on my elbow, my hand touching his thigh as I lean over him, and his hand snaps out, grabbing my shoulder.

"Elena—" his voice is a low warning. "What did I say?"

"You said no sex." I slide my hand up, fingers toying with the leather of his belt. "That's fine. We won't do that. But this—"

I tug at his belt buckle, and he lets out a low groan, his eyes closing as his hand tightens. "Elena—"

"I want to make you feel good, too," I murmur, slipping the buckle free. "Let me make you come, Levin. Please—"

I reach for the button of his jeans, and this time, he doesn't stop me.

Levin

I've reached the very end of my self-control.

I'd been afraid I would. I knew I was dancing with danger when I let myself touch her as intimately as I just did. Still, I'd reasoned it away, telling myself that it was for her, just to give her something.

Now her hand is on my cock, and I don't think I can stop her again.

"I want to make you feel good, too," she murmurs as she undoes my belt, her fingers tugging open the button at the top of my jeans. "Let me make you come, Levin. Please—"

Hearing a beautiful woman beg me to let her make me come, when I know to the very depths of my soul that I should tell her no, has to be one of the worst tortures that god or man could ever devise.

"I want to find out—"

"What it feels like," I finish through gritted teeth. "I know. You said that earlier." *Goddamn it.* Her fingers are already tugging down my zipper, curiously slipping inside to seek out my hard, aching cock, and I'm beyond the limits of my ability to stop her. How any man is meant to stop a woman so desperate to pleasure him, I have no fucking idea.

I haven't wanted anything in years as much as I want this. Everything about her turns me on in a way that I haven't experienced in so long. I'd forgotten what it was like to want someone so much, to the very depths of my being.

When her hand touches me, I'm fucking lost.

"You're so big," she breathes as she frees my cock, her hand sliding down the length of it. I'm dripping pre-cum already, pearling at the tip and sliding down my shaft long before she touched me, and I'm slick with it in an instant as she strokes me, letting out a small hum of pleasure that goes straight to my cock.

"That's what every man wants to hear," I force out between gritted teeth, with a little bit of much-needed humor. I can feel myself throbbing in her fist, so close already, and now my self-control is being used up for something else—to make sure this isn't over too soon.

If I'm going to overstep yet another boundary I've set for myself, I might as well make sure I get to fucking enjoy it.

"I've never seen anyone else." Her hand strokes me again, experimentally, and she shifts, nudging my legs apart on the blanket so she can kneel between them. "Does this feel good?"

Her hand slides up as she asks it, palm sliding over my swollen cockhead, and I let out a sharp hiss of pleasure as I nod, momentarily unable to speak.

"What about this?" Her hand tightens a little, sliding down to the base in a long, slow stroke that has my eyes rolling into the back of my head.

"That's perfect, *ptitsa*." I groan, a low sound deep in my throat as she slides her hand up and down again, over the taut flesh. "Slow—just like that. That feels fucking incredible."

"I want to make you feel good, too." Her teeth sink into her lower lip, as if she's concentrating very hard on stroking my cock. It's so fucking adorable that I would have kissed her if it didn't mean that she'd stop–and also that it would put her into a position far too easy for me to end up fucking her in.

If there's one line I can't cross tonight, it's that. *I can't fuck her. I have to stop before that happens.* Not that it likely will matter–with the way she's touching me, I'll finish before we can get that far.

She strokes me for a few moments longer, her fingers teasing along my length as she traces the pulsing veins, her thumb finding the soft spot beneath my tip and toying with it until my hips jerk and thrust into her hand, my entire body shuddering from the pleasure. And then, just when I think I'm going to lose my mind from the teasing, she leans down, brushing her lips over my cockhead, and I *know* I'm going to lose my mind.

"What about this?" she whispers, and I can't find my voice for a moment.

"Yes–" I manage finally, my hand fisting in the blanket as the other rises up to touch her hair, stroking the silky fall of it as her lips brush over me again, her tongue flicking out to lap up some of the pre-cum still dripping. Her lips part, sliding down over the tip of my cock as her tongue swirls against my sensitive flesh, and I forget how to speak–until her teeth catch on the edge, and I let out a grunt of pain.

"I'm sorry!" She pulls back, her hand still closed around my shaft, and the last fucking thing I want her to do is to stop.

"It's alright, *ptitsa*," I murmur, my fingers running through her hair. "It happens."

"I want it to feel good for you–"

"Oh, it does," I assure her, a small laugh catching at the back of my throat. "It feels fucking incredible."

"Will you tell me what you like?" Her voice is hesitant, uncertain, but she's still touching me, her hand moving along my length in a slow slide that threatens to make me forget how to speak again.

"I'll try," I tell her hoarsely, swallowing hard as her palm slides over my tip again. "Just go slow, *ptitsa*. Slow feels just as good–maybe even better."

"Like this?" She leans forward, her lips brushing over me again, this time over my cockhead and beneath it, her tongue flicking out to tease that soft spot until I gasp. "Was that good?"

I nod, my hips jerking as she does it again. "That's good," I manage, trying to find the ability to speak as she takes the tip of my cock in her mouth again, her tongue making circles that I don't think she has any concept of how good they feel. "So good–"

Elena lets out a low, satisfied hum that vibrates over my flesh and makes my hips jerk again, and I have to fight not to thrust into her mouth. I don't want to make her go any faster than she's comfortable with. I let her slide down a little at a time, slowly, as she takes me inch by inch into her mouth until my cockhead brushes against the back of her throat, and she jerks back, coughing a little.

"That's alright," I tell her quickly, giving her a moment to recover. "You don't have to take it all."

"I want to," she insists, and I laugh hoarsely, my cock throbbing in her fist. I feel like I'm being fucking edged, she's getting me there with such a perfect, torturous slowness, and I'm both desperate to make it last forever and to come all at once.

"What you're doing feels amazing," I tell her gently, my hand still stroking her hair as she dips her head again, tongue swirling around the tip before she starts the slow slide downwards, sucking me a little more firmly this time.

I can feel her getting a little more confident, her hand moving at the base of my cock as she sucks and licks as far down as she can before I reach the back of her throat. It feels *too* fucking good, and I know

I'm going to come before very long. I don't know how much longer I can stop myself from letting go.

"I'm almost there," I murmur as she slides up again, her tongue still flicking all the way up the underside of my cock, and driving me insane with pleasure. Her blowjob technique could best be described as *exploratory*, but I'm enjoying it every bit as much as I have every woman who knew how to suck my cock like a professional– maybe more, because Elena is clearly so delighted to be learning how. "I'm so close–*fuck*, Elena–"

I breathe her name as my cock throbs, dangerously close to the edge, and she takes that as a sign to double her efforts. Her hand tightens around the base, stroking me as much in sync with the rhythm of her mouth as she can with her inexperience. The combination of her enthusiasm and the warm, wet pleasure of her mouth drives me to the very brink.

"Elena–" I warn her, wanting to give her time to pull back before I can't control it any longer. "I'm going to come–I can't–*fuck*, I'm coming, I–"

To my astonishment, she doesn't stop. She slides down a little more, sucking my cock as if it's the only thing she wants to be doing, her hand moving along my shaft as I throb and pulse between her lips. I feel her jerk with surprise when the first hot spurt of cum coats her tongue, but she still doesn't stop, and when I feel her *swallow*, I'm completely fucking lost.

I come harder than I have in years, groaning her name aloud as my hand flexes in her hair, struggling not to grip it too tightly as my hips jerk and buck. I do everything in my power not to shove my cock down her throat as I fill her mouth with my cum, and she swallows every fucking drop.

My entire body is shuddering with the force of the orgasm, and she keeps going, licking every drop of cum off of my cock until I finally grasp her arm, breathless and over-sensitive.

"Too much," I gasp, hips twitching away. "Too sensitive–"

"Oh!" She backs up, her hand wiping at her mouth in an automatic gesture that's as adorable as her biting her lip had been earlier. "I'm sorry—"

"You have *nothing* to be sorry for," I tell her as firmly as I possibly can. "That was fucking incredible, Elena."

"Was it? I didn't know—"

"Come here." I reach for her, adjusting my clothes back into place and helping her tug her shorts back up before I pull the blanket over us both, maneuvering her so that she's lying in the crook of my arm with her head on my chest. "You did such a good job," I tell her gently, pressing a kiss to the top of her head as she snuggles against me, holding her with one arm around her. "That felt amazing."

"What you did felt amazing too," she mumbles sleepily, as I feel her body go lax against mine, all of the tension drained out of her.

I should fall asleep immediately, too. But I lie there awake for longer than I should, feeling the warm weight of her against my chest, pressed against me in a way that feels far too good.

I'd missed this more than I've ever been willing to admit—the feeling of someone next to me, holding someone as I fell asleep, the knowledge that I'll wake up tomorrow with them curled against me.

When I sleep, it's dreamless and heavy, and for the rest of the night, Elena stays in my arms.

———

In the morning, when the bright, harsh sun wakes me up first, Elena's head is still pillowed on my chest. I don't move for a long time, letting her stay that way, until she finally groans in her sleep and rolls over to her other side, taking the rest of the blanket with her.

I take *that* as my cue to get up, moving carefully so that she can sleep a little while longer. A quick perusal of the supply bag confirms what I noticed last night—we're already low on both rations and bottled water. If our only chance is waiting on someone to come within view of the shore to rescue us, we're likely to run out of both before that happens.

I hate the idea of frightening Elena. But she'd asked me to be honest with her, and I know she's not going to let me leave her on the beach while I go off foraging. I know her well enough by now to know what her reaction to that would be.

I also know how she's going to feel about the other conclusion I've come to—that what happened last night can't happen again. But I also suspect that she expects me to say that.

When she finally wakes up, bleary-eyed with her hair tangled from the night before, she sits up slowly, narrowing her eyes at me.

"Are you going to tell me how adorable I look first thing in the morning?" she asks grumpily, taking the ration pouch that I offer her. "Because I don't feel adorable. I feel like there's sand in my mouth."

I hand her the water bottle without a word, refraining from commenting on what *had* been in her mouth last night. As tempting as it is, I know it's not wise to talk about it unless I want to have to explain to her right now why we can't have a repeat.

The moment I think about it, my cock twitches. That part of me, at least, is clearly not on the same page.

She also *does* look adorable first thing in the morning.

Elena eats a few bites of food in silence, watching me from where she's sitting cross-legged on the blanket. "Is there something you want to talk about?" she asks finally, shifting uncomfortably. "You look upset."

"I don't know if *upset* is the right word," I tell her slowly, taking a contemplative bite of my own breakfast.

"Worried, then." She leans forward. "What's going on?"

There's no point in beating around the bush. "We're low on supplies," I tell her frankly. "I think it would be a good idea to look around and see if there's any source of fresh water, anything that might be safe to eat that we could bring back. If we're going to try to hang on until there's some kind of rescue, we need food and water."

Elena's eyes widen slightly, and she swallows hard, but she nods. "Alright," she says finally, taking a breath clearly meant to steady herself. "So after breakfast, then?"

As I look at her, I wonder if I'll ever stop being surprised by how tenacious she is.

I wonder if I'll get the time to.

"Yes." I take a quick sip from the water bottle, handing it back to her. "That way, we can take our time. The less strain we put on ourselves, especially in the heat, the better."

I have some survival skills. The Syndicate taught us how to last in situations like this, but on our own, and not in any great depth. The kind of jobs we were meant to do were jobs that required us to get in and get out. Wilderness survival was not high on the list.

But I'm determined to keep Elena alive if there's any possible way. And if not—

I can't let myself think about that.

We set out after breakfast, walking up the beach to the jungle-like treeline up ahead. "Stay close to me," I warn Elena. "I don't know what's out there." I hand her the knife, handle pointed towards her, as we near the trees. "Just in case. I have my gun."

She swallows hard, but nods, taking the knife and holding it tightly in one hand as we find a path through the trees, and walk into the soft, slightly muddy ground just beyond.

"That's a good sign." I nod at the ground. "There should be fresh water somewhere, then. It hasn't rained in the last few days. We just need to look for it."

"Do we have any way to purify it?" Elena frowns. "What if—"

"We'll have to take our chances," I tell her honestly. "It might not be the safest water, but it's better than salt water or none. It'll be the best chance we have."

She nods, and I can see the nervousness in her eyes. "We'll just take the chance then," she says, as bravely as I think she can. "Let's keep looking."

There are a few possibilities for food that I see—some berries and a fungus growing at the base of a tree we pass, but it's nothing that I know for certain won't poison us. If it comes down to it, I think I might choose the risk of poison over starvation–but for me, there's a faster way out than that if I know there's no hope of rescue.

I can't think about that as long as Elena is still alive, though. And I'm not willing to test uncertain foods on her.

"I think I hear something!" she calls out as we walk a little further past the trees, dodging a tangle of vines as she picks her way through the increasingly muddy ground. "There might be–"

We push through the tangle, and that's when I hear it, too–the unmistakable bubbling sound of a stream.

"Thank *fuck*," I murmur, reaching for her arm to make sure she stays close as we make our way toward it. Food we can go without for a while, if we have to, but we wouldn't last long without water. It's a risk, without any way to purify it, but it's better than nothing. "Do you have the other water bottles?"

Elena nods, pulling them out of the bag we'd brought with us. "Here you go," she says, setting them down next to me.

I crouch down by the stream, cupping my hands and lifting them to my mouth to take a small sip. It tastes fine at first impression, clean and clear, and all we can do is hope for the best. I twist the cap off of the first bottle, dunking it into the stream to fill it, and I see Elena out of the corner of my eye, picking her way down the path.

"Don't go too far," I call out after her. "We'll head back as soon as I'm done with this."

"Alright!" she shouts back, and I go back to filling the bottles, screwing the lid tightly back on each one as I put it into the bag.

When I look up, Elena is nowhere to be seen.

"*Fuck*," I breathe, looking down the path. "Elena!"

I call out her name, but there's no answer. I can feel my jaw tense with frustration as I sling the bag over my shoulder, following her footprints as I head in the direction I saw her walking off in. *I told her not to go too far,* I think, with a slowly building irritation as I see the footsteps going further off the path.

"Elena!" I call out again, sliding my gun free as I glance around. I don't think there's much chance of there being any other people out here, but there's absolutely a chance of there being other things that could hurt her. I clench my teeth with frustration, trying not to let my mind run away with too many possibilities before I know there's a reason to panic.

And then I hear her scream.

I know it's her–a high, thin, reedy sound that I recognize as her voice. "Elena!" I shout her name, turning in the direction that I'm fairly certain I heard it coming from, and then I hear the scream once more.

"Levin! Help!"

I break into a run in the direction of her voice, my chest seizing with fear. I hear her shriek again, and then I turn a corner around another tangle of vines to see her sprawled in the dirt, tears running down her pale, fear-stricken face.

"Levin!"

Her ankle is twisted under her, but she's trying to crawl forward. She twists as she sees me, pointing with a look of horror on her face, and I see in an instant what she's so frightened of.

Moving towards her in a sinuous slither is what looks like a boa constrictor, big enough to kill her if it gets to her, its tongue flicking out as it gets closer.

Elena shrieks again, pulling herself forward in the mud, but it's gaining on her. *Not for long*, I think with a sudden, furious surety as I aim the gun, finger curling around the trigger.

"Elena! *Do not move!*"

She freezes in place at the sound of my voice, even though I know everything in her must be screaming for her to keep trying to flee as the massive snake gets closer. I aim as carefully as I can, wanting to be absolutely sure that I don't hit her by accident—and I squeeze.

Elena lets out a startled cry as the gunshot goes off. It misses the snake's head by an inch, and it hisses, recoiling as I aim once more—and this time, I hit it, the bullet striking it squarely in the head.

The snake goes still in the mud, and I see Elena collapse forward, all the blood draining out of her face.

As I break into a run once more, the only thing in my mind is making sure that she's safe.

Elena

I'm so stunned I can't move, my ears ringing from the gunshots as I lie there shaking. Dimly, I see Levin running towards me, shoving his gun back into his belt as he leans down to scoop me up into his arms. I curl against his chest, trembling all over as he starts to carry me away from the snake's corpse, one hand holding my head against his shoulder as he walks.

"You're alright now," he murmurs, his fingers brushing against my hair. "You're fine."

I'm not sure that's entirely true. My ankle is throbbing, pain shooting up my leg, and I wonder faintly if it's broken.

Levin scoops up the bag from where he dropped it, shouldering it as he keeps me carefully balanced in his arms, walking as quickly as he can back towards our makeshift campsite.

He doesn't say a word until we're back. He carries me to the edge of the water, setting me down on the sand as he helps me rinse off the mud, and then he picks me up again, taking me back to the blankets.

Once I'm settled, he sinks into the sand with a long sigh, looking at me with one half-raised eyebrow. "What happened, Elena?"

Guilt swamps me as I see the expression on his face. "I'm sorry," I whisper. "I didn't mean to wander off so far. I got distracted, and before I knew it—"

"I know," he says gently. "Nothing we can do about it now. What happened?"

I swallow hard, my stomach knotting all over again at the memory. "I saw the snake in a tree," I whisper, feeling faintly sick. "It slithered out and came after me. I thought I could outrun it—it was so big—and maybe I could have, but I tripped when I tried to run. I thought it was going to get me—crush me—"

Nausea clogs my throat at the thought, and I have to stop, reaching for one of the water bottles. Levin rubs my back with one hand, in slow circles until I can speak again.

"Is it broken?" I ask faintly, nodding down at my ankle.

"I'm not sure." He shifts, moving towards my feet as he gently picks my leg up and sets it in his lap. "This might hurt a little," he warns as he turns my leg to one side, gently prodding at the swelling flesh around my ankle, pressing his fingers up my foot and wiggling my toes until he sees what hurts and what doesn't. He's right that it *does* hurt—I cry out despite myself when he touches the area around my ankle bone, and I can't help another low moan of pain when he tries to rotate my foot a little.

"I don't think it's broken," Levin says finally, carefully setting my leg back down on the blanket. "I can't be sure, obviously—we'd have to go to a doctor for that. But I'm fairly certain. We still need to try to keep it stable."

He leans over, rummaging in the bag. "There are medical supplies in here—I think there were some bandages."

It takes a moment, but he fishes out a thick bandage that looks like it might work to stabilize my injury. "This won't feel good either," he warns as he props my leg up in his lap again. "But it should feel a little better after this."

I bite my lip as he winds the bandage around my foot and ankle, not wanting to make him feel worse than he already does. I can tell he doesn't enjoy the fact that I'm in pain, his touch as careful and soothing as it can be as he wraps up the injury.

"There," Levin says finally, helping me readjust when he's done. "I'm going back up to the trees to find the snake," he says, after a moment's hesitation. "I know it doesn't sound very good, but that's food. It'll help us put off going through what's left of the rations."

Privately, I don't know if I'm going to be able to stomach that, but I nod. I know it's what makes sense, even if I don't have the slightest idea how I'm going to eat it.

"Try to sleep a little," Levin suggests. "If you can."

I'm not sure how I'm going to manage that, either, but I roll onto my good side, grateful at least that the twisted ankle is on the same side as the still-healing cut from the plane crash. The sand feels even more lumpy and uncomfortable than usual, and it's too hot for a blanket, so I roll it up and tuck it under my head as a makeshift pillow.

I didn't think I could fall asleep, but I must have, because when I open my eyes again, Levin is sitting by the fire, and I see a thick shadow further off down the beach that I know, with a shudder down my spine, must be the corpse of the snake.

"I thought you wouldn't want to see it too close," Levin explains, when he sees where my gaze goes. "I'll see about cutting it up and cooking it as soon as I can."

I nod, feeling that sick lump in my throat again. *You'll eat it if you get hungry enough*, I tell myself, sitting up with my leg stretched out in front of me. But as the night goes on, and I go to sleep to the smell of Levin butchering and cooking it, I'm not so sure that's true.

I sleep through most of the next day, the pain from my ankle keeping me up most of the night and leaving me exhausted. Levin wakes me up to feed me a bit of a ration pouch and give me some water before I fall asleep again, waking up at twilight to see him fiddling with the radio.

"Any luck?" I ask faintly, and he looks up with a tense expression on his face. I can tell he doesn't want to answer.

"No," he says finally, setting it aside. "Nothing."

There's a moment of heavy silence, and I press my lips together, fighting back the tears welling up in my eyes. I hadn't really expected a different answer, but it's still hard to hear.

"I want to come sit by the fire with you," I say finally. "I would really like–to be held for a little while."

It feels strange to ask, but Levin just nods. He gets up, helping me up from the blanket, and then down to sit with him on the sand next to the fire, facing the water with my back to his chest as I sit between his legs.

There's a long silence as I sit there, feeling the warm solidness of him against my back, one of his arms wrapped around my waist and over my stomach. "I'm scared," I whisper finally, and I feel Levin let out a long, sharp breath behind me.

"I wish there was more I could do," he says quietly. "This isn't something I foresaw happening."

"I know." I swallow hard, still fighting back the tears that I desperately don't want to let fall. "It's weird, in a way–I was so terrified of Diego. More scared than I am of this, maybe. It's so different. It feels less–immediate. More ephemeral. Like there might still be a way out. It didn't feel like that, when I was in that cell."

"It's not over yet," Levin says quietly. "Unappetizing as it is, we have food for a little while still, and we won't run out of water. We have a chance."

"Even if we don't—" I bite my lip, squirming back a little so I'm closer to him. "Maybe this is better than whatever he had planned for me, when the plane was supposed to land. But—" I let out a long, slow breath, feeling the fear worm its way through my veins, cold and as sinuous as the snake had been. "I'm really afraid of dying."

"I'm sorry." Levin's arm tightens around me. "I'm not giving up yet, Elena. If there's a way out of this, I'm going to find it. But I know—" He sucks in a breath, his hand splaying over my hip as he holds me close. "I know that feeling. It's long gone for me. But I still remember what it felt like."

Of all the things he's said about his past, that one sinks in the most—the idea that he's been living a dangerous life for so long that he's beyond the fear of dying. I feel a shiver go through me, and Levin mistakes it for cold, reaching for the blanket to tuck it over me as he holds me, his other hand gently running through my hair as I lean back against his shoulder.

The sun is setting over the water in a blaze of color, and I feel my eyes mist over as I watch it. I can't help thinking how different it might be in other circumstances—how romantic this could be if we weren't here stranded, on the verge of losing everything. How I could be sitting here happy and in love, instead of terrified and fighting back panic.

What if I could pretend, just for a little while? What if we could both pretend? Just to make all the bad things go away for a night. Why would that be so bad?

"I'm glad that I'm not alone, at least," I whisper, turning my head so that my lips are almost brushing his throat. "You make me feel safe."

"It would be better if I could *keep* you safe," Levin says darkly, but I feel the tension suddenly running through him as I shift in his arms, my breath warm against his neck. His arm tightens over my waist, and I feel his breathing quicken just a little.

I shouldn't take advantage of the situation. I know that. I hadn't meant to, when I asked to come sit with him by the fire. But suddenly, all I can think about is how good he feels so close to me, his arm wrapped around me, as I breathe in the warm salty scent of his skin and feel his chest rise and fall against my back.

I shift against him again, and I feel his breathing catch as I feel the thick, hard ridge of his cock starting to press against the base of my spine. He's getting aroused by how close I am, and that, in turn, makes my heart skip and speed up in my chest, my skin flushing with a heat that has nothing to do with the balmy night air or the fire in front of us.

Slowly, I reach out, my fingers brushing against the side of his knee as I run my hand up the inside of his thigh, almost up to where the top of mine is pressed against him, before he reaches down, covering my hand with his and stopping it from going any further.

"Elena."

There's a warning in his voice, but I can hear the hoarse rasp in it, too, a sound that I'm slowly learning means desire. I lick my dry lips, my pulse lodging in my throat as I wrap my hand around his, brushing my thumb over the back of it.

I feel him stiffen behind me, hear him swallow hard, his breath ruffling the hair at the back of my neck, and another quick shiver goes down my spine.

All around us, the world is silent, the sky fading to the dark blue of almost-night as the fire crackles in front of us. It feels as if we're the only two people left in the world, and at this moment, I'm not entirely sure that I would mind if we were.

"I don't want to die without finding out what it's like to be with someone," I whisper softly, swallowing past the lump in my throat as I trace a pattern, slowly, on the back of his hand.

"Elena, I don't think—"

"I thought I'd only ever be with a man who was picked for me." I plunge forward, forcing the words out as my heartbeat quickens almost painfully in my chest, tingles of nervous desire running over my skin. I've never felt anything like this, the kind of wanting that makes me feel as if I'm vibrating from the inside, blissful and terrible all at once, a longing that desperately needs to be fulfilled. "But I want to pick *you*. And there's no one stopping me now."

I twist slightly in his arms, and I feel him breathe in sharply again as I shift against the hard pressure of his cock. "I want it to be you," I whisper. "I know you'll take care of me. Please, Levin—"

I can *feel* him wanting to give in. The air throbs around us with tension, and I feel his hand flex against mine, the deep shudder that goes through him.

"I've never been a girl's first, Elena." The words sound forced out between his teeth, as if he's having a hard time even talking about this, as if even giving it consideration will tilt us over the edge into doing it.

I can't help hoping that's the case.

"But you know how to make it good." I bite my lip, feeling my pulse quicken again. "You want to. I know you do. I can feel it." I squirm against him, just a little, as if to make my point, and Levin's hands come down on both sides of my hips at once, holding me very still between his legs.

"If you keep doing that," he murmurs, his voice a rasping growl, "I'm going to lose what little sense I have left for the two of us, Elena."

I feel his fingers flex against me, the moment where he fights his desire to pull me harder against him, instead of holding me still. I tilt my head back slowly, leaning it against his shoulder as I arch my back just a little, moving in his grasp as I grind backward against him, just a little, as much as I can with how tightly he's holding me.

"I want you," I whisper. "It's just us out here, Levin. Who has to know? We might not even make it long enough for anyone to ever find out."

"God, Elena—"

He groans my name, and one hand comes up to gently touch my face, turning it towards his. I see the glint of his blue eyes in the darkness, the way they rake over my face, full of a heated desire that tells me that he's lost the war with himself. His palm presses against my cheek, his breath sucked in between his clenched teeth as his face suddenly softens, and he leans down.

When his lips brush against mine, I give in to it completely. I reach up, cupping my hand around the back of his neck as I twist towards him, parting my lips for the hot slide of his tongue.

This is what I've been waiting for.

Elena

I feel the moment that he gives in to it, too, the moment that he pulls me tightly against his chest, the hand pressed against my face sliding into my hair as he deepens the kiss. One moment it's only a brush of lips, the warmth of his breath against my mouth, and then his tongue is tangled with mine, his mouth slanted over my lips.

He groans, the sound vibrating over my skin, and his hand strokes over my hair as he kisses me deep and slow. I gasp as his teeth graze against my lower lip, reaching up to grasp his shirt in my other hand. I want him closer, as close as he can possibly be, and there's nothing that could make me want to stop now.

All I want is him.

A warm breeze ruffles my hair as he brushes his lips over mine again, shifting me so that my legs are hooked over one of his, his other arm holding me against him. My hurt ankle is stretched out in front of me, out of the way, but I don't think I would have noticed. All I can think about is how he's making me feel.

How much I want to feel more.

His hand brushes up my thigh, up to the edge of my shirt, his fingers caressing just beneath it as he kisses me. He sucks on my lower lip lightly, tugging it between his teeth as his hand moves a little higher, sliding over the taut skin of my lower stomach.

"We're going to take this very slowly," he murmurs against my lips. "And if you want to stop, Elena, tell me. I don't care how turned on you think I am. I don't care if I'm on the verge of being inside of you–hell, I don't care if I *am* inside of you. Tell me, and I'll stop."

He brushes his thumb over my cheekbone, looking down at me in the dim light of the moon. "I won't want to, and it'll be one of the hardest goddamn things I'll ever do, but I'll stop. Just say the word."

"Is there a word other than stop that you want me to say?" I ask softly, and he shakes his head, his fingers skimming over my hair.

"We're not going to play those kinds of games, Elena. Just say stop, if it's too much. And I will."

I nod, swallowing hard. *There's no way I'm going to want to stop*, I think as his lips press against mine again, firm and warm, his hand sliding higher. His palm presses against my ribs, higher still between my breasts, and I gasp as he cups one in his palm, tugging the cup of my bra down so his fingers can toy with my stiffening nipple.

"You're so responsive," he murmurs hoarsely against my lips. "Everything I do–the way you react–it's so fucking good. Feeling how much you want me–"

"I do want you." I arch up, both of my hands fisting in his shirt as I deepen the kiss. "I've wanted you since the day I met you. In the office–"

"Well, now you have me." His tongue slides into my mouth again, hot and insistent, and I hear a soft moan escape me as his hand tightens on my breast.

For tonight, at least. The unspoken words hang between us as the moments drag on, Levin's kisses and the slow slide of his hand over my skin, heating my blood with an aching desire that makes me feel as if I'm going to lose my mind.

He breaks the kiss suddenly, his arm sliding under my knees as he lifts me, standing up and carrying me back towards the blanket. "We're not doing this in the sand," he murmurs, gently laying me down atop it as he leans over me. "I can't find a bed for us, but at least there's this."

"I don't care about a bed." I reach up, wanting to pull him down for another kiss. "This is fine."

"You deserve better." His hands are already tugging my shirt up, though, sliding it up my body as I lift up a little so he can pull it over my head. "You deserve a soft bed and candles, roses and champagne, and everything else you could dream of. All the romance your heart desires."

"I was never going to have that." I pull at his shirt, dragging it upwards. I want to see him without it, all that hard muscle I've felt beneath my hands. "You think whatever man I was going to be married off to was going to give me rose petals on the bed and candles?"

"Probably not." Levin reaches up, dragging his shirt over his head, and I suck in a sharp breath, forgetting whatever I was going to say next at the sight of him.

His chest and abs are impressively muscled, lines of it cut deeply down his sides and into the waist of his jeans. I could outline each ridge of his abdomen, trace a path down, and most of that muscled flesh is covered in tattoos—black and red, mostly, inked from his neck down to his hips and spreading over his arms.

"Not what you'd expected?" Levin looks down at me, his face suddenly blank, as if he's worried about my reaction. "Elena—"

I reach up, pressing the tips of my fingers against his lips before he can ask me if I want to stop. "You're so–" I can't even think of the right word to use. *Handsome* doesn't feel like enough to describe him. He's like something out of a fantasy, an inked statue carved from stone, and I reach down without thinking, hands fumbling with his jeans. I can see the outline of his cock pressing against his zipper, and I'm suddenly desperate to see the rest of him, to touch him. I remember how good he felt in my hand, in my mouth, how he *tasted*, and I want more.

"So are you." His voice is almost reverent as he unhooks the clasp of my bra, dragging the straps down my shoulders as he tosses it aside.

His mouth presses down between my breasts, his tongue tracing a path there as he slides both hands around the curve of them. I let out a soft, shuddering breath, hands curling in the blanket as my back arches at his touch.

Slow is also torturous. Every stroke of his fingers and flick of his tongue against my skin makes me feel as if I'm going to come out of it, as if my skin is too tight, my body aching for more of him–and it's also exquisite, pleasure tingling over every inch of me as he teases my nipples to stiff peaks and then rolls his tongue over each of them, sucking my flesh into his mouth as I squirm and whimper underneath him.

I know he must be aching just as much. I slide one hand down as I fumble with his zipper with the other, my palm sliding over the thick ridge of his cock. I hear the breath he sucks in, the sharp jerk of his hips, pushing himself against my hand as I let out another soft moan at the feeling of his tongue against my sensitive nipple.

"Not yet," he murmurs hoarsely as I try to reach inside of his jeans. He twitches his hips out of the way, reaching for my hands and gently pinning them down at my sides. "You're not ready yet, Elena."

"What? I–" For a brief second, I think *he's* changed his mind, that he's about to tell me we have to stop. But then he starts to kiss his way down my stomach, and I realize he has something else in mind.

My stomach tightens with anticipation at the realization of what he's about to do, and I hear his low chuckle as he feels it. His hands are at the edge of my shorts, undoing them, pulling them down, and I squirm under his touch as his lips graze past my navel and then lower still.

"Remember what I said," he murmurs softly, sweeping his mouth between my hipbones. "If it's too much, tell me."

I can't speak. I can barely think as he tosses my shorts and panties aside, leaving me completely bare as his hands smooth up my inner thighs, spreading my legs open slowly. His lips press against the soft flesh there, sliding higher to the crease of my thigh, and I feel as if I can't breathe any longer.

Gently, he brushes his thumbs upwards over the soft flesh between them, spreading me open almost delicately as he leans forward. I hear his low groan as his tongue flicks out against my clit, and I let out a cry of pleasure at the sudden, new sensation.

It feels so fucking good. His tongue presses against me, wet and hot, sliding over my drenched flesh as he opens me wider, spreading my thighs with light pressure from his arms. His tongue circles my clit in slow circles that leave me gasping, my head thrown back against the blanket and my fingers digging into it as I feel that knot of pleasure in my lower belly tightening.

My heart is fluttering in my chest, my breath is caught in my throat, an orgasm building that I know will be more intense than anything I've felt before. I'm almost afraid of it, but I don't want him to stop. It feels too good.

He groans as his tongue slides over my clit again, and then lower, sweeping over me as his hands tighten against my thighs. "You taste so sweet," he murmurs, his tongue circling my entrance before sliding back up to flutter against my aching clit. "So fucking good–"

I can feel myself flush at the thought of him tasting me, of it turning him on. I can feel that it is, from the way he's holding me, the low sounds that vibrate over me as he presses his mouth tighter against my pussy, his tongue working faster now in the rhythm that he's realized feels the best.

I'm so close. I can feel it building, tightening, that burst of pleasure that will crash over me at any moment. Then, Levin's lips tighten around my clit, sucking the throbbing flesh into his mouth, and I lose all semblance of control.

I forget where I am, everything except the waves of pleasure bursting over me as I let out a moan that turns to a high-pitched cry, bucking and writhing under him as his mouth keeps sucking, licking, driving me into spasms of sensation that I never knew were possible. I come hard, riding his face as he holds me against the blanket, and all I can think is that I never, ever want him to stop.

When the ripples of pleasure start to recede, I reach for him, gripping his muscled upper arm as I try to tug him up my body. "Levin, please–" I gasp, and he looks up from between my thighs. I can faintly see his lips glistening from how wet I am, and it sends another pulse of desire through me.

"Not yet," he says gently. "I'm going to make sure you're ready for my cock, Elena. I don't want to hurt you."

"What does that even mean?" I gasp, my head falling back as his hands gently stroke my inner thighs. "I'm ready. I–"

"No. You're not." His hand slides up, his fingers gently teasing my entrance. "You're so wet, *ptitsa*. But you need a little more."

I feel one finger press into me, just slightly. "I'm going to make you come for me like this, Elena. One more, and then you can have my cock."

His voice is taut with need as he says it, and I can feel the tension in the other hand on my thigh, how hard he's trying to hold himself back, to go slow.

"Fuck, you're so tight," he whispers as his finger slips into me, slow and gentle, his thumb pressing lightly against my sensitive clit. He rolls it lightly under the pad of his thumb as I squirm a little, the intrusion of his finger feeling a little strange—and good.

"More," I whisper, and Levin chuckles.

"Greedy girl," he murmurs, but there's a hint of amusement in his voice. "Take my fingers first, and come for me like a good girl, Elena. I have to be sure you're ready for me."

I feel myself tighten around his finger as he slides it deeper, curling it inside of me, and he groans, his jaw tensing.

"*Fuck*, I want to be inside of you," he murmurs, his finger moving ever so slightly inside of me. A strange ripple of sensation goes through me, and I arch my hips upwards, wanting more of it. More of *him*.

"That feels good," I whisper, and I move a little more, wanting him deeper. I reach up, grabbing his arm again as I tug him down, wanting him to kiss me.

He leans forwards, and I feel a second finger pressing against me as his lips find mine, brushing over my mouth as he lets out a low moan.

"God, Elena—" His second finger pushes inside of me, and I clench around him, shuddering as I gasp and arch upwards. His thumb is rubbing over my clit faster now, and I feel his fingers starting to move as well, thrusting slowly inside of me as he opens me up for him, readying me for what we both want.

"I—" My hands curl against his chest as he leans into me, the weight of him pinning me to the blanket as the kiss deepens. I moan into the kiss, my hips moving with the rhythm of his fingers as he pushes me closer and closer to a second climax. I can feel myself trembling, tensing, arching upwards to press against him, and I reach up to grip his arms as I start to shudder as the pleasure begins to unfurl through me.

"Fuck, *fuck*—" Levin breathes the words against my mouth as I clench around his fingers, grinding against his hand as I cry out, my entire body tensing underneath him. Everything feels swollen, sensitive, almost too much—and I still want more.

I want *him*.

"Now," I whisper, my hands sliding up to his shoulders, tugging at him. "Please, Levin. I don't want to wait any longer. Please—"

"How am I supposed to say no to that?" His mouth crooks in a half-smile as he reaches down, pushing his jeans off, and I see his cock spring free, thick and so hard that it brushes against his abdomen as he reaches for it.

He leans over me, his mouth hovering over mine, and I can feel the tension running through every inch of him. "You're sure, Elena?"

I don't know how he can still ask me that. I can feel how much he wants me, can see it in the long, hard line of his cock, the tension in his jaw, *hear* it in the hoarse thickness of his voice. But he still hovers over me, looking down at me with an expression that tells me he's going to wait until he's absolutely certain.

"Yes," I whisper, reaching up to touch his face. "I'm sure."

He swallows hard, a shudder rippling through him, and I feel him nudge against me, his swollen tip pressing against my entrance. I can feel how big he is, and even after two orgasms, I'm not entirely sure how he *can* fit inside of me. I can feel the pressure, burning as he starts to push himself inside of me, and Levin leans down, cupping his hand against my face.

"This is the hardest part," he says gently. "It will feel better after this."

And then he leans down, capturing my mouth with his, and thrusts.

Just an inch, maybe. Not all of him, not yet. His tongue slides into my mouth as the tip of his cock pushes into me, and I feel the stretching, burning pain of the first time—mitigated by the sweet pleasure of Levin's mouth on mine, his thumb brushing over my cheekbone as he tilts my chin up so he can kiss me more deeply.

I feel him go very still, holding himself there as I tighten and flutter around him, and his forehead presses against mine as he breaks the kiss, groaning.

"*Fuck*, you feel so fucking good—"

A shudder ripples down his spine, and I feel him clench the blanket next to my head with his other hand, fighting to stay still. I know he's letting me get used to him, giving me time, but I want more. I want to feel him lose control.

I arch upwards, hooking my unhurt leg around his as I squirm beneath him, trying to get him to slide deeper. Levin lets out a trembling breath, then he kisses me again, and I feel him thrust again.

I let out a small cry as I feel him go deeper, almost too much, and Levin freezes again. "Are you alright?" he murmurs against my lips, and I nod shakily.

"It's a lot," I whisper, and he chuckles.

"What every man wants to hear." He smooths my hair away from my cheek as I shiver underneath him, kissing me lightly. "I'll go slowly, Elena. I promise."

He keeps his promise. He slips into me, inch by inch, letting me get used to the feeling of him inside of me. Slowly, the pain gives way to the strange new sensation of him filling me, and as he slides in completely, going very still again, I let out a gasp.

"That feels good," I whisper, looking up at him as I cling to his shoulders, trembling with mingled pleasure and nerves. "You feel good."

"Does it?" Levin kisses me softly. "Are you ready for more?"

I nod, tilting my chin up. "Yes," I murmur against his lips, arching beneath him. There's no one on the beach but us, no one for who knows how far, but it feels like a sacrilege to speak above a whisper, anything beyond what he and I could hear.

I gasp when he starts to move, sliding out of me slowly, almost to the tip, and then back in again the same way. Each thrust is long and slow, turning any remaining pain to pleasure as I feel desire washing over me, drenching me with it. I cling to him as he kisses me harder, my nails biting into his shoulders.

"Elena—*fuck*—" He breathes my name against my mouth, his hips moving against mine as he sinks to the hilt again, and then I feel him speed up just a little, his strokes faster now.

It's impossible to make him lose control. I can feel him almost vibrating with the tension of holding himself back, keeping himself from fucking me as fast and hard as I know he must want to. Still, he keeps a slow pace, letting me get used to every new sensation.

With that comes the building pleasure from before. He grinds against my clit each time his hips meet mine, and I arch up, my breasts pressing against his chest as I lean up to kiss him, moaning with every stroke of his cock inside of me. It all feels so good—the sensation of him filling me up, thick and hard, bare skin on bare skin, warm lips against mine. I'm lost in the newness of it, the intensity, and as Levin shudders above me, I press both of my hands against his face, deepening the kiss.

"I won't last much longer," he groans against my mouth, his forehead pressed to mine again as he sucks in a breath, hips jerking as he sinks into me. "You feel too good—*fuck*—"

"I'm close too," I whisper, sliding my hands down to press against his chest. I want to feel all of him, to memorize all of this. "Just a little more—"

"I want you to come for me again." He kisses me, fast and hard. "Come on my cock, Elena. And then let me fill you up—"

"Yes," I whisper against his mouth. "Yes, *please*. Please make me come. I want all of it. I want everything."

I've never meant anything more in my life. And I know, as Levin surges inside of me, groaning as he fucks me harder than before, a tiny fraction of his control slipping, that I would do anything to keep him with me.

For this to not be the only night I spend with him.

Levin

I'm losing my mind.

She feels so good, better than I'd imagined. Hot and wet and tight, seizing around my cock with every thrust, and I'm so close to coming that I can barely hold it back. I've *been* close since the moment I felt her clench around my cockhead, but I wanted to make it last.

I wanted to take it slowly, to make it good for her, as good as it possibly could be. I've never been anyone's first before, but I've been with plenty of women–enough to know how to make sure it hurt her as little as possible. It had taken every ounce of my self-control to go as slowly as I had, but it was worth it.

Feeling her tremble underneath me, hearing her soft gasps and moans as I slid into her inch by inch–it all came close to undoing me again and again. And now, I'm on the very edge, wanting nothing more than to feel her come one more time before I lose myself.

Her lips are on mine, her nails sinking into my shoulders, her body moving under mine with quick, uncertain movements that tell me she's close too. Everything about her is so innocent, so curious, and I never would have thought that would turn me on as much as it does. But she makes me feel as if I'm going insane with need.

I tried not to, I think as I kiss her again, trying to push away the guilt. *How could I keep telling her no, after what she said?*

"Levin—"

She gasps my name again, her breasts brushing against my chest as she writhes under me, and I feel her tighten and flutter around my cock, sending a jolt of pure pleasure down my spine. My hips jerk against hers, my cock throbbing as I struggle to hold back, and I kiss her hard, thrusting my tongue into her mouth the way I want to shove my cock inside of her.

Next time, I think, and then close my eyes with a shudder, because I know there shouldn't be a next time. This should be it. Once, so she knows what it's like. Anything else—

Anything else is dangerous.

"I–I–" She moans against my mouth, her entire body going taut, and I feel a wave of heat flood me as I feel her start to come, trembling and clenching around me as she climaxes on my cock, her hips rolling against mine as she clings to me. "Levin, *Levin!*"

Hearing her shriek my name against my lips undoes me. My cock goes harder than I knew possible, throbbing as I drive into her one last time, seating myself as deeply in her as I can as I kiss her hard, feeling the first wave of my climax seize me as I fill her with the hot rush of my cum.

"Oh *god*," she moans, her hands pressing against the back of my head as my cock pulses inside of her again and again. I come harder than I have in years, *more* than I can remember having come in a very long time. I can feel the heat of it, and I slide my arm beneath her, holding her against me as we both shudder together.

I don't ever want to slip out of her. She presses her forehead against my neck, her hands against my chest, and I don't want to let her go.

As I feel the last tremors of her climax go through her, I turn onto my side, still holding her against me. I'm still inside of her, and I feel her turn her head, her cheek against my shoulder.

I press a kiss to the top of her head, one hand stroking her hair as she curls against me, sliding down between her shoulder blades. I want her closer—as close as she can possibly be, and that terrifies me.

I've spent the last twelve years being the guy who rolls out of bed almost as soon as he comes and goes straight to the shower—leaving either the fee for the night or cab fare on the nightstand, depending on how I met the girl in my bed. It's been that long since I've held a woman in my arms after sex, since I've had the desperate urge to stay inside someone, to keep that intimacy.

Elena makes me feel all of that, and more. I feel a fierce surge of protectiveness, a desire to keep her close and safe, and with that comes a frustrating wave of helplessness—because out here, it doesn't seem as if I have very much control over that.

She shifts against me, pressing her lips to my throat, and I feel my cock twitch inside of her, coming back to life in a way that hasn't happened to me in a long time, either. She lets out a soft, humming moan, her hips arching against mine as if to urge me on, and I chuckle against her hair.

"Not tonight," I tell her gently. "You'll be too sore in the morning if we go again. Besides, you need to rest."

"I can sleep when I'm dead," she mumbles against my throat, clearly going for gallows humor, but it has the opposite effect on me tonight. I can feel the arousal fade as I wrap my arms around her instead, resting my chin atop her head as I roll onto my back and gather her against my chest.

"Sleep now," I suggest, hand stroking soothingly down her arm. "You need the rest for your ankle to heal."

She makes a small, disappointed sound in the back of her throat, but it's only minutes before I feel her breathing even out and hear the soft snores fill the air as she falls asleep.

Normally, I'd be passed out too. Usually, nothing knocks me out faster. But as I lie there and watch her sleep, all I can feel is the crushing weight of guilt.

When she rolls onto her side, away from me, I get up. Pulling my jeans back on, I walk a little ways down the beach, sitting on the sand within eyeshot of her in case she wakes up. I need a minute to think, and I can't do it with her so close to me.

I've tried to reassure Elena by telling her that we have food and water for now, such as it is, to try to mitigate her fear. Still, I know she's smart enough to understand the danger we're in. Truthfully, I have no idea if we're going to make it.

I have no way of contacting anyone, and the radio won't work. I don't have any means of fixing it, either. By now, I know that the Kings, Viktor, and Luca will be trying to find out what happened to Elena and me, but it's going to be like trying to find a needle in a haystack. Our flight would have been logged as heading to Boston, with no record of where Diego had paid the pilot to actually go.

I've failed again. I'm not going to be able to protect her.

I know what my motivation was in coming to rescue Elena. I don't need someone to psychoanalyze me to know that I'd been trying to redeem myself for what happened to Lidiya by helping her—that's all I've ever been trying to do, over and over again…with Ana, with Sasha, and now her. I want to make up for losing the woman I loved, somehow, as if that failure can ever really be redeemed. As if I can ever do enough penance to make up for not having been there for her.

At least I got Liam to Ana, and Max to Sasha. I think of Max, back in Boston with his now-wife, and all the many hours we've spent half-arguing over the ways we don't see eye to eye. A priest—even a former priest—is the last sort of man I'd have thought I'd make friends with, and yet Max has always been a good counterpoint to my nihilism.

The situation I've found myself in now has me wishing I could feel more about things the way he does. I wish I could believe that I'll see Lidiya again, that something good could come out of the end other than snuffing out a life lived in blood, danger—and, ultimately, failure.

What happens when the food is gone? I can try to hunt with the small bit of ammunition I have, but that will only go so far. I'm not a survivalist, and if we're not found, this only ends one way—with us dying of starvation. It's not a good way to go. It is, in theory, something that ends with me having to decide at what point all hope is lost, and whether or not I'll need to take steps to make the end easier on us.

Just the thought is horrifying enough that I know in an instant that I won't be able to do it. For myself, maybe, but not for her. I won't even be able to spare her that.

I glance over at where she's still sleeping, curled on her side. I know she cares for me—maybe more than she should. But I also know I'm not worthy of it.

I hope that I made her happy, for the night at least. It can't happen again, but I wanted to give her something good. To give her the chance, at least, to find out what it's like to be with someone who cares about her, who she wants in return. She was right that it wasn't something she would have gotten otherwise, and I wanted her to have some small part of this awful situation to feel as if it were for the better. For there to be something in all of this that would make her happy.

I can't save her. But I could at least give her that.

Elena

I wake in the morning thoroughly sore—and very happy. As I blink awake in the sunlight, I stretch experimentally, feeling soreness in muscles I didn't know I'd use—and a very pleasant, lingering soreness between my thighs.

Levin is sitting by the fire, heating up chunks of the snake meat. I wrinkle my nose at the smell, and he catches sight of my expression as he hears me shifting on the blankets and looks over at me.

"There's still rations," he says, nodding at the bag. "I thought I'd eat the meat for now, and leave you something you'd prefer. It won't keep forever anyway; we don't have any way to keep it cold. I might as well start in on it.

"Thanks." I press my lips together tightly, feeling suddenly shy as I look at him. I'm struck with an immediate wave of memory—the sensation of his arms around me, his lips on mine, the heavy pressure of his body above me as he'd touched me in all the ways I'd fantasized about for the very first time.

I'm not a virgin anymore. I don't entirely know how to feel about that. I'm not sad about it at all—I know that. I'm glad that if I ever do go back home to my father, it won't all be idle speculation about whether or not I'm still "pure." I won't be, and that will have been entirely on my own terms.

It had been everything I could have hoped for. I didn't need a bed or a fancy room or all the things Levin had thought I should have. All I needed was what I'd gotten–tenderness and pleasure, and someone who would care about what it was like for me.

I start to gather up my clothes, keeping the top blanket tucked above my breasts as I do. There's no real reason to be shy–Levin has seen every inch of me by now, had his hands and his mouth all over me, been literally *inside* of me–but I can't help feeling a little self-conscious, out in the daylight like this.

"Are you alright?" Levin glances over at me as I struggle to get my clothes back on without dropping the blanket, trying not to jostle my hurt ankle too much. He starts to stand up, his brow creasing. "Don't do too much–"

"I think I can make it. I'm just going to go down to the water and, um–clean up. From–" I feel my cheeks flush, and when he looks away quickly, I feel a drop in the pit of my stomach.

I don't want to think that he regrets it. I don't want there to be even a chance of that, because I *definitely* don't.

"Of course." Levin clears his throat. "I can help you–"

My cheeks heat even more at the thought. "No, that's okay. I can manage. I'll just be careful."

It's a lot harder to make it down to the water's edge than I thought it would be. I have to almost hop through the sand, dragging my hurt ankle, and I glance back to see Levin looking at me with a distressed expression on his face. I know he wants to help, but when I see him try to stand again, I wave him off.

"I'm fine!" I yell back, and I can see the sigh he lets out as he sinks back down to sit in front of the fire. I know he wants to help, but for this, I need my privacy.

It's even more awkward trying to clean up. I end up taking my shorts and top off, wading into the chilly water to give myself some semblance of a bath. The saltwater stings between my thighs, and I let out a small hiss of pain, clenching my teeth as it hits both the soreness there and the still-healing cut on my side.

For someone who has spent her entire life without any injuries other than a stubbed toe or bumped elbow, this is a lot to take in all at once.

I glance over my shoulder a few times as I clean up, to see if Levin is watching, but he's not. In fact, he seems to be studiously *avoiding* watching, and somehow that feels worse.

I'd hoped that he would wake up and want me again. That this would mean we would spend whatever remaining time we had enjoying each other, rather than simply waiting for the end. But it doesn't seem like that's going to be the case.

If anything, he seems more distant than before. And without that to distract me, I can feel the fear starting to creep in again, chilling me down to the bone as I finish rinsing off and dry myself with the blanket, wishing to the very depths of my soul for a hot shower and a real towel.

One of the ration packets and a bottle of water is waiting for me on the other blanket when I finally limp my way back up. As soon as I come within view of the firepit, Levin is on his feet, heading towards me despite my assurances that I can make it on my own.

"Just because you *can* doesn't mean you should have to," he says firmly. "I gave you your privacy just now, so you can accept help with this."

When his arm goes around my waist, I wonder why I argued so much. I feel instantly calmer, safer, the moment he's touching me, and I can't help but lean into him, savoring the warmth and scent of him so close to me, the solidity.

I miss it the instant it's gone, when he helps me down to the blanket and steps quickly away.

"Last night—"

The minute the words come out of my mouth, I see his face shutter. "Do you feel alright?" he asks, and I swallow hard, feeling that disappointment flood through me again at the emotionless way he says it.

"I'm fine," I manage. I reach for the food, fighting back tears that I know are pointless. I have no reason to be upset. He hadn't promised me anything–hadn't even really done more than give in to my desire for one night. "We don't have to talk about it."

Levin nods wordlessly, biting into his own food. I look away, unable to stomach the sight of it, and my ankle throbs at the memory.

How many more days do we have? I'm afraid to ask how many of the ration pouches are left, how long there is before I'll have to stomach the slowly spoiling meat or starve.

"Is there anything else we can do?" I ask, hearing the edge of desperation starting to color my voice. "Can we make a bigger fire? Send up smoke that someone might see? Is there a chance that might help? Or are there flares in the bag—"

The words start tumbling over each other, a tinge of panic creeping in, and Levin quickly shifts closer to me, touching my hand gently. Just that touch is enough to calm me a little, a warm tingle running over my skin at his touch, but he pulls back quickly.

"The fire could work," he says slowly. "But there would have to actually be someone in range to see it. That's a big *if*, and we might not get too many chances at that. There aren't any flares, I looked."

"Hasn't someone seen the wreckage by now? Someone flying over?"

"Someone would have to actually be looking. There's no reason for anyone *to* look. There's no record of us flying out here."

"Oh." I bite my lip, once again fighting back the tears. "So I guess the fire, then. If we get desperate."

"Pretty much—"

Levin breaks off suddenly, getting to his feet. "*Bladya!*" he swears under his breath, striding past our tiny campsite and a little further down the beach. "Shit! Elena, come here!"

I'm on my feet in an instant, heedless of my hurt ankle, letting out a gasp of pain as I put too much weight on it. I look towards him, towards where he's gesturing, and I suddenly feel faint as I see what he's seeing.

Is it some kind of trick? A mirage? Our desperate imaginations?

But both of us can't be having the same hallucination, and we're not so bad off yet for that to be what's happening. Which means that what I see Levin pointing at–the outline of what looks like a huge cargo ship–is real.

It means we could be rescued.

"Wait here," Levin says quickly, his voice taut. "There's some high rocks further down the beach. I'm going to try to flag them down."

"I'll come with you—"

"No." He shakes his head. "Please, Elena. Wait here. Your ankle is hurt, and it will take longer if I need to help you–and I can't let you struggle your way down the beach on your own," he adds as he sees me open my mouth to argue. "Please, just wait."

I give in, retreating back towards my blanket. I hate the idea of being left to sit and wonder what's happening, especially when it's a fucking *life-and-death* situation, but I know he's right. I'd just slow him down, and risk the chance of us being rescued at all.

That doesn't mean that I don't want to sulk about it, just a little.

Instead, I sit down on the blanket, knotting my hands together in my lap as I try to stay calm. If the ship sees Levin, we might be able to get out of here. But depending on who it is, flagging them down could be dangerous, too. Or–

Don't think about it, I tell myself as the minutes tick past. I'm afraid to think that we might be rescued, to hope for it, but there's also no point in thinking of all the ways it can go wrong.

I sit there, feeling as if I'm on the verge of coming out of my skin, until I see Levin coming down the beach. I'm on my feet again in an instant, ignoring the throbbing in my ankle as I watch him come back. He looks stunningly handsome, even a little sunburned and dirty. I remember with a flush of heat how he looked last night, when I'd finally gotten his shirt off and seen his muscled torso covered in tattoos.

"They're coming," Levin says breathlessly when he's within earshot. "They saw me; the ship is headed this way. I'll help you down the beach. We should hurry."

I can hear the hope in his voice, and my chest tightens, a flurry of emotion filling me as I nod. I limp towards him, grabbing onto his arm as soon as I can, and he wraps his around my waist, helping me slowly towards where the ship is coming in.

It feels like an interminable wait until the ship starts to come in to shore. When it's close enough, a few men take a smaller boat to approach the beach, and Levin steps in front of me, gesturing for me to stay behind him.

"Let me talk to them," he says quietly, and I nod, the lump in my throat making it impossible for me to speak anyway. The panic I feel at the approaching men feels much worse than the still-ephemeral fear of what will happen to us without rescue–because this feels like a much more immediate potential danger.

"What's going on here?" one of the men asks as he approaches, barking out the words. I take another cautious step behind Levin, entirely fine with being out of the way. I'd rather they *didn't* notice me.

"We were stranded a few days ago. Plane crash." Levin's tone is brusque, to the point. "Where are you headed?"

"Rio." The man narrows his eyes. "You're looking for a ride, I'm guessing?"

"I can get money for you, once we're there," Levin says smoothly. "The men I work for will pay handsomely for it. We won't take up much space. Just a corner, until you dock in Rio."

"We?" The man cranes his neck, his eyes taking on a glint I don't like when he sees me behind Levin. "Oh, I see. Well, then. Might be some other way to pay for your passage—"

"I don't think so," Levin says sharply, his hand twitching towards his hip. His gun is at his back, but the man seems to recognize the gesture, because he backs off a little.

"What kind of payment are we talking?"

"Name it," Levin says smoothly. "All I need to do is get in contact with my boss once I'm in Rio. Then you'll be paid."

"I'm usually in the business of getting at least part of it up front."

Levin shrugs. "You can take the chance, or you can leave us here and be sure of getting nothing."

His tone is so calm that they might have been discussing splitting a check after dinner, instead of whether or not Levin and I will be left on the beach to die. But Levin doesn't so much as flinch, staring the man down until he finally nods.

"A corner," the man says flatly. "I hope you have something to eat and drink on the ride, and I won't be bothered keeping my men off the girl. You handle that yourself, big man."

Levin nods. "Understood," he says coolly. "Elena, grab the bag."

I swallow hard, surprised he'd ask me to walk back up the beach, but I suspect that it's so I either don't hear what he says next, or so that I'm out of the man's line of vision long enough for him to finish the conversation.

Either way, I limp up the beach to get the bag with the remaining rations in it and the blankets, gathering them up and then slowly making my way back. By the time I do, Levin is waiting for me, with the other men waiting impatiently by the boat.

"Let's go," the one who negotiated with Levin barks out, and I look at Levin nervously.

He nods. "It's our best chance," he says quietly, low enough for only me to hear. "If we don't—we might not get another one."

"It's dangerous?" I whisper, knowing the answer even before he gives me a small nod.

"Yes," Levin answers honestly. "But this is the kind of danger I can protect you from, Elena."

That's all I need to hear. I give him a small nod in return. He gently helps me towards the boat, the cold water splashing over my feet and calves as he helps me get in and sits next to me, his jaw clenched as he looks warningly at the men around us.

No one tries to touch or interfere with me, at least. The boat approaches the larger cargo ship, and once again, Levin gets between me and the others, helping me up the ladder one rung at a time. It's excruciating on my injured ankle, but I force myself to ignore it, reminding myself over and over of what Levin just told me.

It's our best chance.

The man wasn't lying when he said we would get a corner. He leads us to a lower part of the ship, pointing to an area with slightly fewer boxes, crates, and other cargo. "Find a spot," he says coldly and then turns to leave.

I look at Levin, hardly able to believe we're actually off of the beach. I'm not sure how much safer we are, but we're *headed* somewhere, and that has to count for something.

"Here." Levin wraps his arm around my waist, taking the bag from me and guiding me to a corner by a stack of crates. "We might as well get comfortable."

He folds the blankets, making a spot for me to sit before helping me down. The instant I'm sitting, he lets go of me, backing away and putting a significant distance between us—at least a foot, which means he's smashed up against another stack of cargo.

It's very clear that he doesn't want to touch me unless he has to. That he's going out of his way *not* to unless I need the help. And now, with the immediate fear of being stranded on the beach without a way out receding, it hurts more than it did before.

That's the only excuse I have for what I say.

"You only had sex with me because you thought we were going to die, didn't you?"

The words come out sharper than I'd intended for them to, and I see Levin's face go very still the instant I say it, his jaw tightening. He says nothing, looking away, and somehow that just makes me even more upset than before.

"Well?" I fight back the sudden burn of tears in my eyes. "You might as well tell me the truth."

I see the tension that ripples through him, the clench of his hand as he swallows hard, his Adam's apple bobbing in his throat. I can see him trying to decide what it is that he's going to say exactly.

"Or just sit there, and we never talk about this—"

"Yes!" Levin turns towards me, his blue eyes flinty. "Is that what you want to hear, Elena? The truth? Yes, I wouldn't have done it otherwise. I was supposed to take care of you, not fuck you." His jaw clenches harder, the muscle in the hollow of it leaping. "And I failed at both," he adds bitterly.

I stare at him, feeling a flash of regret for how I'd spoken to him. "You didn't fail," I whisper, softening my voice as much as I can. "We're going to be safe now. We're on this ship. Going to Rio. We're fine—"

"We're not out of the woods yet," Levin says tightly. "I still have to get us home."

He stands up then, pushing himself to his feet as he looks down at me. "I *will* keep you safe, Elena. I'll do everything I can. I'll fight and kill whoever I have to in order to get you back to Boston and your sister. But—"

Levin swallows hard, taking a deep, resolute breath. "I won't touch you again, Elena. Not like that. I can't."

"Why?" The question comes out before I can stop it, more pleading than I want for it to, and I wish I could take it back. I see the hint of regret in his eyes, and that upsets me more than anything, because I don't regret a single second of it.

What he does is worse than an answer. He looks at me for a long second, as if considering what he could possibly say, and then he shakes his head, turning away from me.

He walks away, towards the stairs, leaving me alone for the moment. I don't doubt that he'll stay close enough to make sure I'm safe, that no one will be able to touch me. I'm not afraid for my own safety, not with him here.

What I feel is so much worse, hollow and empty, a longing and a sense of loss that I can't describe, because I've never had the opportunity to feel it before.

I watch him go, and a part of me almost wishes that we were back on the beach. That I could rewind and go back to when he held me in his arms, and I felt closer to him than I've ever felt to anyone in my life. When I learned what it was like to be wanted in that way.

I don't want anyone else. I want more of *him*.

But he doesn't want the same.

We're going to Rio. He'll get me home. And then I'll be with family again. It will all be fine.

But as I watch him walk away, all I can think is that I've never felt so alone.

It's going to be a long trip home.

Want to dive deeper into Levin's mind? Click here to subscribe to my mailing list and gain instant access to a HOT Savage Assassin bonus scene from Levin's POV!

Ready for the next book in The Savage Trilogy? Click here to read what happens next in Levin and Elena's Bratva romance!

Printed in Great Britain
by Amazon